DECEPTION

Forgotten Colony, Book Two

M.R. FORBES

Chapter 1

Guardian Alpha Caleb Card stared at the door.

He had tried the control panel beside it multiple times, and multiple times it had refused to open. Then he had returned to his stasis pod and checked the event log. Then he had discovered he had been in hibernation, not for the single year he was expecting, but for over two hundred years.

Then the door had started opening.

His stasis thaw had registered in the log as remotely operated. Had the door been opened remotely too, or had it been programmed to open after he reviewed the logs?

Was someone playing some sort of strange game with him?

He had no idea what was happening, or why he had been in stasis for so long. Where were Shiro and Ning? Dead? Or in one of the nine other chambers? The Marine module had been designed to house ninety Marines in stasis at one time, with ten maintaining watch over the starship. That had been the plan anyway. But the trife had ruined that plan and left the Space Force Marines with only six survivors.

Now, they might be down to four.

Caleb broke out of his momentary hesitation. He would figure it out later. He sprinted to the door, suddenly afraid it would decide to close again before he could make it to the other side. The last thing he wanted was to wind up trapped in the chamber again.

He made it to the door and through, out into the Marine module's armory. He came to a stop on the other side, scanning the racks of rifles positioned between the doors. He grabbed a standard-issue carbine from the rack and put it on the floor, positioning it so the hatch wouldn't be able to seal again if it tried to close.

It didn't seem like it was going to close, but he wasn't taking any chances. He was still confused and definitely frightened. His heart raced, his body shook with cold and fear. Waking up from stasis had been a shock. Discovering something had gone wrong was an even bigger shock. He was a Marine. A Guardian. It was his duty to protect the Deliverance and the city of forty-thousand resting in its belly. He glanced back into the stasis chamber.

At least he didn't have to do it alone.

He was about to return to the chamber when he noticed the smell. It caused him to freeze in place. It was pungent and rank, drifting over from somewhere nearby. He recognized it. Death. Recent? Anything that died two centuries ago should have finished decomposing by now, even in the climate-controlled air of the ship.

A ship that was still operational after all of these years. Caleb wondered if he should be thankful for that. Maybe he would be better off if the Deliverance had run out of power and died, taking him with it.

He grabbed another carbine from the rack and a magazine from a shelf on the opposite side of the aisle. The sound of the magazine locking into the gun seemed magnified, echoing in the room. If there were danger nearby, it would know someone was in here.

But how could there be danger? The Guardians had killed all the trife, he was sure of it. They had scoured every last nook and cranny of the massive starship. It had taken nearly two months, but they had been ninety-nine percent confident the creatures were gone. If one had turned up, Shiro would have woken him.

But what if the trife had caught Shiro off-guard? What if it had killed him?

The pod had been programmed to wake him in a year. Its programming had failed.

Or someone had changed it.

That made more sense, didn't it? Someone had altered his pod. Someone had changed the date. He knew there was at least one person on board who could have done it. A man he knew only as Harry, a computer programmer who had been with Doctor Valentine's research team.

Had Harry done it?

Except there was no need to go through the network to cancel the thaw date on the pod. Anyone with access to the chamber could have done it from the terminal, including Privates Shiro and Ning. But why would they? What purpose would that serve?

There had to be a reason, and it had to be related to the smell.

Caleb reached the corner of the armory, coming around it with the carbine up and ready to fire. He swept the weapon across the aisle, but he didn't see anything. He started down it, coming to a stop about halfway when he reached the door to another of the stasis chambers. He stared at it curiously, new fear putting pressure on his chest.

The door was dented in like something had hit it repeatedly. But what could do that kind of damage?

He glanced to his left, at his artificial arm. The trife queen had bit his original, damaging it beyond repair. This one had the strength to make dents like that. Doctor Valentine's Cerebus armor could probably have done it too.

But why? Was this door sealed too? Was someone inside?

He reached for the control panel, activating it and trying to open the hatch. He wasn't surprised when it didn't budge. He decided to leave it for now. There was too much he didn't know to get fixated on any one thing.

He moved along the wall, turning left at the corner. The exit was up ahead on his right. He could see the hatch was open, and the smell of death and decay had gotten stronger. He made his way along the aisle, moving slowly. The floor was cold on his bare feet, but at least it helped him stay quiet.

He reached the open hatch, leading with the carbine as he cautiously emerged from the armory and into the short corridor. He swung left and right, checking his position. Clear.

The smell was getting stronger to his left, down the corridor leading to the CIC. His arms prickled, his skin crawling. He had a bad feeling about all of this. A momentary panic hit him. What if they hadn't killed all of the trife? What if the trife had gotten into Metro? What if he and the Vultures were the only humans left alive on the ship?

The contingency if they were overrun was for someone to contact Command on Proxima and tell them what happened, and request assistance getting the trife off the ship or the colonists away from the ship past the trife. That wasn't the kind of thing that took two centuries to execute.

Unless they had tried and failed?

How could that have happened?

Caleb stared down the corridor toward the CIC. The hatch leading to the central command room was closed. Sealed and locked? He hoped not, but either way he was done operating solo. His team was still in stasis. Still alive.

He needed their help.

He turned around, moving back into the armory. He hesitated near the hatch, considering whether or not to close it. He was nervous it wouldn't open again if he did, but he also knew the Guardians would be vulnerable while they were coming out of stasis. He reached over and tapped the control panel, relaxing slightly when the hatch slid closed without complaint. It wouldn't open from the outside without a passcode.

Unless whoever opened the stasis chamber door could open that door too?

There were only so many things he could control, and that wasn't one of them. He took a shortcut through the armory, passing between the shelves of military equipment – guns, shells, magazines, knives, and more. It didn't look like the inventory had diminished over time. Whatever had happened out there, nobody had come here searching for firepower.

But somebody had come here. Somebody or something had dented the door to one of the stasis chambers.

Caleb approached the chamber. The door was still open. Everything had remained as he had left it during the few minutes he was gone. He was about to go inside when he heard a loud groan from the side of the room, followed by grinding and popping. The noise echoed in the space, loud enough to wake the sleeping Guardians on its own and causing Caleb to fall to a knee, pivoting and aiming his rifle in the direction of the sound.

He found himself facing the dented hatch. It was sliding open, or at least trying to. The dent was hitting the wall, the motor fighting to overpower it and causing the awful noise as it bounced back and forth.

Caleb didn't move. He held the rifle steady, aimed at the opening. He waited there for a moment, in case something was inside and came out.

The motor on the hatch lost the fight. It made one last terrible grinding noise, and then the heavy panel settled into place, smoke spilling out of its track.

Caleb stood and walked toward the door, keeping his carbine ready to fire. The inside of the chamber was dark, the interior lighting either malfunctioning or shut down because there was nothing active inside. He hoped it was the latter.

He reached the door, trying to look in. He didn't see anything moving. It was hard to see anything at all. He held the gun forward, waving it in the room to activate the sensors. A few of the lights along the ceiling activated, casting the chamber in an eerie, dim glow.

There was nothing in the room. Nothing awake, anyway. But the door had opened for a reason. Caleb stepped through, approaching the first stasis pod. It was empty. He moved to the next. Also empty.

He reached the third. The cryogel inside the pod was crystallized, making it hard to make out what was beneath it. A person, that much was obvious. A woman. Not a Guardian then. Sho and Flores were the only females on his team.

Who was it?

He circled the pod and tapped on the control surface for its terminal. It took a few seconds for the display to activate, and Caleb drew in a sharp breath when it did.

What the hell was Doctor Valentine doing in stasis down here?

Chapter 2

Caleb stared at the display. According to the terminal, the occupant was one Doctor Riley Valentine. The pod was in optimal working condition. Her vitals were good.

Caleb navigated the computer, opening the log. He checked the timestamp on the first line to determine when she had entered hibernation.

Two years after he had gone under.

If there had been a problem, why hadn't she woken him? And why had she come down here to go into hibernation? The Research module had its own pods. She didn't need to use theirs.

The dented door was a clue. He didn't need to be a scientist to figure that out. Something or someone had chased her, and she had locked herself in here. The chambers all required a passcode, the same as the armory door. She knew it. Her assailant didn't.

But who was her assailant?

Or rather, who had her assailant been? The chase occurred two hundred thirty-four years in the past. Whoever it was, they had to be dead by now.

But his pod had activated. Then his chamber door had opened. Then hers had opened. Someone was orchestrating the sequence of events. In the present? Or had all of this been programmed to occur two centuries earlier?

Doctor Valentine's hibernation had started two years after his.

He had questions.

She had answers.

There was only one thing to do.

He navigated back out to the main menu, tapping on the command to manually thaw the pod. A box popped up on the display, asking him if he was sure. He confirmed without hesitation.

The pod began to hum loudly, the display switching to a countdown timer of the thaw sequence. Caleb took a step back, splitting his attention between the timer and the pod. Condensation started rising from the sealed lid as the cryogel's temperature was slowly adjusted from a deep freeze to a warm bath. The process wasn't quick, and Caleb leaned back against the empty pod on the other side of the aisle, with nothing to do but wait.

The minutes ticked down. The cryogel became evident in the pod, the glass defogging as well. Caleb straightened up and stepped forward, looking into the pod to confirm the occupant really was Doctor Valentine. Her expression was peaceful, her arms folded beneath her breasts, her legs straight. Her eyelids fluttered gently in the flow of the gel, which was filtered continuously out of the pod, cleansed, and replaced.

A loud thunk signaled the next phase of the thaw. The cryogel began draining from it, sinking away from Doctor Valentine. Caleb stepped away, moving closer to the exit. He didn't want her thinking he had been standing there staring at her naked body the whole time.

The machine thunked again, and the display message changed.

THAW COMPLETE. SUCCESS!

Caleb waited. He was beginning to settle into his new predicament, his heart rate starting to slow, his adrenaline rush fading. He was switching over to acceptance, curious about what Doctor Valentine would have to say and growing eager to figure out how to proceed. If there was a problem, he wanted to solve it.

"Doctor Valentine," he said a minute after the thaw finished. He was using his own experience to assume she could hear him. He figured his voice would be less jolting than having her sit up and find him standing there. "Can you hear me?"

He heard her clear her throat. "Guardian Alpha Card. Is that you?"

"It is."

"Where are you?"

"Near the door."

"Are we safe?"

Caleb couldn't help but laugh. "Doctor, I have no idea. I was hoping you could tell me. There are a lot of things I'm hoping you can tell me."

"Come here. Help me up."

Caleb walked over to the pod. Doctor Valentine's eyes were open, looking up at him with a peacefulness he found disconcerting, all things considered. He hadn't noticed how blue her eyes were before.

He held out his hand. Riley reached up and took it, and he pulled her into a sitting position.

"How do you feel?" he asked.

"Scared," she replied.

"You don't look scared."

"Looks can be deceiving. You have no idea how deceiving."

"What does that mean?"

"How long?" she asked instead.

"Two hundred thirty-six years."

She nodded. "And we're safe in here?"

"The armory door is closed and sealed. Is that enough?"

"It should be."

"What the hell is going on here, Doctor?"

"Please, call me Riley." She looked up at him, her eyes locking on his. "I know all of this is jarring. It is for me too. I want to get you up to speed, but we have problems."

"I figured that much. What about Metro? Are the civilians safe?"

"I honestly don't know."

Caleb's fresh calm vanished again. "What?"

"I'm sorry, Alpha. I wish I could tell you everything is great. It isn't. I wish I could tell you Metro is secure. I can't. It's been two hundred years. I have no way of knowing what we're waking up to, any more than you do."

"But you know what you went to sleep to."

"Yes."

"Let's start there."

"Are your people still in stasis?"

"Yeah."

"We need to wake them."

"I need answers first."

"We don't have time for answers yet, Alpha. Time isn't on our side."

Caleb laughed out loud. "Are you kidding? We just spent more than two hundred plus years asleep. What's that supposed to mean?"

Riley stood up in front of him. He was surprised her

skin wasn't covered in goosebumps. He had been freezing when he came out of the pod. Wasn't she cold?

"Help me down," she said, reaching out toward him.

Caleb offered his hand. Riley took it and stepped over the edge of the pod, using him for balance as she dropped to the floor. He turned away from her while she picked up her clothes and started dressing in the same bland pants and shirt he was wearing.

"I take it the trife weren't all dead?" Caleb asked.

"Those trife are the least of our concerns right now," she replied.

"What does that mean?"

"The Deliverance is rated for a two hundred year duty cycle. We're thirty-six years past it."

"Which means what?"

"Which means we have to get the ship to the surface before it runs out of power. As you can imagine, landing a vessel of this size and weight inside an atmosphere with Earth-like gravity takes a lot of energy."

"I can imagine. And since we've been out here longer than expected, we have less energy to land with."

"Exactly."

"You said Earth-like. What happened to Proxima?"

"We aren't near Proxima."

Caleb closed his eyes and sighed. "Seriously, Riley. This would be a whole hell of a lot easier if you would stop making me ask you for every little detail."

She came around in front of him, fully dressed. "Maybe, but I don't want to tell the same story five times. We should wake your team."

"Hold up there, Doctor. I'm not dragging my team into this until I know what this is. You were just in stasis too, so you know hibernation is a hell of a lot better than coming to in the middle of a nightmare."

"Let me ask you a question, Alpha, and we can decide to proceed after that, okay?"

Caleb nodded. "Go ahead."

"Do you want to give the people in Metro the best chance to survive or not?"

"You said you don't know if they're still alive."

"Which means we should assume they are, don't you think?"

Caleb's jaw tightened. He had forgotten how condescending Doctor Valentine could be. Maybe he shouldn't have woken her up.

"Okay. You win. Let's go wake the others."

Chapter 3

Caleb and Riley woke the Guardians as close to the same time as they were able. It left the stasis chamber echoing with hums and pops and gurgles, each of the machines running through their thawing processes almost in unison.

Caleb remained near the door to the chamber. Riley stood beside him. They didn't speak to one another, each lost in their own thoughts while they waited. Caleb wondered what the doctor was thinking. About what had happened, whatever that was? About how to move forward? They had never been friends, and he didn't expect they ever would be. Right now, as before, they were reluctant allies.

Flores was the first one to sit up, rising in the pod and taking a moment to look around. She drew back slightly when she saw Caleb, her face twisting when the saw who he was with.

"Alpha," she said. "What's going on?"

"It's time to get up," he replied. "Take it easy. I'll explain when everyone else is ready."

Flores looked the other direction. Washington and

Sho's pods were open, the Marines awake inside. Sho sat up at the sound of Caleb's voice, wiping the gel out of her remaining eye so she could see him better.

"Sarge. I was right. No dreams. Nothing. How long has it been?"

"We'll get to that," Caleb said.

Washington sat up last. He still looked disoriented. Caleb remembered in training how they said the more muscle mass a Marine had, the longer it took for them to regain consciousness. Washington had enough muscle mass for four of him.

"How are you feeling, Wash?" Sho asked.

Washington shrugged before motioning like he was going to vomit.

"Stay over there then."

Washington smiled and looked at Caleb. He offered a wave that Caleb returned. Like Flores, his face dropped when he saw Riley Valentine.

"I feel like I just closed my eyes," Flores said. "It might have been nice if you at least got to have a dream or two maybe. I was hoping for some time with Antonio Banderas."

"Who?" Sho said.

"He's an actor. Was an actor. I'm pretty sure he's dead by now. Sexy, sexy in his younger days."

"To each their own, I guess," Sho said. "I like people I can actually meet and talk to. We're all awake now, Sarge. So...how long?"

"Get dressed first, and then we'll debrief."

"It can't be good if you're standing hip-to-hip with her."

"Yen, you're still a Guardian and a Marine."

She caught herself, stiffening up. "Yes, Alpha."

Caleb watched the trio pull themselves from their

respective pods and begin to dress. He was as eager as they were to hear what Doctor Valentine had to say for herself. What had happened here, and what could they do to fix it?

A little more time to settle in had taken away his earlier panic. He couldn't do anything about anything that had already occurred. Now he just wanted to get to work.

They lined up in front of him when they finished, standing at attention.

"Guardians reporting for duty, Alpha," Sho said.

"At ease," he replied.

They relaxed their posture slightly, waiting impatiently for him to start explaining as if he had much more of a clue than they did.

"Well, Doctor Valentine," he said, turning to Riley. "We're all here. What are we looking at?"

Riley drew in a deep breath, preparing to speak. She didn't even get the first word out before a deep crack echoed across the chamber,

"What the hell was that?" Sho said.

Caleb glanced at Riley, whose face had suddenly paled. The same crash came again, shaking the floor beneath their feet. Caleb turned around, facing the door to the armory.

Something was slamming into it. Something big and heavy.

"It heard us," Riley said. "It knows we're here."

"It?" Flores said. "What it?"

The crash came again. Caleb turned back to the Guardians. "Armor up, Marines. Move!"

They snapped to, joining Caleb as he rushed out into the armory and over to the rack of combat armor. Each suit was custom sized, leaving Washington and Flores to get dressed in their original, battle-scarred SOS. Sho and

Caleb were both more average in height and build, and they picked out unused suits and quickly pulled them on.

Whatever was on the other side of the door hit it four more times while they dressed, clearly not ready to give up on getting through the passage.

"I need a SOS," Riley said, joining them.

"What happened to the Cerebus armor?" Caleb asked.

"Gone," she replied simply.

"Take that one," Sho suggested, pointing to Goth's armor. The dead Marine didn't need it anymore, and Goth and Riley were close to the same size.

Riley didn't argue, grabbing the suit from the rack and unclasping the front of it. She turned around and stepped into it, getting the rubbery black material over her legs and arms and pulling it up over her back. She pulled the front together and closed the clasps, the artificial muscles activating as soon as the seals were closed.

Caleb grabbed helmets from a separate rack, intending to hand them out to his Guardians. He changed his approach when the door cracked again, the rending of metal creating a deafening scream in the room.

"What the hell is running around out there?" Sho asked.

Caleb ran over to the rifles. The P-50 plasma rifles were all accounted for, but they didn't dare fire them in here. They were liable to ignite the ammunition in the room and blow themselves to pieces. He grabbed for the carbines instead, tossing one to each of the Guardians and then one to Riley.

The door shuddered again, collapsing inward with a resounding thud that shook the floor.

Caleb grabbed a carbine while Sho and Flores snapped magazines into their weapons. A fresh crash sounded from the opposite corner of the room, and then he heard heavy footsteps rushing along the perimeter.

"Wash," he said, grabbing a magazine and tossing it to the private. He took one for himself, sliding it into the gun at the same time their attacker came around the corner.

"What. The. Hell?" Sho said.

The thing standing a dozen meters away from them was a trife, but it was no trife Caleb had ever seen before. It was bigger than the queen, with thicker muscles and heavier, stronger bones. Its head was smaller than the queen's, but its mouth and teeth appeared to cover more of the overall area, and it opened wide in an ear-splitting scream.

"Fire at will!" Caleb shouted, raising his carbine and letting loose.

The rounds of four Marines poured into the creature, bullets punching into flesh and sending pieces of the demon flying away from it. The trife screamed and backed away, vanishing around the corner. Caleb could hear its feet moving from them and then down one of the adjacent aisles.

He turned to Riley. "You didn't shoot."

"You're wasting your ammunition, Alpha," she replied. "Don't you think we tried to shoot it?"

"What do you mean? It's wounded."

"Not exactly."

Caleb didn't have a chance to ask her what she meant. The trife appeared in the center aisle of the room, rushing toward them a second time, its shoulders shoving the heavy shelves of equipment aside.

Was it his imagination, or had all of the creature's wounds already healed?

He raised his carbine and started shooting again, along with the rest of the Guardians. Their rounds peppered the creature, but this time it didn't slow. It rose high over

Caleb, right in front of him, intelligent eyes looking down as it swept its claws across his path.

He reached up, catching the limb with his artificial hand, the strength of the synthetic muscles enough to stop the blow. He twisted, yanking the trife toward him and firing point blank into its chest.

The bullets went through the demon and out the other side. It screamed again and collapsed.

Caleb let go of the arm, breathing hard. He glanced over at Riley. "Not that hard."

"We can't stay here," she said. "It'll heal."

"What?"

"We have to go, Sergeant. Now!"

"Guardians, grab as much gear as you can. P-50s and MK-12s, and all the ammo you can carry. Make it fast."

The Marines responded to the order, grabbing the rifles and the ammunition from the nearby shelves. Caleb stood over the fallen trife. He put the carbine against its head and pulled the trigger, spreading its brain across the metal floor.

"What about now?" he asked.

"That'll slow it down a bit more," Riley replied.

"Are you kidding? What is this thing?"

"I told you, it's a long story."

"Tell me it's the only one on the ship." Riley bit her lip. Caleb drew a deep breath and closed his eyes. "Tell me this isn't happening."

"I'm sorry, Sergeant," Riley said. "We had... complications, after you went into hibernation."

"Why didn't you wake us up earlier?"

"It was too late. I barely made it to the pod alive. When things went sideways, they did it at light speed."

"That thing got through the armory blast door. How do we know it didn't get into Metro?"

"It shouldn't have, but I can't tell you for sure that it didn't. My last contact with Governor Lyle ended with them reinforcing all of the hatches and welding them closed. The city was on total lockdown."

"That was over two hundred years ago, Doctor."

"Don't you think I'm aware of that? Do you think any of this is easy for me?"

"What do you mean?"

"You're going to find out anyway," she said. "What happened here was my fault. I caused it."

Caleb's jaw clenched along with his gut. "What?" he hissed.

She didn't have time to answer.

Another harsh scream sounded nearby.

Chapter 4

"How many of them are there?" Sho asked. She had snapped a P-50 to the back of her armor and had an MK-12 in her hands. A long knife sat against her leg, right below a standard-issue pistol.

"There were eight of them when I went into hibernation," Riley said. "The good news is they can't reproduce."

"What's the bad news?" Flores asked.

Caleb noticed the trife at his feet begin twitching. He fired another round into its chest, just in case. "That's the bad news."

"We were hoping time would kill them off," Riley said. "It hasn't."

"Bullets can't kill them, and you thought time would?" Sho said.

"It was the only option we had left. Can we talk about this later?"

Caleb was still reeling from her statement of guilt. How had she caused this? She was a geneticist. Had she created a new kind of trife?

Why in hell would she do that?

"Guardians, pair up and take the flanks," Caleb said. "Valentine, go with Washington."

Riley didn't argue, following the big Marine along the left side of the back wall, while Flores and Sho took the right. Caleb dropped the carbine, replacing it with an MK-12 and snapping a P-50 to his back. He grabbed an extra cell for the plasma and a pair of magazines for the rifle, dropping them into the hardened carry packs on the armor.

A second huge trife appeared in the armory doorway, partially obscured by the shelves between it and Caleb. He wanted it to keep its attention on him, so he fired a round into its shoulder.

It hissed and shifted, tracking the source of the noise and pain. Caleb shot it again, just to make sure it knew who had done it.

The monster screamed and rushed him, bashing the shelving aside in its charge. Caleb didn't need to tell the other Guardians to hit it from the sides. Rounds began punching into both its arms, spitting back flesh and blood. It didn't matter. Nothing was going to slow it down.

Caleb watched it approaching. He only had a few seconds to spare. He crouched low, ready to move in either direction.

"Come on, you ugly bastard," he hissed.

The trife screamed and rose up, prepared to drive both sets of claws down on Caleb's smaller form. Caleb dove forward, sneaking through its legs, rolling on his shoulder and turning to its back. He opened fire, digging a dozen slugs around its spine as it rotated its torso and backhanded him.

The blow knocked him backward, sending him sprawling. The trife screamed again, the sound painful in Caleb's ears. He rolled over, pushing himself to his feet. The

Guardians moved in around him, washing the creature in rifle fire.

"Back up!" Caleb shouted. "Out of the armory!"

The Guardians did as he said, keeping the pressure on the trife as they retreated. They had delivered enough damage to slow it down, leaving it bleeding profusely from countless wounds. It stumbled to its knees, reaching up and covering its head with its claws to protect it.

Caleb retreated with the Guardians, nearly tripping over the destroyed hatch to the room as he did. He hopped onto it, backing up until he was out in the corridor, the others standing nearby, ready to continue their assault on the trife.

"Run!" Caleb said, shifting his finger to the MK-12's secondary trigger.

"Alpha, you'll blow the entire armory," Riley said.

"Headshots don't kill these things. Do you have a better idea?"

Caleb didn't want to blow the armory. He had no idea how large a detonation he would create, or what kind of damage he would do. The Marine module was on Deck Twenty-nine, right above the hangar. The Marine module was designed to be isolated from critical systems, the hangar was nearly sixty feet high, and the hull was thick. The ship should be able to absorb the blow.

He hoped.

Riley responded by breaking toward the CIC, along with the rest of the Guardians.

Caleb counted to three, giving them a head start, holding off as long as he dared. The trife was already healing, rising on repaired legs to resume the chase. There was no more time.

"Regenerate from this," he said, squeezing the trigger.

The small silver explosive thunked out of the larger

barrel, arcing into the trife's chest and bouncing onto the floor.

Caleb didn't see what happened next. He pivoted to the right, sprinting away from the armory as fast as his augmented legs could carry him. The other Guardians were up ahead, already through the door and out into the command center. They had to get further, at least through the module's blast door and into the ship's passageway.

He glanced over his shoulder when he heard the trife's scream. The demon slammed into the wall across from the armory, scrambling to change direction and catch up to him.

He heard the crack, and then the trife was bathed in fire and shrapnel, the detonation from the explosive tearing it apart. It bounced off the wall and flopped to the floor, even as the fire redirected, spreading down the corridor in Caleb's direction.

He raced through the door to the CIC, vaulting the command station as the first of the secondary explosions rocked the armory, causing the entire area to shudder in response. The backwash caught up to him as he neared the exit, the force of the explosion lifting him and throwing him through. He managed to turn his body, taking the brunt of the impact with the opposite wall on his artificial shoulder, hitting it hard enough to dent the metal.

Sho was waiting near the door, and she slapped the control panel the moment he was through, the blast door sliding closed behind him and choking off the rest of the explosion.

Caleb fell to his knees, breathing hard. Deck Twenty-nine was shaking, the ordnance in the armory still going off. The rest of their equipment was destroyed. The Module was destroyed. The stasis chambers and pods were destroyed.

At least the two mutant xenotrife had been destroyed with it.

"Alpha," Riley said. "We can't stay here. This chaos is going to bring more."

"More?" Sho said.

"I'm fairly confident those two are dead. There are six others."

"We just lost our armory. How the hell are we going to kill them? Flip them the bird?"

"Enough, Private!" Caleb snapped, getting to his feet. "We need somewhere to hole up and figure all of this out. Doctor, what do you suggest?"

She hesitated a moment before pointing down the corridor, toward the central lifts. "Follow me."

Chapter 5

"This is apropos, considering this entire trip has gone to shit," Sho said, hopping onto the counter in one of the crew heads on Deck Nine. The bathroom was spotless despite the passage of time, the lack of people to use it and the efficiency of the ship's filtration systems keeping it free of dust and debris.

"I wish I could get into laughing right now," Flores replied, leaning against the counter beside her. "Alpha, I'm about this close to having a nervous breakdown." She spread her thumb and forefinger less than an inch apart.

Washington pointed at Doctor Valentine and then shrugged, turning his hands over, palms up.

"I think we all want the same thing," Caleb said. "Hopefully we can get through a debriefing without any more interruptions. Before Doctor Valentine takes over, let me answer the question I know is at the front of your minds. How long have we been sleeping?" He paused for a second, giving them a chance to prepare. "Two hundred thirty-six years."

Washington tried to whistle. It came out as a burst of air.

"Damn, that's a long time," Sho said.

"It felt like ten seconds," Flores said. "I'm not sure I'm happy to be awake. Did any of you ever see that movie Aliens? This is like that, but worse."

"At least those aliens stayed dead," Sho said. "I never thought I'd be living the real thing."

They fell silent, looking at Caleb expectantly. They were good Marines, ready to accept the facts and eager to do their duty.

"Doctor Valentine, I'd love it if you could give us some idea what led to this," Caleb said.

Riley nodded. "Please, call me Riley. Although, you'll probably have a worse name for me once I'm finished with this story."

"Which might also be apropos to our location," Sho said.

Riley breathed deep and blew out. Her expression was contrite. It was a big change from how she had approached things before they had entered hibernation.

"I know you already guessed some of the truth behind my team and me. Command called us the Reapers. We were Space Force Special Operations, a group of elite former Marines culled from the rest of the armed services. Like I told Caleb, I was originally a member of MARSOC, first as a Marine Raider, and then in operations. I already had my doctorate by then. After school I became a Marine, and then an officer."

"You can't be more than thirty years old," Sho said.

"I'm thirty-seven," Riley replied. "I finished my doctorate at twenty-one. I was a little ahead of my class."

"No shit," Flores said.

"And then you went into the service to run with the

wolves?" Sho said. She pointed at Caleb. "You two never met?"

"I think Riley was already out of the Raiders by the time I went in," Caleb said.

"You were a Raider too?" Riley asked.

Caleb nodded. "Only for a year. Then the trife came."

"If I had known, I wouldn't have been such a bitch to you."

"It doesn't matter now. All of that is gone."

"Right. I joined the Marines because I was bored with science," Riley said. "I wanted to test myself physically."

"Is there anything you aren't good at?" Flores asked.

"Two hundred years ago, I would have said no," Riley replied. "Things change. Anyway, my people were all special forces, all elite level Marines at the top of their game, all with secondary skills suited for the specific task. We had two primary directives. One, find a way to even out the balance in the war between human and trife. Two, solve the mystery of their origins."

"That's a pretty tall order," Sho said.

"It was, and I don't know if Command ever expected we would fill it completely. It didn't matter. We had every resource at our disposal. Transportation, equipment, intel, troops. We probably knew more about the hot spots around the globe than half the governments in the world."

"So how did you wind up in the basement of the Department of Health and Human Services office in Atlanta?" Caleb asked.

"That's a really long story," Riley said. "Did you know General John Stacker?"

"I've heard the name. He refused to help defend the generation ships. He was convinced we could win the war on Earth."

"He got wind of a discovery that was made about a

year into the war. If you saw any news reports, what you always heard was that the trife came down as dust from a meteor storm, part of a two-pronged attack that included a virus which killed over half the human population within six months.

"The reports also called it an alien disease, like its existence was somehow coincidental. It was bullshit the government fed them to keep the remaining population calm. Or maybe I should say a little less panicked. You probably don't know this, but every person who survived the virus, including all of you, are lacking a specific genome key that was traced back to a single dispersal out of Africa nearly fifty-thousand years ago. A hereditary trait that wasn't always passed on, could skip generations, and was pretty much ignored until the trife arrived and we started looking for answers."

"What does that mean?" Sho asked.

"We don't know for sure. There are multiple hypotheses. One is that human life evolved from the same origins as the virus millions of years ago and essentially arrived from the same place in the universe to the planet Earth years apart. There was a time when I accepted that one. The one I subscribe to now is that our enemies first visited Earth fifty-thousand years ago in preparation of the day when they would attack. They keyed their disease to that genetic marker. Maybe they even took some of the people back with them. Then they waited."

"Waited for what?" Caleb asked.

"For us to evolve. Advance. Become a threat. They left us alone as long as we stayed contained, looking up at the stars but not trying to touch them. Then we started sending people to the moon. Then we started sending probes out beyond our solar system. Then we invented inertial dampening, gravity generators, powerful fusion reactors, and ion thrusters. We attracted their attention with our technology and they decided it was time to put a stop to it."

"Why not just give us a warning and let us get on with our lives?" Flores asked. "Or if the ultimate plan was to destroy us, why not do it fifty-thousand years ago before we ever had a chance to spread out and multiply?"

"I can't speak for an intelligence I've never directly met," Riley said. "I guess that not all life forms manage to stay on the positive logarithmic scale."

"Meaning?" Flores said.

"If you look at human history, there are thousands of points in time where we could have fallen apart, broken down, or otherwise lost our technological advances. Look at the dark ages, for example. Or even the number of tribes sharing the planet, still surviving as hunters and gatherers, living in thatched huts and walking around in loincloths. If we hypothesize that Earth isn't the only planet undergoing a similar evolution, then it stands to reason other intelligent life has failed to live up to even a portion of their capabilities. Just because a race has the potential to one day go beyond their world and to the stars doesn't mean they ever will."

"But we did," Caleb said. "We're out here right now. Their plan failed."

Riley smiled. "It did worse than fail. It was one of the greatest motivators in our history. The impetus that sparked the cooperation of every government on the planet in designing, building, and launching the generation ships and carrying us to the stars."

"Oops," Sho said.

"Oops is right. Getting back to General Stacker, he was privy to intel suggesting the newly minted Space Force had found something strange in relation to the arrival of the trife. A piece of alien technology too advanced to be an accident. When we tried to get access to it, we were met with all kinds of blockers and denials, and finally told that what we were looking for didn't exist. That the communications we had intercepted were fabrications."

"You didn't believe that?" Caleb said.

"No. I've run into walls before. The officers we interviewed were afraid. Whatever they found, it scared the shit out of them, and they wanted to make it go away...and fast. For the Reapers, it only made us more curious. We couldn't make any headway with the officers in question, so we started running some searches of our own. We mapped the meteor storm in new ways and with new filters, trying to track down objects that didn't fit the standard profile of the space rocks carrying the trife embryos and virus. We identified a suspicious site in Peru."

"And that's where you found whatever it was you were hiding beneath the tarp," Caleb said. "The package that got Banks and Habib killed."

Riley nodded. "Not exactly."

"What was it?" Sho asked. "And what does it have to do with the trife? Or with the mutant trife that just attacked us? Or with going to sleep for two hundred years?"

"I'm getting to it. The backstory is important because I believe it has a direct correlation to everything that happened leading up to my hibernation, including my culpability in this disaster. Where was I?"

"Suspicious site in Peru," Caleb said.

"Right. We didn't normally run ground operations ourselves. We had all of Space Force at our disposal. We made an exception and took a hopper to Peru. We spent two weeks in the Peruvian Amazon, scouring the area for clues. And then we found it."

"Found what?"

"A shard of foreign alloy about the size of his fist." She pointed to Washington. "It was alien, made of materials we had never encountered before, and definitely not naturally occurring. It was our first physical evidence of a life form more intelligent than the trife, which we also directly connected to the trife.

"In any case, we ran every analysis in the book against the material. The elements it was composed of were about forty-percent identical with elements available on Earth. The rest of it was undiscovered, unique material. More than that, we discovered that at a microscopic level, the piece was layered with tracks and pads resembling the composition of a circuit board. What we had found was at least a part of an alien computer, or more likely a piece of an alien satellite or probe. We postulated its intent to be some sort of a guidance system or sensor array monitoring the initial invasion."

"Damn," Flores said in disbelief.

"Riley, this is all captivating," Caleb said. "It honestly is. But we have current problems we need to deal with. Can you skip ahead a little?"

"Bottom line, we used the composition of the probe to build a sensor to detect like materials. The result of our scan is what brought us to Georgia, and the basement of the Department of Health and Human Services."

"What was it?" Caleb asked.

"That's what I said," Sho said.

Riley paused, still hesitant to reveal the nature of her top-secret package. She stiffened, seeming to remind herself that her secrecy was part of what had gotten them into this situation.

"A spacecraft. A piloted spacecraft."

Chapter 6

"Piloted?" Flores said. "As in, something was behind the stick, controlling it?"

"At some point in time, yes. But we found the craft buried under six feet of dirt. It had been on the planet for at least a thousand years, and it was empty when we discovered it."

"You're saying there was an alien walking around on Earth a thousand years ago?" Caleb said.

"It was on the planet. It probably died almost as long ago. We never found a body, assuming there was a body to be found."

"So the thing under the tarp was an alien spacecraft?" Caleb asked.

"Yes."

"It wasn't very big," Caleb said.

"No. The cockpit would have been a tight fit for the occupant, but we think it also served as a stasis pod for its passenger. The material inside shared properties with our cryogel."

"So it could have come from anywhere," Caleb said. "What kind of engines does it have?"

"The thrusters are small. We don't think the aliens use them to travel over distances. It was probably just a single-occupant landing craft. Anyway, we only discovered it about a month ago. Or maybe I should say, a month before we boarded the Deliverance. We were only starting to really dig into the craft itself. Do you remember the Reapers' other directive?"

"Balance the war between human and trife," Flores said.

"That was our priority, considering the imminent launch of the Deliverance. We were working with multiple teams across the globe to find ways to even out the balance of power. The main advantage the trife have is their ability to reproduce quickly. They can replenish an army in a week where it would take humans years.

"We took a number of approaches, from robots like the Butchers to improved weaponry like the plasma rifles we're carrying, to the combat armor we're wearing, to the artificial limbs we gave the Marines to get them back out into the field.

"As a geneticist on a diverse team of special operations veterans, our approach was twofold. One, improve Marine longevity. Two, undermine the enemy's position. When you picked us up, we were in the middle of launching a fresh round of trials on the first branch."

"Let me guess," Caleb said. "Regeneration?"

Riley nodded. "The combat armor is effective where the plates sit on the underlying spider-steel bodysuit. But as you know, the trife claws have evolved to be able to pierce the bodysuit, and they learned where to attack to get the best results. We can pretty much assure that a trife will try to slice your neck and cut a vital artery to kill you or go for the joints in an effort to disable. If we could negate that damage by enhancing a human's healing factor, we would have nearly unkillable Marines."

"But you tried robots," Caleb said. "How is that different?"

"The problem with robots isn't their overall effectiveness. One Butcher can stand up to hundreds of trife. But robots require manufacturing. They require reliable supply chains. They're made up of multiple components that come from different places. They also require a power supply. Thirty percent of our Butchers were lost not to irrevocable damage, but to power loss. They simply ran out of juice to keep fighting. A human? All we need is a man, a woman, and time."

"Proxima," Caleb said. "If you perfected the science--"

"Given enough time we would have an unstoppable army. But we had to get the science right first. We wanted to have it done before we left Earth. If we could have proven the alterations worked, we never would have left."

"But it's been over two hundred years," Flores said. "Why haven't we touched down on Proxima?"

"Too dangerous. Harry altered the programming for me before he died. The ship isn't capable of sending or receiving communications without my direct authorization. We can't land without my say-so either, assuming we're close to being somewhere we can land."

"Which is why you were in stasis?" Caleb said.

"Yes."

"So we kill the remaining uber-trife and we're home free, right?" Flores said.

"Not quite," Riley said. "You're missing a lot of the story."

"Yeah, like what the hell did you do to Pratt?" Sho said.

"And what happened to Shiro and Ning," Caleb added. "Not to mention, how were you planning on testing your genetic alterations without any…" Caleb trailed off as the truth made itself apparent to him. His eyes narrowed as he stared at Doctor Valentine, a new sense of disgust clouding his vision. "Son of a bitch."

"No, just the bitch," Riley said.

"What?" Flores said. "Did I miss something?"

Washington was nodding. He looked horrified.

"I had full authorization from Command," Riley said. "They approved the whole thing, top to bottom. Sacrifice the few for the sake of the many."

Flores put up her hand. "Wait. I'm still not following."

"The breach into Metro wasn't a total accident, was it?" Sho asked, catching on. "The trife didn't get through that seal on their own."

Riley's eyes dropped to the floor. "No. They didn't. We placed what we called a blocker under the door. It was basically a small circuit that overrode the lock on the blast door and kept it from freezing closed. Somehow the trife knew there was a flaw in the door and they took advantage of it."

"Whoa. Wait a second," Flores said, her voice raising. "Are you telling me Command authorized you to experiment on the civilians in Metro?"

"Flores, keep it down," Caleb snapped. "We aren't alone in here."

"Yes, Alpha," Flores replied tensely.

"Our orders were to find a way to change the balance of the war," Riley said. "We knew if we didn't solve the equation before we had to evacuate we would have to solve it after we launched. It wasn't ideal, but what choice did we have?"

"Choice? You could have chosen not to go after innocent civilians."

"At what cost, Private Flores?" Riley said. "We were trying to save everyone on the planet. We had to do something."

"You did something all right," Sho said. "You did something to Pratt and Ning, and then you lied to us about it."

"You were getting slaughtered. It made the decision an easy one. I gave Pratt and Ning two of the samples with the hope they could help you kill the trife. Pratt's was the more promising approach, the best we had at the time. It did improve his healing factor. Unfortunately, it also made him paranoid."

"And Ning?" Caleb asked.

"We gave him an alternate sample that caused fewer alterations to the genes. It seems all it accomplished was to make him sick."

"And half-paralyzed," Sho said. "Don't forget that."

"What happened to them?" Caleb asked. "What happened to Shiro and Ning?"

"Dead," Riley said. "Killed by David Nash."

"Who the hell is David Nash?"

Chapter 7

YEARS EARLIER...

David's body quaked. He didn't want it to, but he was afraid. More than afraid. Terrified beyond anything he had ever felt before. His bladder had already emptied, leaving a damp spot on his pants and a puddle on the seat of the chair.

He didn't want to be here. He wished he had never joined up with Espinoza. He wished he had never followed him to the mountainside where the starship Deliverance was hiding.

And he absolutely, positively wished he had never stepped foot on this starship from hell, where the trife weren't even the most dangerous and frightening monsters on board.

Wishes weren't worth a damn thing. Desire and hope had no place here either. He knew how things were going to end. The same way they would have back on Earth. With him dead, killed by his nightmares.

Why couldn't he have just succumbed to the virus like his parents? He wasn't strong. He wasn't healthy. He wasn't smart or talented or anything else that had value in this new life. He was next to nothing. A speck of dust on the ass of the universe. He wasn't good for anything.

Well, he was good for one thing. He was a human and had a heartbeat. That was all Doctor Riley Valentine needed him to be.

He had tried to keep track of how long he had been here, tucked away in a cell in the back of the place they called Research. He had scratched marks into his sheets, creating runs in the cotton for each day he believed had passed. It was hard to be confident in the crawl of time without any identifying information. He had settled for basing it on his scheduled escorted trips to the bathroom. Every day included four excursions. They would feed him after every third journey to the head, and on the fourth he would defecate. They were always polite but stern, letting him talk but refusing to talk back.

He did everything he could think of in an effort to form a rapport with at least one of them. He told jokes. He talked sports and movies. He tried to get the men in the group to admit that Doctor Valentine was gorgeous. Every word he spoke fell on disinterested ears. He was a prisoner, useful for only one thing, and they made sure he knew it.

It had been over a year. His twenty-second birthday had come and gone. He didn't know exactly which day it had been, not that the team in Research would have given him a cake or anything. He hadn't gotten a birthday cake in nearly six years, even before the trife had ruined everything. His mother told him he was too old to care so much about his birthday.

"When you get older," she would say, "you'll realize there's nothing special about it. It's just another day. Make the most of all of them, Davey. Don't wait for that once a year."

She had meant well, but he still missed the cake.

The door to the room slid aside, and Doctor Valentine walked in, flanked by Doctor John Byrnes and their head of security, the one Doctor Valentine called Mackie. Mackie was cute too. Not as pretty as Doctor Valentine, but he knew he was too scrawny and ugly to be picky. She had a handsome face and a shapely body. What more could someone like him have wanted?

Of course, sitting in a puddle of urine and shaking like a leaf in a windstorm wasn't likely to score him any dates. He looked weak because he was weak.

He just wanted to go home.

"David," Doctor Valentine said. "How are you feeling?" He noticed her noticing his wet groin, but her eyes didn't linger and her expression didn't reveal any negative judgment.

"Scared," he admitted.

"I know this hasn't been easy for you," she said. "Honestly, when I was in school I never expected holding someone prisoner would be part of my job description. But we don't always get to choose the shit life throws at us, do we?"

"No, we don't," he replied. "I never expected demons to overrun the Earth."

She laughed, causing him to blush. "Me neither. My goal isn't to hurt you David." She moved past the chair to the counter behind him. He hated when she did that. "It's actually the opposite. I want to heal you. That's why everything has taken so long. I'm trying to be as certain as I can that the alterations will be effective."

"Alterations?"

She came back to the front of the chair. "Have you ever heard of CRISPR?"

"No."

"It's a method of genetic editing. You may not have heard of it directly, but you may be familiar with some of its applications. For example, it was used to wipe out the mosquitos that carried malaria, and to create fruits and vegetables that stay ripe for weeks without spoiling."

"Wow."

"Exactly. My team and I have been working to create a tool like CRISPR that will allow us to make better humans. Humans that can resist the trife, fight back against them, and ultimately defeat them."

"I saw Sergeant Pratt heal from his wounds in seconds," David said. "Was that CRISPR?"

"Sort of. Our methods follow the same principle, but we do it by injecting prepared plasma into your bloodstream."

David could hear Mackie moving behind him, doing something on the counter. "You're going to inject me with something?"

"Yes. This is the next evolution of our original sample. We've spent the last year working on it, but there always comes a time when you have to let your babies fall or fly. Today we'll find out which it is."

"I'm going to die."

Doctor Valentine smiled. "Oh, I wouldn't think of it that way. No matter what happens, you're doing a great service to the rest of humankind. The most successful people become successful because they've learned from failure."

"I'd rather help myself."

"At least you're honest. I'm sorry, David. We need you."

David shifted his hands. They were shackled to the chair, limiting his movement. "Like I have a choice?"

"True. Choices are for the strong. You? You aren't strong, are you?"

"I'm a survivor."

"And how do you survive, David?"

David remembered Corporal Carlyle, the Marine who had helped him during the trife attack. He remembered how he had left the man to die, taking advantage of Carlyle's bravery to run.

"Any way I have to," he replied, swallowing hard. He could feel the heat of his embarrassment on his face. He hated to feel so weak in front of her.

Doctor Valentine moved in close to him, leaning over to put her face near his. David's heart began to pulse to have her so close to him. His face began to burn even more. "Uh. Um. What are you doing?"

She put her lips to his ear, breathing into it. He could smell her breath, minty and fresh and hot. "Distracting you," she replied.

Something stung his neck. He grunted in pain, struggling against his restraints. Too little, too late. Doctor Valentine stood up, her expression a mix of amusement and disgust. She thought he was weak and pathetic.

He hated that.

"What's going to happen to me?" he asked, his voice cracking.

"If things go well, you'll show positive alterations in your healing factor, agility, and general intelligence. If they don't go well? You probably won't wake up."

David's fear burned through him. He closed his eyes, fighting to hold it in check. He didn't want to lose control of his bladder again. He already looked weak. Doctor Valentine already thought he was a joke.

She stared at him in silence, waiting. He stared back at her, his eyes getting heavy. Everything was going to go away. He was terrified it would never come back. As bad as his situation was, dying was worse.

He might not have a choice. Choices were for the strong, and that wasn't him.

He sucked in one last breath and the world faded away.

Chapter 8

David didn't know how long he'd slept. When he woke up, he felt good. Better than he had in a long, long time.

Better than he ever had.

He took a deep breath – deeper than he could recall ever having breathed before – finding it easier to breathe than he could remember. He put a hand to his stomach, feeling his stomach expand as he sucked loads of air into his lungs.

Lungs?

"Congratulations, David."

David turned his head toward the voice and realized he wasn't in his cell. He was in the research lab, the chair adjusted so he was lying flat. They had changed his soiled pants and taken his shirt so they could put sensors on his body, but otherwise he hadn't moved.

"How do you feel?" Doctor Valentine asked.

"Good," David said. "I feel good. Better than good."

"Your damaged lung has regenerated. You should be able to breathe like a normal, healthy young man."

"It's amazing," he said. "I was so afraid you were going to kill me, but you didn't."

"No, we didn't. The better news for both of us is that your brain activity is stable. No signs of delusions or paranoia. No signs of rejection of the altered DNA. As near as I can tell, the editing went flawlessly."

"That sounds great."

"There is one complication."

"What's that?"

"We do have to test your stimulus-response."

"What does that mean?"

Mackie appeared from behind the table. She had a scalpel in her hand.

"We have to cut you," Doctor Valentine said.

David looked at the scalpel, and then back at her. He was breathing better than he had in his entire life. If his lung had regrown, why shouldn't his skin?

"Okay," he said. "Go for it."

Doctor Valentine smiled, surprised by his willingness. She nodded to Mackie, who lowered the scalpel to his arm.

She pressed down as she sliced, cutting deep. It hurt more than David thought it would, the blood pouring easily from the deep cut as Mackie dragged the blade through.

"Ow. Damn," David said, looking over at the wound.

Mackie drew her hand back. All three of them watched as first the blood stopped flowing, and then the flesh and muscle quickly knitted back together.

"You did it, Riley," Mackie said, staring at the unblemished flesh.

"We did it," Doctor Valentine replied. "David, how does it feel?"

"It still hurts a little. It feels okay now. Better than okay. I've never felt better in my life."

"Everything looks good so far. I'm pleased with the way things are turning out."

"Me too," David said. He felt so damn good. So strong. His body was tingling like it was on fire. He could breathe normally. What else could he do? "Is this all I get? Super healing? Or is there more?"

"There's more," Doctor Valentine said. "You should see improvements in your hand-eye coordination, your agility, your endurance, and strength. The genes play a massive role in your capabilities and limitations. A larger role than most people realize."

"I can't wait."

"It shouldn't take long. We need to keep you under observation for a while. Sergeant Pratt exhibited a lot of the same improvements, but the alterations had a negative effect on his mental state. I have a theory that the age of the subject is important. Older brains struggle more to handle the change. It's easy to feel invincible, but you aren't invincible. You aren't a god. You're just a more optimal human."

David nodded. "I see. I don't know, Doctor. I feel pretty powerful right now, to be honest." He flexed his arms, pulling against the metal restraints holding him to the chair. "I feel like if I tried hard enough, I could bust right out of these bonds."

"What would you do if you got out of them?"

David paused. "Hmm. I don't know. If I were that strong? What do you think I should do with it?"

"If everything goes according to plan, I'd like to work on making similar alterations to one of the female civilians in Metro, and then introducing the two of you. Would you like that, David?"

David's heart started thumping. He was already

aroused – a side-effect of the sudden rush of energy and strength. "I might if she looks like you."

"I'm sure I can find someone who looks like me," Doctor Valentine said. "In the meantime, if you're willing, once we've finished our evaluation I can let you walk free in Research. You can become part of my team."

"Really?"

"Yes. I never wanted to keep you prisoner, David. But you need to understand how important this work is."

"Oh, I do, Doctor. I understand. You can't make an omelet without breaking some eggs, right?"

"That's not what I meant. The human race is at war, David, and before we didn't have any weapons to stand up to our enemies. Now we have one. You. And if we can make more, and they can have children with the same genes, then by the time we reach our destination, we could potentially have thousands. You'll be directly responsible for saving humankind. How does that feel?"

"It feels great." David smiled. Everything felt great. Everything felt easy. He pulled against his restraints again. Breaking them would be so easy. And why should he be a prisoner anyway? He was special. Important. He kept watching Doctor Valentine. Riley. That was a pretty name. She was a pretty woman. "Doctor Valentine?"

"Yes, David?"

"Maybe you could take the CRISPR? Then you would be like me, and you and me could test your theory. About making super babies, I mean."

She smiled. "I'm too old to take it. I'm almost old enough to be your mother."

"I think you should take it. Do you have any more?"

"We always keep extra so we can replicate it. I'll find someone for you. Someone closer to your age. Metro has a database of every passenger. I can show you their profiles. You can pick the woman you want."

"Hmm." David didn't mind the idea, but it didn't really excite him. Riley excited him. "I really want you, Riley."

Doctor Valentine's expression changed when he used her first name. She stiffened, glancing over to where Mackie was standing. The other woman was looking back at her, concerned. Her hand started drifting behind her back.

"I don't mean any harm," David said. "You're just so beautiful, that's all. Beautiful and smart. I think we'd make a good couple. You said I'm special. That I'm optimal. So why don't you like me?"

"I never said I don't like you," Doctor Valentine replied. "I told you, I'm too old."

"I think I should decide that."

David pulled at the restraints. They broke easily beneath the force, the metal bending out of shape before snapping. He kicked his legs out, one at a time, breaking the bonds.

"Mackie," Doctor Valentine said, backing up.

"Are you afraid of me?" David asked. "Why? You'd rather be afraid of me than be like me? You'd rather be afraid of me than be *with* me?" He felt the heat of Mackie's arm coming toward him. He turned and reached up, catching her wrist before she could jab him with a needle. He turned his wrist and pushed, throwing her to the floor. "I wasn't going to hurt you. But you want to hurt me? Why? You made me."

He turned back to Doctor Valentine.

"Look what you did, David," she said, pointing to Mackie, who was slowly getting up. "We're trying to help you. All we've done is try to help you."

"I'm trying to help you, Riley," David replied. "You can have optimal babies. You can make your own army. Isn't that what you want?" He lunged for her, moving too fast for her to get away. He grabbed her wrist and held it tight. "Where's the CRISPR? I want you to take it."

"I'll go insane."

"Is that what you think? That I'm insane?"

"No, but you're mind is younger. Didn't you listen to what I said?"

"Do you think I'm stupid too?" He squeezed her wrist, and she cried out in pain. "If I break you enough you'll have to take it, won't you? If you don't want to die."

He heard a crack behind him and felt something punch into his back. It was followed with a second something, and then a third. He glanced back over his shoulder.

Mackie had drawn a gun from somewhere, and she had shot him three times. She was preparing to shoot him a fourth.

He let go of Riley, moving toward Mackie. She fired twice more, the rounds hitting him in the chest. It hurt. A lot. But the action enraged him, and he kept going, reaching out and grabbing the weapon from her hand as it fired into him again.

"I didn't do anything to you," he said. "I wouldn't have hurt any of you." He swung his hand into her, throwing her sideways into the chair. Her head bounced off the side of it, and she collapsed to the floor.

David whirled around to face Riley. Only she wasn't there. She had let her friend take the beating so she could run.

That was okay.

He didn't mind chasing her.

Chapter 9

YEARS EARLIER...

The door to the lab closed in front of David. He came to a stop, staring at it for a moment. Riley wasn't getting away that easily. He looked around the room. They had left him with all kinds of equipment and heavy machinery. One looked like a square metal box. He walked over to it and started lifting the heavy machine with little effort. He knew he would never have been able to pick it up before his change.

He had no trouble doing it now.

He raised it over his head, turning back to the door. She couldn't run from him like that. He wanted her to take the CRISPR. He wanted her to be like him. Then they would be together, and they would be happy. Why didn't she want that? She wasn't too old, no matter what she thought.

The door slid open again. Doctor Byrnes and Doctor Craft flanked the doorway, rifles in hand.

"David," Craft said. "Put the centrifuge down and put your hands up. It's going to be okay."

"Where's Riley?" he asked.

"I'm here, David," she said, appearing behind them. "You don't have to do this. We don't want to hurt you, and you don't want to hurt us."

"You know what I want."

"I can't do that. David, if you make me take it you're going to kill me. Is that what you want?"

"No. I love you." He noticed Craft's expression when he said it. "I do, Doctor Craft. I love her. She's perfect."

"I'm not perfect," Riley said. "Far from it."

"You're trying to trick me, aren't you? You think I'm an idiot." David stepped toward them, still holding the heavy centrifuge. He had forgotten they had already shot him in the back. It didn't hurt anymore. In fact, he felt even stronger than he had a minute ago.

"David, don't move," Doctor Craft said.

"Or what, Paul?" David said. "You're going to shoot me? Go ahead." He smiled, taking a step toward the doctor.

Craft did fire, a single round that hit David in the chest. His breath escaped him, and he stumbled forward, the machine in his arms suddenly heavy again.

"Paul, damn it!" Riley shouted.

David recovered his strength and threw the centrifuge at Paul, who tried to get out of the way. It caught him in the shoulder, spinning him around and knocking him down.

The violence caused Doctor Byrnes to start shooting, unleashing a volley of slugs. David put his hand up in front of his face, tears coming to his eyes from the jolting pain in his chest and hips and arms. He cried out, rushing the other doctor.

He reached him, dropping his hand away and grabbing the rifle, tearing it out of the man's grip and throwing it back into the lab. John tried to backpedal away. Too slow.

David punched him in the face, the blow shattering his teeth and knocking him to the ground.

"David, stop!" Riley said. She had backed away from him again.

He turned toward her. "I can't. Not until you take the CRISPR. Just do it, Riley. Nobody has to get hurt. We can be together. I'll take care of you. I'll be gentle. I promise."

He heard the gunfire before he felt it. His head whipped to the left. Harry was there, shooting him again. It hurt so bad. He needed to get away from it. He looked the other way. He was in a small corridor. There was a door at the end of it that looked thicker than the others.

A second barrage joined the first, Doctor Gu appearing behind Harry, sending more rounds into him. He fell to his knees, turning and taking the rounds in the back. He wasn't sure how much more he could take.

"Hold your fire!" Riley screamed. "Damn it, stop shooting!"

They didn't hear her. Or they didn't listen. She was trying to help him, but they didn't listen. He stumbled away, diving for the room, desperate to escape.

"David! Stop!"

He threw himself down on the floor behind the wall, finally escaping the gunfire, which stopped as suddenly as it had started. He reached up to the control panel, closing the door and cutting them off. They would have to get close to open it, and if they did, he would do to them what they had tried to do to him.

He looked down at his body. He couldn't believe how bloody it was. He couldn't believe how torn his clothes were. They had tried to kill him. He couldn't believe he was still alive. He pulled his shirt off, looking down at his chest. He was still skinny, but muscles were bulging out from his stomach, rippling across his torso. The same was true of his arms. He stared at his body as he watched torn skin wither and die and fall away, replaced by fresh skin that blossomed and replaced it, all within seconds. His body was still on fire, still burning with anger, hate and joy, and love and lust.

They had made him unstoppable. Invincible. Riley had lied to him.

He *was* a god.

He smiled at the idea. Maybe not an actual god, but he had power no other human possessed. He was more perfect than they could ever be, and he could tell he was getting stronger by the minute.

He remained against the wall, listening. He could hear Riley yelling at her underlings through the door. She was on his side after all. She was trying to help him. They were the enemy. Her enemy too. They didn't listen to her. He would show them in just a minute. He wanted to make sure he was healed first.

He looked around him. The room he was in resembled the lab, but it was smaller and had fewer machines in it. There was something in the center of the room however, held up by a pedestal jutting up out from the floor. It had a dark tarp over it, though he could see it was folded up on the other side. What was it? Curious, he got up, walked over to it and around to the other side, still listening for the scientists to make sure they weren't near the door.

There was a machine of some kind under the tarp. He couldn't see much of it, but the scientists had opened up a panel on it, revealing a dark sphere inside. It wasn't all that interesting or impressive, except for the fact the sphere was floating.

"What the heck?" David said, leaning down to get a closer look at it. He started reaching out, intending to run his hand around the sphere, to prove it was actually floating and wasn't some optical illusion. He had no idea what the machine was or what it did. He didn't even care. But it fascinated him. How did it float?

His hand came within a few inches of the sphere when it started to react, glowing blue lines activating across its surface. He yanked his hand back, momentarily afraid as the sphere began to spin.

The door slid open. He had forgotten about it, mesmerized by the floating sphere. Riley stood in the doorway with Harry and Doctor Gu.

"David," she said calmly. "I'm sorry for the misunderstanding. Please, come back to the lab with me. I'll take the CRISPR. I'll be with you. Everything will be okay."

"Really?" he said. "You aren't trying to trick me?"

"No. I don't want to trick you. I need you. All of humanity needs you. You're the key to our future."

"Yes I am, aren't I? You made me special. You made me important. That's why I love you."

"I love you too, David," Riley said.

His whole body tingled at the words. "What is this thing?"

"It's another of my projects. I'll tell you more about it later, okay? I need you to come back to the lab with me. I need you to watch over me after I take the CRISPR. It's going to knock me out, and I want to be safe."

"Oh." He smiled. "Okay. Sure. Did you know your project is turned on? The sphere thing is spinning."

Her face changed. "What?"

"It's spinning. And glowing."

She seemed very interested in that. "Can I come around to see it?"

"Of course."

Harry and Doctor Gu didn't look happy when Riley entered the room and went around the machine. David realized they must be jealous because she was choosing him over them. He liked the way that felt, to have them envious of him. He had spent his whole life wishing he was someone else. Someone special, healthy and strong. Now he was all that and maybe more.

"It's active," she confirmed, glancing at the scientists. They seemed nervously excited by the prospect. "David, how did you activate it?"

"I just put my hand near it," he said. "Like this."

He reached out the way he had before, putting his hand close to the sphere. A bolt like lightning shot out into his fingers. He tried to pull his hand away again in response. It hurt.

His hand didn't move. More bolts lashed out from the sphere to his hand, and he tried harder to pull it away. "Riley, help," he said, suddenly fearful.

"What's happening?" she said, eyes fixed on the sphere.

David continued pulling, but he couldn't get free. "I can't get my hand out. I'm stuck, and it hurts."

The energy was swallowing his entire hand, and he couldn't free it. Riley grabbed his arm and tried pulling with him, but it was no use.

"What is it doing to me?" David asked.

"I don't know," Riley replied. "It's never done this before."

"But it's your project." He froze. "You tricked me, didn't you? You said you weren't going to trick me, and then you lied to me to get me to touch it. You knew it would do this."

"I didn't. I swear."

"Aahhhhh. It hurts."

David felt his pain turning to rage. He lashed out at Riley, slapping her in the face with enough force to knock her down. She turned away and then looked up at him accusingly.

"I'm sorry," he said. "I'm sorry. It hurts so bad."

"I'm sorry too, David," Riley said. She produced a gun from behind her back and stood up.

"You can't kill me with that."

"Don't be too sure."

She stepped forward, putting the barrel to his temple and pulling the trigger. He heard the round fire. He felt the heat of it on his scalp. He was aware of it shattering his skull and piercing his brain, and of the machine suddenly releasing him.

He fell to the floor, and everything went dark.

Chapter 10

"Only David wasn't dead," Riley told Caleb and his team. "Blowing his brains out didn't kill him. We thought it had. We took his body and put it in storage so we could do an autopsy later. The alien craft released him, but it stayed powered up. We had never gotten it to turn on before, so we wanted to study it first."

"Haven't you seen like, any horror movie ever?" Flores asked. "You don't leave the bad guy alone like that. You toss him out the airlock."

"We had no reason to believe destroying his brain wouldn't kill him, and I wanted to study the effect of the gene alterations on the rest of his system. Every failure is a learning experience."

"I'm learning a lot," Sho said. "Thank you for that."

"Settle down," Caleb said. "Riley, what happened to the other Reapers?"

"It took about an hour. I was running tests on the sphere, using sensors to collect data. Harry and Bo took Paul and Gina to sickbay to get them patched up. They were both bruised and lacerated from the event. I heard a commotion in the lab, and I went running out there. David was awake and alive. Only he wasn't the same. He didn't speak to me at all, even when I tried to get his attention. He ignored me and went right for the sickbay. I shot him in the back. He still didn't pay me any mind. The other Reapers heard him, and they came back to fight. He killed them, one after another like it was nothing. No effort at all. Harry was with me, and we ran. We got out of Research and into the ship. We realized there was a problem and we had to figure out a way to manage it."

" Why didn't you wake us up," Caleb said.

"So you could die too? I saw how easily he went through my team. They were Marines, Caleb. As well-trained as you and I. We decided to go to the bridge. We called Governor Lyle, and I explained what had happened. I told him he needed to seal off Metro as tight as he could, so nobody could get in or out. At the same time, I had Harry hack into the stasis pods and erase the thaw dates. We decided to wake you first, and we set the pod to thaw you either when the ship was clean or when the power started to reach critical levels."

"When it was too late to do anything about the problem? Why didn't you go to Shiro and Ning?"

"I did. I left Harry alone on the bridge. I went down to the Marine module. Shiro and Ning weren't there. I tried to find them. I used the ship's sensors. I used the cameras. At first, it was like they had disappeared. Then I got a hit on one of the corridors, and when I switched to the closest camera, I got a shot of David carrying Shiro back toward Research. His neck was broken."

"David killed him?"

"That's what I said before. He killed all of them."

"So where did the monsters come from?" Sho asked. "The mutant trife."

"Harry and I hid on the ship. We managed to stay out of sight for weeks. David got close to us a few times. We could hear his footsteps in the corridors. And sometimes he would shout out for me. *Riley, come out. I love you.* He went to the bridge. He knew we had been there. He didn't know what we had done. Then a month went by, and there was no sign of him. We thought maybe the alterations had burned him out. There was a precedent for that. It had happened to a lot of the earlier subjects. We went down to Research.

"Let me guess," Flores said. "He wasn't dead."

"No. He knew we were coming. He unleashed his hounds on us. It was the first time we saw what he had done to the others."

"To the others?" Caleb said. "You're saying the trife are the Reapers?"

"And Shiro. And Ning. He took our research and used it to combine trife DNA with human DNA. He created hybrids, and somehow he brought them back to life. I think the alien spacecraft has something to do with that. We had enough time to put a fallback plan in place. We ran for the Marine module, for the stasis chamber. I made it, barely. Harry didn't. I went into the pod with the hybrid still pounding on the blast door. Part of me was hoping I would never wake up."

"But I woke up, and I woke you up, and here we are," Caleb said.

"Here we are," Riley said. "Two hundred thirty-five years later. Two thirty-six for you. The Reapers are still alive. It stands to reason that David is still alive too. And since you weren't thawed because the ship's sensors registered the ship as clean, it means the power levels are reaching critical."

"And we have no idea where we are in space. We don't

know if we're near Proxima. We don't know if we're close to anything. Even if we somehow manage to deal with the Reapers, there's a good chance we're going to run out of power and die anyway. Is that right?"

"Not completely right. The tests I was running with the alien craft suggest that its power source has enough energy to replace the Deliverance's multiple reactors and then some. That was part of the reason we set up the thaw the way we did. We hoped that David and the Reapers would die, we would wake up, and then we could connect the alien ship to the interchange and keep the lights on, so to speak. Failing that, wake up the Guardians and hope they can fix my mistake."

"I'm honored that you thought of us, Doctor," Sho said. "Really."

Caleb glared at her. She smirked and looked at the floor.

"What makes you think we can fix this when your team couldn't?" Caleb asked. "Like you already said, they were trained Marines too. Better trained than we are, according to you."

"They were caught off-guard, and pinned in the Research module. You have the entire ship outside of Metro, and you were smart and quick enough to grab the P-50s."

"We weren't smart or quick enough to grab our helmets," Flores said. "The ATCS would come in handy right now. So would the comms."

"The rifles are more useful than the headgear," Sho said. "You can't kill a mutant Reaper-trife with a hat."

Flores smiled. "True enough."

"So you think the plasma rifles can do better against the Reapers?" Caleb asked. "Why didn't you try to use them?"

"One of them was always guarding the armory. I barely got past it, and it cost me Harry. You saw the door to the stasis chamber. Anyway, the Reapers can recover from most damage. You can destroy their brain, and it'll regenerate. I don't think they can come back from being burned to ash."

"You don't *think*?"

"I haven't had a chance to prove it. The mechanism behind the accelerated healing factor is complex. It's based on studies done on lizards. Caudal autotomy. They can intentionally shed their tails when threatened, and then grow them back again. We used our splicing technique to introduce the related gene pairs into human DNA. Obviously, something like that takes a bit of trial and error, and we failed multiple times."

"With human subjects?" Sho said.

"Yes."

"Where did you get them?"

Riley glared at her as if she was mad Sho had asked the question. "There's no law left on Earth, Private. There are no rules. No civilization."

"What about morals?"

"There weren't many morals left even before the trife came. We took people off the streets. Scavengers. Survivors. If we had been successful, we would have turned them into superhumans. Forced evolution. Even David Nash understood the value of what we were trying to accomplish."

"I don't believe you can stand there and justify any of what you were doing."

"Okay," Caleb said, interrupting. "Sho, enough. We're about two hundred years past the expiration date on judgment. Riley, go on."

"My hope is that if we destroy enough connective

tissue the target won't be able to restore it all. It takes time and energy to heal. Like the trife, a Reaper's energy comes from radiation. In this case probably the alien power source. We corner it, wound it, cut it off from escaping and keep putting the pressure on, and we can take it down. Alternately, we can try to blow it to pieces or get it out of one of the airlocks, but the first is extremely dangerous depending on where we are in the ship. The second is incredibly difficult."

"And you're sure there are only six left?" Caleb asked.

"As long as David hasn't been able to get into Metro, he wouldn't have the bodies to make more. He created them to hunt Harry and me down. Up until an hour ago, he might have even thought I was dead."

"Thank you, Doctor," Caleb said. "Guardians, fall in." The rest of his Marines lined up and came to attention. Caleb was surprised when Riley joined them at the end of the line next to Washington. "You heard Doctor Valentine's account of our situation. Our primary mission is to take out the Reapers. Secondary is to locate and neutralize David Nash. Tertiary is to capture the alien power source. Riley, how much effort will it be to connect the alien reactor to the interchange?"

"Impossible to say, Alpha," she replied, staying at attention. "We will probably need to unseal Metro and enlist their engineers to assist."

"Understood. Then that's step four."

"Alpha, if I may?" Riley said.

"Go ahead."

"David Nash has had over two hundred years alone on this ship. There's no telling what he's spent the time doing, if he's been doing anything at all, or if he's even still alive. It isn't safe to assume the Reapers are the only threat on the Deliverance."

"Good point," Caleb said. "We need to be careful with every move we make from here on out."

"Yes, Alpha," the Guardians replied.

"Also, I just want to apologize to all of you," Riley said. "My successes made me arrogant. My orders made me cold. This is my fault, and I take full responsibility for it."

"Thank you, Riley," Caleb said. "If you're integrating into this unit, then your problem becomes our problem. The Vultures are family, and that makes the Guardians family too. It doesn't mean we don't have our disputes, but we come together when it counts. If any of you don't agree with that statement, speak up now."

Caleb's eyes shifted to Sho. She didn't flinch, staying at attention, her eyes forward. He knew she didn't like Riley. He didn't blame her for that. She would accept her into the fold regardless because this affected all of them and their sworn duty to protect Metro from the outside.

"Good. First order of business. I want to get up to the bridge to review the sensor data and the camera feeds. Ideally, I'd like to set up operations there, but I don't know that we'll get the chance. Riley, is it safe to assume a Reaper is watching that area?"

"Yes, Alpha," she said. "But Harry and I managed to sneak past it on multiple occasions. I can help guide you there."

"Excellent. Guardians, let's move out."

Chapter 11

Caleb raised his hand, bringing the Guardians to a stop at the intersection. He motioned with two fingers, directing Sho across the corridor. She moved across before whirling around and aiming her P-50 down the passage. She signaled it was clear, and the Guardians moved into formation again, silently covering the corridor.

It had taken an hour to get from the head on Deck Nine to their current location, closing on the bridge. They had used the central lift to get from Deck Nine to Deck Six, at which point they had navigated the interlocking passageways in the same manner. There had been no sign of Reapers save for occasional deposits of excrement along the corridors, most of it so old it had hardened into near-stone sprawls against the sides of the walls. Caleb didn't know if trife had to go the same way. He had never seen trife piss or shit, and he had always assumed either they kept it neat like a cat or their biological process dealt with waste some other way.

The reality of their situation was only starting to sink in for him. It was one thing to listen to Doctor Valentine recount the story of how they had wound up on an occupied starship two hundred years in the future. It was another to really absorb it and become comfortable with it. Caleb had calmed considerably since waking, but he could also sense the edge of panic in his gut, the generalized nervousness and frustration of feeling out of his element and underprepared.

But how could he have prepared to fight monsters, real monsters, that made the original trife seem like wind-up toys in comparison?

Prepared or not, that was the job. It was nothing like he had expected. Nothing like he had planned or wanted. But it was reality, and as the head of the Guardians he had to see it through.

The group slowed as they neared the next intersection. Caleb repeated the process, this time raising three fingers and sending Flores across the gap. She jumped across, using the strength of the SOS endo-musculature to carry her across in one hop. She cleared the other side and turned around, crouching and aiming her rifle.

Her expression told Caleb the status of the passageway before he looked for himself. Her face froze and tightened, and she raised her hand, signaling they weren't clear. Caleb rounded the edge of the corridor, crouching at the same level and spinning the muzzle of the P-50 around the wall, tilting his head to get a clear view.

The Reaper was crouched against the wall, motionless. It seemed to be asleep, but it didn't look asleep. It looked more like a Butcher when it was offline. Powered down. It was silent as it sat, eyes open but focused straight ahead, mouth hanging slightly agape, claws resting on the floor. It was terrifying even in its current state.

Caleb raised his hand and signaled Riley over. She crouched behind him, her head next to his.

"What do you think?" he asked, his voice barely loud enough to form the words.

He didn't need to explain what he meant. The door to the bridge was down that corridor. They could circumvent the Reaper by going the long way around, but it would add hours to their trip with no guarantee the thing wouldn't move. At the same time, if they could take it by surprise here and now they could reduce the population to five with minimal effort.

"We can close in on it from three sides," she replied just as quietly. "Sho and Flores on the right flank. Washington and me on the left."

"Or go past it?"

"You may not get another chance like this. It was far enough away from the module it didn't notice the explosion."

Caleb nodded. He raised two fingers and then pointed across the corridor. Sho paused beside him before leaping across without catching the Reaper's attention.

Caleb went through a series of hand gestures, silently signaling the Guardians on their plan of attack. Sho and Flores acknowledged the orders and began moving away, heading for the adjacent corridors that would re-intersect with the passageway further aft. He looked back at Washington and Riley, and they responded the same way but heading down the opposite side.

Caleb remained static, ears open for the sound of gunfire in either of the alternate approaches as he prepared to launch his own assault. Just because there was a Reaper here didn't mean there wasn't a second nearby. That was the risk they had to take regardless of anything they did. There were no guarantees, and without access to sensor data they were running almost blind.

He reached the four-minute mark of the five minutes

he gave the others to get into position before he slowly rose from his crouch. The Reaper hadn't moved a muscle the entire time he had been observing it. In fact, he was starting to wonder if it was even alive. Maybe things didn't always have to be as hard or as cut and dried as they seemed.

Something bumped into his foot.

It took every ounce of Caleb's control to keep from making a sound or any quick motion. Maybe whatever had touched his foot was still there. Maybe it wasn't. He hadn't heard anything approaching, and he would guess anything that meant him harm would have attacked, not nudged him for attention.

He slowly started turning his head, eyes pressed into the corner of the socket to check on his foot without moving more than he had to.

He looked down. There was a baseball laying right up against his heel. It was worn and weathered, the red stitching coming out slightly. Someone had written on it. A signature.

What the hell?

Caleb wanted to reach for it. He stopped himself. He didn't know where the ball had come from. It looked so familiar to him. Regardless, it was harmless. The Reaper wasn't. He turned his head back toward the creature.

It was gone.

Caleb's heart began racing the moment his eyes fell on the empty passageway. Where the hell had the Reaper gone? In which direction? Had it heard Sho and Flores or Washington and Riley? Had it left to chase them, while he was staring at a damn baseball?

He moved out into the corridor, raising the P-50 and walking quickly down the passage. He listened for an indication of the Reaper's direction. It was too big to move silently. But he didn't hear the tapping of claws or the pounding of feet. He didn't hear hissing or screaming. The thing was too big to hide on the ceiling or in the shadows. It was too bulky to move without a sound. It didn't make any sense.

Unless it was still there.

He stopped moving, staring at the spot where the Reaper had been. Could the creatures make themselves invisible? Or was there something else going on? Something potentially worse.

Caleb aimed his weapon at the spot. He was still ticking the seconds off in the back of his mind, the practice so ingrained he didn't lose count even with the strange occurrences. He checked the plasma rifle, making sure it was set to stream.

The clock in his mind touched five minutes. He squeezed the trigger.

Superheated gas poured out of the muzzle, launching into the bare wall in a ball of red and orange and blue fire. Caleb still didn't see anything, but he heard the ear-splitting, pained scream of the Reaper as it began to burn.

He kept his finger depressed on the trigger, continuing to blast the Reaper with plasma. Its screams lessened a moment later, the sound shifting position as the demon tried to run.

It didn't get very far. Four Guardians revealed themselves at the intersection behind it, four plasma rifles catching it in a deadly crossfire. Their plasma rifles exploded out toward the hybrid, causing it to hiss and howl in pain.

Caleb adjusted his aim, targeting the same empty space where the others were shooting. He still couldn't see the Reaper. He only knew where it was because of them. He had no idea what kind of damage it was taking, or if it would recover from the barrage. He kept firing, watching the charge counter in his rifle drop.

He noticed Riley signal the others to stop shooting, so he stopped too, releasing the trigger and lowering the rifle to his side.

"Cal?"

He heard the voice behind him. He recognized it immediately.

"Dad?" he said, spinning around.

The corridor was clear. What the hell was happening to him? He turned back. The Reaper was suddenly visible to him, lying in a smoldering heap on the floor. Its head had been completely burned away, its entire right side reduced to ash and dust. The smell of cooked meat and fresh excrement filled the air.

The Guardians stood around the corpse with him, watching it with intensity, waiting to see if it would recover from the damage. Caleb could see part of it changing, the cells regrowing, the demon beginning to knit back together.

"Screw this," Sho said. She snapped her plasma rifle to her back and pulled her MK-12, resting it on the floor and unloading one of the explosive rounds from the secondary magazine. "Alpha, permission to blow this thing to hell?"

"Granted," Caleb replied.

She manually triggered the activation switch on the small silver ball. Then she reached into the Reaper, shoving her hand through its destroyed chest and placing the explosive deep inside. She pulled her empty hand back out, and they all scattered back to the aft intersection, getting clear of the creature before the round went off, muffled inside the Reaper's chest cavity. The force tore the carcass apart, sending bits of flesh, blood, and bone to splatter against the passage. It was disgusting but efficient.

"And then there were five," Caleb said softly. "Nice work, Guardians."

"Alpha, what happened?" Sho said. "You look like you saw a ghost."

Caleb looked past the remains of the Reaper, down the corridor to where his dead father had been standing. What had caused his hallucination? A weird side-effect of stasis or was he starting to crack?

"It's nothing," he replied. "I'm fine. Let's get to the bridge, and hope none of the other ones heard us."

"Roger that."

The other Guardians turned back toward the aft end of the passage. Caleb's gaze lingered for a moment longer. He hadn't just seen a ghost.

He had heard it too.

Chapter 12

The door to the bridge slid open. Caleb paused at the threshold. The last time he had been up here, it was to say goodbye to Sheriff Aveline.

It was weird to think that Lily had been dead for close to two centuries. He couldn't help but wonder how her life had progressed. Had she met a man who treated her well? Had she become a mother like she had hoped? Would he ever meet her offspring?

It was a bittersweet line of thought. He hoped Lily had been happy. He hoped everyone in Metro was still happy. It was better they were beyond welded doors, sealed in from the violence and chaos out here under the threat of attack by the Reapers.

"Well, this is going to complicate things," Riley said.

Caleb snapped out of his head, finding her standing a few steps ahead of him. He looked past her, trying to discern the source of her statement.

It wasn't hard to figure out. The stations on the bridge had been ransacked. The terminals were torn from their wires, the displays smashed and shattered. The holotable had been lifted from its moorings and cast upside down. From his location, only the central command station appeared intact, and it was stained with old blood as though someone had died in the chair and someone else, or something else, had dragged him or her out of it.

He was staring at it when he heard a pair of gasps ahead of him, and then the sound of Washington snapping his fingers, which he did to register surprise. Caleb's head snapped up, searching for the source of their astoundment. It didn't take long to figure it out.

The large displays that hung over the bridge were all intact, and all currently active. They revealed a high definition view of the universe outside the ship, a one-hundred-eighty-degree field of view of the stars ahead of the bow. The left screen showed what appeared to be the light of a thousand stars. The right screen wasn't empty either, revealing a light source that filled the entirety of the view, the cameras outside the hull filtering it down to a manageable level. Caleb recognized it immediately as a star, a sun, and for a moment he started to worry that it was the same Sun that had once warmed him on the beaches in California and toasted him on the sands in the Middle East.

That was because the center display wasn't empty either.

"Please tell me that isn't Earth," Flores said. "Because I don't know about you, but it sure as hell looks like Earth to me."

Caleb couldn't argue. He was thinking the same thing. He was looking at Earth. Their Earth. Wasn't he?

"It isn't Earth," Riley said, matter of factly. "For one, it's too large by at least thirty percent. For another, the continents are all wrong. Third, I see two moons."

"How can you see two moons from here?" Caleb

asked. "Or judge the size? We look like we're close to an AU out."

"Don't you see two spots orbiting it?"

"No. You do?"

"I have twenty-five vision," she replied. "Two moons are orbiting the planet."

"How do you know one of them isn't a space station?" Flores asked. "Maybe we're in a galaxy far, far away."

"You've watched way too many movies in your life-time," Sho said.

"You have no idea," Flores replied. "I had a pretty lame childhood."

"Riley, you're confident that isn't Earth?" Caleb asked, skeptically.

"Yes. Completely."

"Whew," Flores said. "In all seriousness, that makes me feel better. I mean, how lousy would that be if we slept all that time to wake up back where we started?"

"You said Proxima B is a rocky planet with a thin atmosphere," Caleb said.

"It is."

"So that isn't Proxima B."

"It isn't."

"Earth-6?"

"It might be."

"What happened to Proxima?"

"I was asleep too, Alpha. Before I went under, we were headed for Proxima B."

"You're sure?"

"Again, completely."

"You're suggesting something happened to the ship's computer while we were in stasis? Because if you are, I can't even begin to consider what that might mean for us, and for Metro."

"Metro should be fine. If they sealed the doors the way I told Governor Lyle to do, there's no reason for them not to be safe and sound. I had a feeling we might not be in the Proxima Centauri system."

"You did? Why?"

"The majority of the ship's power goes to the engines. If we had been floating close to Proxima, we should have had enough energy for at least another century."

Washington tapped on one of the broken terminals, getting Caleb's attention. He turned his hands over and shrugged, and then pointed to the central display and the Earth-like planet floating in the center of it.

"What's he asking?" Riley said.

"He doesn't think it's a big deal. The ship delivered us to an E-type planet. Is that right, Wash?"

Washington nodded.

"I agree," Riley said. "It isn't worst case, which in this case might make it best case." She smirked at her sentence. "It's possible someone did a hard reset on the ship's computer, forcing a reboot. Since the Proxima coordinates were manually entered, they might have been lost on restart, causing the ship to revert to its original target."

"Earth-6?" Caleb said.

"Yes."

"How do we verify?"

Riley walked over to the command station. She made a face at the blood stains on and around it, but she sat in the chair and activated the terminal. "I'm not that familiar with these systems, but if you give me a little time I think I can get you an answer. I can't promise you'll like it."

"I haven't liked anything that's happened since I woke up," Caleb said. "Washington, Flores, keep watch outside. If you see anything, holler."

Washington flashed his thumb and headed off the bridge with Flores.

Caleb turned back to Riley. "See what you can find out. We need any and all intel you can collect, both with regards to our position in space and the Reapers' positions on board. Everything is important, no matter how trivial it might seem."

"Agreed, Alpha," Riley replied.

Caleb moved away from the command station, heading forward toward the pilot's station to check on its condition. Would they be able to bring the massive starship to the surface without it? He was pretty sure the automated systems could manage the landing, but he would feel better to have backup.

Assuming they ever had the chance to land. It was too dangerous to bring the Deliverance to the surface as long as the people of Metro were prisoners to the city, locked in by David Nash and his roaming hybrid trife.

The whole thing seemed surreal. Caleb and his fellow Marines had fought so hard – and so many had died – in the battle to clear the trife from the ship. To have them back stronger than before because Doctor Valentine had continued her work and she had screwed it all up? It burned his innards to dust. It was almost more than he could handle. She should have told him she had found the man he had seen being chased by the trife. He had spent hours searching for him when he was already in her custody the whole time. She should have told him she was going to use him in her continuing experiments.

Damn it. She should have told him how she was planning to use the people of Metro.

He wanted to say he couldn't believe Command would approve something like that, but he knew how desperate they had become by the time Deliverance launched. As much as he hated himself for it, he could understand their motives and their decision. He couldn't say he wouldn't have done the same thing himself.

Caleb reached the pilot station and looked down at it. The controls appeared to be intact, spared from the ransacking of the rest of the bridge. If David Nash was responsible for all the damage on the bridge, he had apparently known or guessed they might need this particular station to get onto the planet. It's role was pretty obvious, so it made complete sense he'd wanted to keep it intact.

"Sarge, you should talk about it," Sho said, coming up behind him and taking him by surprise. He shook slightly, a shiver running down his spine.

"Talk about what?" he asked.

"Sorry Sarge. I didn't mean to scare you. I was just thinking you should talk about whatever it is you're still thinking about. We're a team, remember? Closer than family. What happened to you out there? If we hadn't popped out of hiding when we did, that Reaper would have torn you apart before you even noticed it. You seemed distracted by something behind you, but there was nothing there."

"There was something there, Yen. Or at least, my mind was convinced there was. First, I felt something hit my foot, and when I looked down there was an old autographed baseball there. My father gave it to me when I was twelve years old. A family heirloom. Priceless." Caleb smiled. He couldn't stop himself when he remembered the rest of the story. "Of course, I didn't understand what that meant, so one day I took the ball out and just started bouncing it off the brick wall of my house and fielding it when it came back. My dad came home while I was still playing. He stopped me, grabbed the ball, and stood there staring at it. I thought he was going to ground me. I was sure I did something horrible. But then his face broke, and he started laughing, harder than I had ever heard him laugh in his life. He tossed the ball back to me and he said, hold on, Cal, I'm going to grab my glove."

Sho smiled in response to the story. "You always said you had a great dad."

"The best." Caleb froze. "But I never would have expected him to show up here, especially considering how long he's been dead."

"Show up here? What do you mean?"

"I saw him, Yen. I saw my father. I heard him call my name. It was so real. For a second, I was sure it was real. I had no concept of reality not lining up with him standing there in front of me, even though I knew it was impossible."

"Do you think maybe it had something to do with stasis? Do you think you're having some kind of side-effect?"

"It's no side-effect I've heard of. They warned us about grogginess, difficulty getting aroused, painful urination, and fluid on the lungs. They didn't say anything about hallucinations."

"Well, that hallucination almost got you killed, Sarge."

"I know. Something is going on here." Caleb glanced back at Riley. She had her eyes fixed on the command station's display. "I feel like she isn't giving us the whole story."

"What makes you say that? You know I don't like Doctor Valentine, but she hasn't exactly painted herself in the best light."

"I don't know. Maybe I'm wrong. It's just a gut feeling."

"I think you should tell her what you're experiencing.

Maybe she knows something about it. She is a doctor, after all."

Caleb nodded. "Yeah, you're right. We're all in this together, right?"

"That's right."

"I'll share with the whole group once Riley is done gathering intel. Thanks for putting it out there."

"Anytime, Sarge."

Caleb looked back at Riley again. He didn't know what he was more worried about: that she would know what was wrong with him, or that she wouldn't.

Chapter 13

"Alpha, I've got it," Riley said, finally looking up from the command station's terminal.

It had been nearly thirty minutes – too long for Caleb's liking – since Riley had started her investigation into their location. He wanted to stay on the move, especially up near the bridge. They might have killed the Reaper in the area, but that didn't mean another wouldn't come along.

Caleb and Sho both approached the terminal. "Do you know where we are?" Caleb's eyes fell on the lines of white text running down the display.

"Here," she said, pointing to a series of numbers. "These are the original coordinates to Earth-6. I know because I was there when Harry updated them to redirect us to Proxima." She typed something into the console, and the screen changed, revealing a log not that much different from that of the stasis pod's. "This is a log of events recorded by the computer. Look here." She scrolled down the list a little bit and then pointed. "There. The computer was hard reset about fifteen years into our journey." She typed into the console again, changing screens. "These are the logs of the firing events on the main and vectoring thrusters. If you line them up, you can see the Deliverance reached a point where it began a slow change in course and started to accelerate again. And here, you can see where she finally started the deceleration process, about thirty years ago."

"How long have we been out here?"

"The ship has been in a stationary position for the last nine years, save for the occasional firing of the thrusters. I don't have full telemetry, and I probably wouldn't be able to read it all if I did, but my guess is this location keeps it clear from passing celestial bodies and in an orbit that maintains its position relative to Essex."

"Essex?"

"Earth-6. E-6. Essex." She smiled. "Unless you want to call it Earth-6 for the rest of our time here."

"Essex is fine. Why didn't we land?"

"Like I said before, I have access keys to the mainframe to override Harry's programming. I can start the landing sequence any time, but I don't recommend it right now."

"Right. We either touch down without any living trife on board, or we don't touch down at all. What about power?"

Riley ran her hand across the control surface, tapped on it a few times, and brought up a schematic of the main reactors feeding into the interchange. There was a bar on the left side of the diagram with only a sliver of red at the bottom.

"We're down to six percent, Alpha." She looked over at him, her expression hard. "We're going to need every last drop of it to get the ship to the surface. Essex's gravity is slightly less than Earth at nine point six, and that'll help a little, but not enough."

Caleb considered for a moment. "Do we have access to any of the systems controlling power output? Would we be able to turn off non-vital systems?"

"Like what?"

Caleb thought about it. "We have five Reapers left on board, plus David Nash. Is that right?"

"I don't know about David."

"Okay, let's go with five reapers. How long do you think it'll take to hunt them down? A day? Maybe two?"

"Let's be conservative and say a week," Riley said. "It's a big ship."

Caleb nodded. "Fine. A week. Let's assume we find them and kill them all, and that they don't kill us. What can we turn off in Metro that they can live without for a week? What about the atmospheric generators?"

"Sarge, you want to shut down Metro?" Sho asked. "Those people might have no idea what's going on if you do. What if they panic and try to unseal the doors?"

"I don't want to shut it down, but we might need the energy."

"There's the alien power source," Riley said. "We just need to go down to Research to get it."

"Essex is right there," Caleb said, pointing at the primary display. "If we can do this without relying on alien tech we don't understand, then we should."

"Do you think it's better to traumatize the people in Metro?"

"It might be, but okay. Let's not go that far just yet. Can we access system control?"

Riley navigated to a screen with a line of text on the left side, a scale showing power draw in the center, and a toggle on the right. Every toggle was currently in the active position.

"Here it is," she said.

Caleb leaned over to see the list better, putting his face next to Riley's. He could still smell the cryogel on her skin. He didn't like it. He probably smelled just as bad. He started reading the list. Other than the bridge, the engines, the gravity generators, and Metro's subsystems like the atmospheric generators and filters, there weren't many things pulling a lot of power.

"We could turn off the gravity," Sho suggested. "That would really freak them out."

"That would freak me out," Caleb said.

"You never did zero-g as a Raider?"

"I never liked it much."

"We can't touch the inertial dampening," Riley said. "We'll kill everyone on the landing."

"What about air filtration?" Caleb asked. "There are only five of us out here. We can probably survive on the current air for a few weeks at least."

"Good idea." She leaned over and toggled off the external air scrubbers. "Same goes for water filtration too, I assume?"

"Yeah. Turn that off too."

"This should buy us a day or two at least," Riley said, tapping a few more of the toggles. "What about switching over to emergency lighting only? On a ship this big, all those lights add up."

"We need to be able to see," Sho said.

"It'll cut two-thirds of the lights in the main corridors. Secondary passages will use the sensors to activate the lights."

"That could be interesting," Caleb said.

"What do you mean, Sarge?" Sho asked.

"He means the sensors controlling the lights could give us early warning of Reapers nearby. Of course, it can also do the same for them."

Caleb shook his head. "I don't think they need it. I bet they can smell us from further away than the lights would flash. Turn off the lights."

Riley tapped on the toggle. Almost immediately, half the lights in the bridge went off. "Done."

It only took a moment before the main door slid open and Flores peeked in. "Tell me you did that?"

"Confirmed," Caleb said. "We're shutting down non-critical systems. Stay alert out there."

"Roger that." She went back out into the corridor.

"If the Reapers have any intelligence left, they'll know someone's on the bridge after this," Riley said. "We have to hurry."

"Okay, we gained a few days. We'll have to split the difference on the time we need to hunt down the Reapers."

"Assuming they don't hunt us down first," Sho said.

"If we die, the ship is going to run out of power and everyone in Metro will die too," Riley said. "We either kill the Reapers or it's game over for everybody."

"Roger that."

"Can you get us over to the camera feeds before we go?" Caleb asked. "I want to – "

The main door to the bridge slid open a second time. Flores and Washington both ducked in, the door closing behind them.

"It's getting loud out there," Flores said. "Something's coming. Maybe two somethings."

"Damn they got here fast," Riley said. "We need to go."

Riley turned off the command station display and locked the terminal before jumping out of the seat. Then the Guardians readied their rifles and turned back to the door.

"Wash, open it," Caleb said.

Washington hit the door control and it slid open again. Immediately, he could hear the sound of claws on metal coming at them from both flanks.

"We have to go through one of them," Caleb said. "Cut left, stay in a tight echelon formation and keep you fire lines clear. We hit it with everything we've got and we keep running. We can't fight two at once."

Then they ran.

Chapter 14

The port side corridor led around toward the hull. It skirted the outer edge of the ship and connected to branching corridors that cut back toward the central lifts and the outer Metro seals. The Guardians raced along the passageway, headlong in the direction of scraping and clamoring ahead.

Caleb's experience with the baseball and his father was momentarily forgotten as he led the charge toward what he assumed would be another Reaper. He could hear one of the creatures behind them too, closing on the position faster than they could escape it.

The first one came around the corner in front of them, careening into the wall, using it to help redirect itself without losing too much speed. It was similar to the others, a powerful black mass rumbling at them, mouth opening to scream in challenge.

"Open fire!" Caleb ordered. He raised his MK-12 and squeezed the trigger, sending a dozen quick rounds into the monster. The Guardians behind him did the same, the din of gunfire nearly deafening in the tight confines.

Caleb didn't slow from his run, racing directly toward the Reaper as the bullets ate into its flesh. It screamed again, also refusing to slow down. The creature and the Guardians had no option but to slam into one another. The only question would be which side survived.

Caleb let out a loud, guttural shout as the Reaper neared, snapping his rifle to his SOS and spreading his arms. Bullets continued to pepper it from behind, ripping into its flesh while it covered its face with a large claw.

They came together in a crash of bodies. Caleb lowered himself as it tried to swipe at him, ducking and grabbing it with his artificial limb and pulling as hard as he could. He felt the weight of the Reaper try to resist him as he shoved it to the side and into the wall. He fell to the floor on top of it as the bullets immediately ceased. His face landed right on top of its face, and he barely had time to draw back when the large teeth snapped down in front of him.

"Keep going!" Caleb shouted. "Don't slow down."

He managed to find purchase shoved against the wall, and he drew back his replacement fist and slammed it into the Reaper's face. Teeth snapped and broke beneath the blow, the jaw cracking and the neck forced to the side. The creature fell limp for a moment, and Caleb used the opportunity to jump off it and sprint away, following the other Guardians down the passage.

"Cal. Cal, wait."

His father's voice reached him from behind, weak and tired. Caleb looked back. His father was on the ground, reaching out for him. His lip was bloody, his clothes torn and dirty. A Reaper was approaching from further back, ready to rip his old man to pieces.

"No!" Caleb shouted, stopping and spinning around to

shoot at the trife. His father was on his hands and knees, struggling to get up. Where had he come from? How had he gotten here? It didn't make any sense, but he had to help him.

He started back toward his father, firing into the oncoming trife. His dad was almost back up, eyes grateful that his son was coming back to help him.

Those eyes changed a moment later. His father shook on his feet, the impact force of multiple bullets rocking him back and away. Caleb froze a second time, heart racing and breaking at the sight. He spun around again to find the attacker, raising his rifle toward a one-eyed woman in combat armor.

"Sarge, snap out of it!" she shouted. "Let's go!"

Snap out of what? She had just killed his father. Caleb glanced back at him, out of the corner of his eye. His dad was on the ground again, on his hands and knees and starting to get back up. He had been shot a dozen times. How was he still alive?

A hand fell on his shoulder. "Caleb, we need to go. It isn't real, do you hear me? Whatever you think you're seeing, it isn't real."

"Not real?"

"We don't have time. Come on!"

She pulled him forward. He didn't resist, joining her as they ran away from the Reaper and away from his father. It wasn't real. He kept telling himself that, but he didn't quite believe it. He was abandoning his father, leaving him behind the same way he had left him behind when the trife came. The same way he had left him and his mother to die without their son to help them.

They reached the end of the corridor. Caleb looked back again, tears in his eyes. His father was gone, replaced by another of the monsters. They were gaining on him and the other Marine. Sho. How had he forgotten Sho?

They went hard around the corner. He lost his balance, hitting the wall. The extra strength provided by the SOS helped them power through the turn and accelerate.

None of the Guardians were up ahead. A new panic hit him. Where had they gone? Had his father been real, and this wasn't real?

"Sarge, here," Sho said, pulling to a stop on the right side of the corridor. The first of the Reapers came around the corner, screaming when it saw them.

Caleb didn't know why they were stopping. He was too confused to argue. He slowed again, following Sho's lead.

A hidden door slid open beside them. Flores was just inside. She leaned out past the edge, gripping her plasma rifle. She unleashed a stream of gas at the Reapers, giving them cause to hesitate while Sho dragged Caleb into the hidden passage. Once they were both inside, Flores retreated from the door and hit the control to close it.

"Keep moving, Sarge," Sho said.

The space was small and narrow, a tight fit behind the smooth walls of the outer corridor. Thick cables and pipes ran along the back wall, barely visible in the dim lighting of the access passage. Caleb could see Washington up ahead, stooped over and crammed into the space, trying to fit through the tight confines to escape the Reapers.

One of them slammed into the hatch a moment later, bashing itself against the metal and screaming, claws scraping against where it had seen its quarry escape in a desperate effort to reach it. The other one joined it a few seconds after that, the two monsters battering the wall.

The Guardians moved slowly through the narrow space. Almost too slowly. The Reapers managed to get the hatch to slide open, and one of them tried to squeeze itself in, pressing itself halfway into the small area. It reached out with sharp claws, hissing as they swung closed on nothing but air.

"Washington, hurry it up," Sho said.

Washington looked back and made a face. He barely fit into the passage and was going as fast as he could.

They kept moving along the maintenance corridor. The Reaper extricated itself from the doorway, joining the other one in following along the wall. It bashed itself against the wall, trying to find some way to reach the people on the other side. Caleb wasn't sure this method of escape had been the best idea. What good would it do them if the Reapers met them wherever this particular passage ended?

They traveled for probably another hundred meters, taking nearly thirty minutes to cover the short distance. Then they came to a sudden stop and instead of exiting outward through the hatch in the wall, Washington shifted and hit a control panel on the inner bulkhead. A door opened there, and he shoved himself through it. The rest of the Guardians followed behind, spilling out into the back of what appeared to be a storage compartment.

The sounds of the chasing Reapers died out the moment the door slid closed behind them.

"This storage area doesn't connect directly with the same corridor the Reapers went in," Riley explained, keeping her voice low. "We should be safe as long as we stay quiet."

"How did you know about this route?" Flores asked.

"This isn't the first time the Reapers chased me away from the bridge. I didn't think two of them would show up there so quickly after we messed with the lights. It's a good thing I've used this path before."

"Roger that," Flores replied.

Riley's eyes shifted to Caleb. "Sergeant Card. What the hell is wrong with you?"

Chapter 15

"That is so messed up," Flores said, once Caleb finished telling them about the hallucinations he was having. "Your dad?"

"That isn't the worst part," Caleb said. "The worst part is that in the back of my mind I know it doesn't make any sense and that it can't be real. But the larger part of my experience is telling me it is, no matter how impossible it seems. I feel like I have so little control over what I think or how I react. You've never heard of that before, Riley?"

Riley shook her head. "Nothing we were working on caused that kind of reaction, intentionally or unintentionally. I don't have a good explanation for you. I would say it could be something internal, but it isn't consistent, though it does seem to happen when you're under stress. I'm assuming you went into stasis in perfect health?"

"I did. I watched almost everyone I knew succumb to the trife virus. I never got it. I haven't been sick since I was four years old."

"Maybe it came from being in stasis," Sho offered. "A side-effect of the long sleep."

"There are no known cases of that kind of reaction from stasis pods," Riley said. "If it were a potential cause, someone else would have come down with the same symptoms, both during trials and out here. None of you see anything strange, do you?"

"Negative," Sho said.

"No," Flores said.

Washington shook his head.

"There isn't anything we can do about it right now anyway," Caleb said. "But the fact is I may be a liability. You can't count on me making the right decisions because I might be basing them on something that isn't there. I hate to say it, but I think one of you should take over as Guardian Alpha."

"Sarge, no," Sho said. "I believe in you. I know you won't do anything to get us hurt."

"I appreciate that, Yen. But I don't even know it, so how can you?"

"He's right," Riley said. "We need to look at the whole picture. Too many lives are at stake to take any chances."

"I'm sorry," Caleb added.

Washington put his hand on Caleb's shoulder and squeezed it lightly.

"It isn't your fault, Sergeant," Riley said. "Whatever is happening to you, we'll get to the bottom of it once we reach the surface. Metro has full medical facilities, even better than what you had in your sickbay."

"I know it isn't my fault. That doesn't make it easier to take."

"So, who's going to be in charge?" Flores asked. "I don't want to do it."

"It's my decision," Caleb said. "Riley, you have the most experience. You were a Marine officer and a Raider."

"She's not even a Guardian," Sho complained.

"What was it you said to me before? We're all in this together, right?"

Sho opened her mouth again but didn't speak.

"Riley, someone needs to be in charge here," Caleb said. "I think it should be you."

He still had that gut feeling he couldn't completely trust her, but Sho was the one who suggested he put more faith in her and tell her about the hallucinations. Not that there had been any way to avoid it after the second one. He had seen a Reaper as his father. If Sho hadn't been so close, he wouldn't be alive right now.

And none of them could argue Riley didn't have the experience. If anything, she was a better natural choice than he was.

"I agree," Riley said without hesitation.

"With all due respect," Sho said.

"Private, you're out of line," Caleb snapped.

"No," Riley said. "It's okay. We need to be able to trust one another. Private Sho, you have my permission to speak freely."

"Thank you… Alpha," she said, struggling to spit out the title. "With all due respect, I have a serious problem with putting the person who created the problem in charge of solving the problem. If she was capable of doing anything about this, why hasn't she already? I'll take a compromised Sergeant Card over a questionable Doctor Valentine any day."

"I've already apologized for the mistakes I made. I screwed up. I admit it. But I also enacted the plan that put the Guardians here today. We've already arrived at Essex. If we can finish mopping up the remaining Reapers, our mission will be complete."

"Our mission will be complete," Flores said. "Your mission was to make better people. You failed in that."

"And then we can get the Deliverance to the surface, and then we can go our separate ways and get on with our separate lives." Riley finished without acknowledging Flores' remark. "Until then, you do what I say, and maybe we can all get through this alive. I know you don't like me. Any of you. I'm the bitch who got Banks and Habib killed. I'm the bitch who screwed up all your hard work getting the trife off the ship. I'm also the bitch that saved your asses from the trife when you were overrun in the water filtration unit near Metro. So technically, you're only here because of me for a couple of reasons."

Sho and Flores glowered. Caleb refused to show anything. In truth, he liked Riley more now than he had the first time they met. Maybe that wasn't saying much.

"I'm with you, Alpha," he said.

Washington thumped his chest, pointed at her, and flashed his thumb. Sho and Flores were slower to come around, but they did after a stern look from Washington.

"Okay," Sho said. "But if you get me killed, I'm going to haunt you like you'd never believe."

"Fair enough," Riley replied with a faint twitch of her lips.

"Alpha," Caleb said. "What's our next move?"

Chapter 16

"This was a good next move," Flores said, taking another bite of the MRE. "Thanksgiving Dinner. I was starving."

Washington jabbed his chest with his thumb and nodded in agreement, taking a large bite out of his Coffee Ice Cream.

"I'm just glad these things were made to last forever," Sho said. "Or we'd really be hungry. I thought the goop in the stasis pods were supposed to keep us fed?"

"They do while you're in them," Riley said. "We've been out for nearly four hours. With your level of muscle mass and fitness, it's no surprise you're hungry."

Flores ran her hand along her bald head. "I can't wait to get my hair back. Especially my eyebrows. Is it just me, or do people look freaky without eyebrows?"

"I think we look like the aliens without any hair," Sho said.

"It reminds me of one of the projects I was brought in to consult on," Riley said. "The military was working on robots with fake skin, the same kind they tried to use on artificial limbs. They wanted to use them in high threat civilian zones, to work with the population instead of actual Marines. Risk mitigation. But they couldn't get the flesh quite right and the robots were attracting the wrong kind of attention. We were trying to use genetics on synthetics. It was interesting work."

"What happened to it?" Caleb asked.

"The trife showed up," she replied.

"That's the most common answer to just about any question," Flores said.

"What about you, Sergeant?" Riley asked. "Where were you when the trife came?"

"Middle East. Not that my answer is surprising. Chasing down some terrorist or another. I can't even remember half their names." He smiled. "The dust from the meteor shower was hard to see against the backdrop of the desert, and we were cut off from the outside world while we closed in on our target. We didn't know anything had happened until one of our squadmates got sick, and then two, and then three. We had to bag the mission, and when we got back to base we found out our guys weren't the only ones getting sick.

"The whole thing seems like a blur now. We were called back to the States to be near a hospital in case we got ill. The military invested so much time, energy, and money into us they treated us like VIPs. I still remember about a month in, calling home to check on my parents. My sister had already died by then. My dad was close to going. My mom had it too. The trife were starting to appear. It felt like the whole world was going mad."

"It was," Sho said.

"They kept me on the base for another month after that, until they were sure I wasn't going to get sick. I've always regretted those two months. Sitting around, doing nothing while millions of people were dying. Those were the hardest two months of my life."

Caleb paused, fighting against his emotions. He wasn't the only one damaged by the invasion. Everyone around him had been too, in their own way. When he looked at them, he could see they were fighting their own painful memories, their own inner demons.

"They sent what was left of the Raiders out to confront the trife, guerilla style. We didn't know anything about them then. We killed hundreds of them in the span of weeks, and it never made a dent. I remember at the time we were calling them hydras."

"Like from those superhero movies?" Flores asked.

"There she goes again," Sho said.

"Like the mythical hydra. Probably for the same reasons. You cut off one head, and two more grow in its place. That's exactly what it felt like. I was on the front lines watching humanity fight a war it couldn't win."

"Against an enemy that had been specifically designed to destroy us," Riley said.

"How do you mean?" Flores asked.

"Like I said, I was already in research when the trife showed up. I made the switch after my sister was diagnosed with Niemann-Pick disease."

"I've never heard of it," Caleb said.

"It's pretty rare, and usually gets diagnosed during childhood. It's a genetic disorder, and it can cause all kinds of problems for the afflicted. Ataxia, dystonia, palsy."

"Come down to grunt level, Doc."

"Difficulty with movement and muscle tone, essentially. I thought if I became a geneticist, I could help find a cure. In any case, before the Reapers I was moved to a team studying the trife. We looked at their genetics through every tool we had. We mapped their entire genome, and we realized one of two things. Either God is real, and He wanted to start over, but since He promised no more floods, He sent the trife instead. Or someone else made them. Their properties were just too perfect. Too controlled. Just like the virus. Not everyone agreed with that assessment, of course, but I'm convinced."

"But if there's another alien out there, and they made these aliens, why bother?" Flores said. "They're obviously more advanced than us. Why not nuke the site from orbit, just to be sure? Or whatever passes as nukes for them."

"The trife only attack humans," Riley said. "I'll repeat that. The trife only attack humans."

"They want to get rid of us without harming the rest of the planet," Caleb said. "So they sent a predator to hunt us down and kill us all."

"That's my theory."

"Who is they?" Sho asked.

"Who knows," Riley replied. "Whoever they are, they didn't want us going into space."

"I wonder if they expected us to destroy half our planet fighting them," Flores said. "Jokes on them if they didn't. Plus we made it to space anyway."

"They're a bigger failure than you, Alpha," Sho said.

Riley's expression changed. She glared at Sho. "There's a line, Private. Go over it again, and there will be consequences."

Sho's face froze. She nodded curtly. "Roger that, Alpha."

They fell into silence for a few minutes, finishing their MREs. Then Flores spoke up again. "So, if the parent aliens wanted to get rid of humans but keep the Earth intact, what do you suppose their endgame is?"

"What do you mean?" Caleb asked.

"I mean, when we left there were still humans on

Earth. They were still surviving, even if they weren't doing it well. Today? Maybe all the people are gone. What if they are? The trife inherit the Earth? Or is there some alternate endgame? Does it have anything to do with the spaceship you found?"

"Good questions," Riley said. "I don't have anything but instinct to answer them. I think the parent aliens, as you called them, are preparing the planet for them to take over when the time comes."

"When do you think that will be? When all the humans are gone?"

Riley hesitated. Caleb noticed the change in her face. The slight narrowing of her eyes, the sudden tightness of her lips. It was gone just as quickly.

"Yes. I think so."

She glanced over at him, eyes fierce and defensive. She wasn't telling them everything she knew, and he had caught it.

Who was Doctor Riley Valentine...*really*? And what did she know that she still refused to share?

"If everyone has had their fill, grab a couple of MREs for your hardpacks and let's get moving," Riley said.

"Roger that, Alpha," Caleb replied. "Where are we headed?"

"Stern side entrance to Metro," she said. "Our first target is there."

"You're sure?"

"Yes. How are we doing on plasma charges?"

"My original cell is almost empty," Caleb said. "But I've got two fresh cells in my hardpack."

"Same for me," Flores said.

"I'm already on my second," Sho said. "About twenty percent used."

Washington held up two fingers. He was on his second cell too.

"We need to be cautious with our ammunition," Riley said. "We can't get more than what we have."

"We might be able to get a little more," Caleb said. "Some of the vehicles down in the hangar have weapons and ammo in them, but probably not plasma."

"If we can get to the hangar after you blew our module," Sho said.

"There are entrances at both the bow and stern. Those should be intact."

"If it isn't plasma, it's fairly useless," Riley said. "Other than to harass them."

"You made them, Alpha," Sho said. "Do you know if there's another way to kill them?"

"There is one other way. But we'd have to get into Research. Harry and I were never able to get close, not in the entire time we were out here."

"That doesn't mean we can't do it."

"No, it doesn't. But if David is still alive, Research is where he'll most likely be. He has control over the Reapers. He'll bring them to him, all five at once. We can't fight five at once. If we can reduce the population by two or three, then maybe we can attempt breaching Research."

"One step at a time," Caleb said. "There's too much at stake to take a risk like that."

"Tango Metro it is," Flores said. "I'm ready."

"Me too," Sho said. "Let's go, Guardians."

Chapter 17

"Caleb," Riley said, getting his attention. "I want you to take the rear. Stay close and watch for trouble, but don't take any action without clearing it with me."

"Roger that, Alpha," Caleb replied. He understood the reason for the order. It was the same reason he had given up command of the Guardians in the first place. He was unreliable. Unpredictable. To the others and himself. That didn't mean it was easy to take. These were his Marines. His Vultures. And his wings were clipped.

The Guardians were on Deck Sixteen, in the corridor leading from the central lift. The lighting here was mostly offline, the overhead LEDs only activating when the sensors picked up their motion, giving them twenty meters of light ahead and behind. It was a benefit in that it would signal them if anything were coming before it arrived. It was also going to make it harder to sneak up on the Reaper.

But not as hard as Caleb initially thought. He hadn't seen Riley grab one of the laser pistols from the armory, and he hadn't noticed it snapped to her SOS until now.

She fastened her P-50 to the rear plate of the combat armor and bent over, grabbing the pistol from above her calf. "Our goal is to get in as close to it as we can without waking it," she said. "Assuming it's where I expect it to be."

"I take it you've encountered it before?" Flores asked.

"We had to get past it a few times. The Reapers go into a hibernation state of their own when there's no activity, to conserve energy. They're somewhat aware of their surroundings, but not completely. You saw that with the last one."

"Until I woke it up," Caleb said.

"Yes. We're going to try not to do that again."

"Roger that."

"We get in close, and we burn it. If everything goes the way it's supposed to, it shouldn't be all that difficult."

"If there's something strange, in your neighborhood," Flores said, her lips splitting into a sheepish smile. "Who you gonna call? Trifebusters."

"You have problems, Mariana," Sho said.

"I've got my proton pack ready," she said, tapping on the P-50. "I ain't afraid of no Reapers."

"Alpha, can you shut her up?" Sho asked.

Washington squeaked slightly, laughing too hard to prevent any noise from escaping.

"It's game time, Marines," Riley said. "Knuckle up." They fell silent and serious in an instant. "I've got point. Once we reach the corner, I'm going to start taking out the sensors to keep the lights from coming on ahead of us. We'll stop for a minute to let our eyes adjust."

"How are we going to see the Reaper if you keep us in the dark?" Sho asked.

"If we come at it slowly, it'll be easy to spot against the bulkhead."

"Maybe for you, you aren't a cyclops."

"Trust me."

"Yes, ma'am."

Riley moved ahead of them, and they fell into a wedge formation, with Caleb taking the rear. He was more nervous than he should be. More nervous than he would usually be. He was waiting to start seeing things again, expecting it to happen with each step they took. Would he wind up as the reason their efforts failed? Was he going to cost everyone in Metro their lives?

He hoped not.

They reached the edge of a t-junction. Riley raised her hand, bringing them to a stop. She leaned out past it, aiming the laser pistol. Caleb didn't see it fire until she turned back to the other side of the junction and used it a second time. The laser itself was invisible, but the weapon put out a tight red beam of light to indicate where it was going. It would be impossible to aim otherwise.

Satisfied, she signaled the Guardians forward into the intersection. The area on both sides of them remained dark, a light scent of burned electronics lingering in the unfiltered air.

They moved ahead in near-silence, careful to step as lightly as they could. The soles of the SOS were medium-soft, designed to comfortably traverse all kinds of terrain, not sneak up on sleeping demons. They would only be able to get so close before the creature might hear them and become alert. It had to be close enough.

Their progress was slow. It took thirty minutes to cross three sections of corridor, with Riley stopping to shoot the sensors along the passage each time. The area behind them was pitch black. The area ahead featured a dim red light from above the sealed hatch leading into Metro. They were closing in on the Reaper's position.

When they arrived, the Reaper wasn't there.

"Stay on target," Riley whispered to them. "This isn't an exact science."

They didn't respond, maintaining the silence. They followed her to the sealed hatch, coming to a stop in front of it. Caleb glanced over at the door. The frame around it was scraped and scratched and scuffed, the Reaper having spent a decent amount of time trying to get through. Maybe it had heard the people on the other side when they had welded it shut? Its efforts appeared to have failed. It was trapped out of the city with them.

"Change in plans," Riley said softly. "I'm going ahead. I'll locate the Reaper and lead it back here. Take position near the door and be ready to blast it."

"You're going to make yourself bait?" Sho asked, a measure of respect in her voice.

"Yes. It may be awake as a result of our activity, which means it may be on the move. We won't be able to sneak up on it that way. I'll track it down."

"How?"

"The lights, for one. It probably won't roam far from here."

"You shouldn't go alone," Caleb said.

"I don't want to risk more than one of us for this. It should be me. Wait for me here. Be ready."

Caleb could tell the other Guardians didn't like the idea. He didn't like it either. He had seen what happened when they split up. Someone usually died. There was no point arguing. He had put her in charge. It was her decision to make.

He signaled his acknowledgment. The other Guardians followed suit. They moved into the short corridor ahead of the hatch, the same one where Sheriff Aveline had helped fight off the trife while the Marines delivered the civilians to the city. It felt like yesterday to Caleb. It *was* yesterday to

Caleb, even though it had happened over two hundred years ago.

"I'm going down the port side corridor, around the outside of Metro," Riley said. "If I'm not back in twenty minutes, it's probably better if you don't come looking for me."

The Guardians signaled acknowledgment and Riley vanished down the passageway.

"I give her credit for having the guts to go out there alone," Sho whispered.

"She's going to get herself killed," Flores said.

"I don't think so," Caleb said. "She survived out here in the beginning. Stay quiet and be ready. For all we know, the Reaper might come back before she does."

"Roger that, Sarge."

Caleb checked his P-50 and then crouched behind Flores and Sho, aiming over their shoulders.

Whatever happened next, he was ready for it.

Chapter 18

Caleb thought he was ready. He was expecting either the Reaper to come around the corner alone or for Riley to come through first, signaling them that it was time to shoot.

The minutes passed in silence. The tension increased with each tick, ratcheting up as they waited for Riley to return. Five minutes. Ten. Fifteen. She had asked for twenty minutes to find the Reaper. It seemed she was going to use every last one of them.

"Stay alert," he whispered to Sho and Flores, making sure they weren't getting distracted by the wait.

Flores shifted her plasma rifle, getting the muzzle aimed out into the corridor again instead of drooping toward her feet. Sho smiled in response to the movement. Caleb was sure Washington was doing the same behind him.

Seventeen minutes passed. Eighteen. The only sound was a soft hum from beyond the hatch. No scratching or clawing, and no sense of imminent danger. Caleb was grateful his hallucinations seemed to have subsided, at least for now. But he wondered...when the action started again, would he relapse?

Nineteen minutes went by. Caleb tracked each second in his head, keeping an accurate count gained by years of experience. Riley had told them if she wasn't back in time to assume she wasn't coming back at all. He couldn't help but wonder if she had used the opportunity to abandon them. To leave them behind while she did...what, exactly? Where was she going to go? There was no scenario he could think of where leaving them where she had made any sense.

After the twenty-minute mark came and went without her return, he started to fear the worst. She knew hunting the Reaper alone was a risk, but it was a risk she wanted to take. Had her gamble failed to pay off?

He knew the other Guardians were thinking the same thing. Sho glanced back at him, taking her eye off the corridor to express the question.

"Eye ahead," Caleb said, getting her to refocus her attention. "We'll give her another minute."

"What if she doesn't come back?" Flores asked.

"We go find her."

"Sarge, she said to—"

"I know what she said. I'm saying we go find her. I'm still Guardian Beta."

"There is no Guardian Beta. Only Alpha."

"There is now. Give her another minute."

"Roger that."

Caleb ticked off the seconds, counting down from sixty. He was sure the others were doing the same. He started getting worried again when he reached twenty. They were going to have to look for her.

He started to shift, to stand upright but paused, hearing a light tapping in the distance. It grew quickly in volume, revealing itself as the rapid cadence of someone running fast and hard.

"Get ready," Caleb said. "Here she comes."

They brought their plasma rifles up, leaving a decent space between each of them so they could fire safely in stream mode. Caleb shifted his finger to the trigger, preparing to squeeze it.

The footsteps grew in volume and intensity, and Caleb nearly lost his focus when he thought he heard four taps instead of two. He leaned over Sho and Flores, turning his head to the side to better hear Riley's approach.

Clomp. Tap. Clomp. Tap. Tap. Tap, Tap. Clomp. Clomp. Clomp.

What the hell?

Trife didn't make a sound like that when they ran.

He recognized the clomp as that of Guardian armored boots. Riley's boots. But the *tap, tap, tap, tap* that came along behind was unidentifiable.

The cadence was growing closer. Caleb was tempted to go out into the corridor to see what was chasing Riley, but he stayed where he was. "Here we go," he said softly as he began putting pressure on the trigger of his plasma rifle, ready to unleash its fury.

The footsteps reached the corner. Then Riley burst past them at an all-out sprint, arms pumping, mouth open to breathe. She whipped past the corridor in less than a second, running faster than Caleb would have given her credit for and offering them little time to shoot.

He began pulling his trigger, freezing in place when he saw what came next. He was expecting a Reaper, large and black and demonic. That wasn't what ran past.

He should have started shooting. He didn't. He watched the thing go by in a blur, turning his head to follow it back out of view.

"Was that?" Sho started to ask.

"I think so," Caleb replied, moving past her and into the corridor. He chased the thing chasing Riley with his eyes, trying to make sense of it.

It wasn't a Reaper running behind her.

It was the Cerebus armor.

"Come on!" Caleb said, jumping over Flores and Sho and taking the lead position in the chase. The other Guardians rose behind him, rushing out into the corridor at his back.

The Cerebus was already dozens of meters ahead, nearing the next intersection. Riley had already gone around it, vanishing from sight.

"They're too fast," Flores complained as they began their sprint.

"You can do it, Flo," Caleb said. "Let's go Marines!"

His legs pumped beneath him, the artificial muscles in the SOS adding power to every step and driving him forward faster than he could run on his own. He barreled down the corridor, quickly breaking away from the other Guardians as he approached the junction. The Cerebus had turned right, which meant Riley had turned right. He slowed to follow, using the wall to redirect himself while making sure to keep the plasma rifle in firing position.

The passage along the port side of Metro was as long as the city, nearly two kilometers from end-to-end. Caleb could see where Riley was in relation to them by the overhead lights that illuminated and dimmed as she and the Cerebus rushed past. Caleb switched his grip on the P-50 and swung it to his back, exchanging it with the MK-12 while still on the run. He found the trigger and aimed wildly, unleashing a half-dozen rounds toward the Cerebus' back, hoping to get its attention.

It didn't pay him any mind, not even when a second

volley threw up quick sparks as the bullets impacted its armored back. It would be easier to hurt the Reapers with conventional rounds than it would be to hurt the Cerebus. Short of using one of the grenades loaded in the MK-12's secondary barrel, he had no idea how to damage the thing.

He wasn't even sure that would be enough.

He stopped shooting but kept running, desperate to keep the armor in his sights. It had to be David Nash inside, chasing down the woman who had turned him into whatever he had become. The woman he had lusted after once the genetic alterations had made him whole. Riley hadn't been completely clear about David's intention. Was it to kill every other human outside Metro? To force her to let him into the city? To coerce her into having sex with him? The way she had described the man, he seemed relatively simple-minded and unintelligent. Could his motive really be as base as that?

Either way, they had to stop him.

He kept running, not gaining ground but not losing any either. However, the rest of the Guardians fell further behind.

Caleb could barely see them as he reached the kilometer mark, the halfway point of the corridor. Broken on the right side by another hatch into Metro, it was sealed and scratched, with a solid red light illuminating the short corridor leading to it.

It had a Reaper waiting at the door.

It was probably hibernating when Riley ran by and before Caleb had opened fire. It was awake now, listening to his footsteps and waiting for him as he crossed the gap. It sprang at him, leaving its feet in a powerful lunge. It reached out and slashed at Caleb's arm at the same time it tackled him, knocking the MK-12 from his grip.

The SOS saved him from the claws, the armor plating

catching the brunt of the assault and deflecting it. But it didn't stop the momentum from carrying Caleb and the Reaper sideways into the bulkhead. Both of them slammed hard against the metal wall, causing them to ricochet off. The Reaper regained itself first, screaming as it grabbed Caleb's artificial arm and yanked him in the opposite direction, throwing him against the sealed hatch.

Caleb hit hard, sending waves of pain down his spine as he quickly regained himself, ducking beneath a heavy claw and coming up with a solid punch from his artificial hand. He hit the Reaper in the mouth, breaking its teeth and whipping its head sideways. Its body followed, and it rolled over and backed up, its screams muffled by the damage to its face.

Caleb used the opportunity to grab his plasma rifle, swinging it back toward the Reaper. The demon hissed as it was hit from the side, a stream of superheated gas washing over it and burning into its shoulder.

Sho led the Guardians forward in a walking crouch, leaving room overhead for Washington to fire on the Reaper. Caleb squeezed the trigger on his rifle, adding more fuel to the fire, melting the creature's flesh and muscle and then bone. Its screams died as it died, dropping to the floor in a gooey heap.

The Guardians stood over it, Flores joining the assault as they spread out around it, all firing into Reaper in the center until it was little more than a pile of ash on the floor.

"Trifebusters!" Flores said, cutting off her stream and raising the P-50's muzzle to her face. She blew on the end of it. "That is how it's done!"

Caleb smiled lightly, turning his attention back to the long corridor. The Cerebus was gone.

So was Doctor Valentine.

Chapter 19

"I'm not sure whether I'm happy about this or not," Sho said. "We killed another Reaper, and our new Alpha is gone."

"I'm not happy about it," Caleb said. "That was the Cerebus armor chasing her. Most likely David Nash."

"At least we know he's alive. Do you think he caught her?"

Caleb shook his head. "I don't know. He wasn't far behind her. One slip and he would be all over her. We already know that armor is higher-end than the SOS. No matter what any of us think of Riley, she knows the Reapers and David better than any of us. We'd be operating blind without her."

"He won't kill her though, will he?" Flores asked. "Why run her down like that if he could have just shot her?"

"No, he probably won't hurt her...badly, anyway," Caleb agreed. "Odds are he's going to bring her back to Research."

"I bet he's happy as a pig in shit that he got her after all this time," Sho said.

"We don't know yet if he got a hold of her. If he did, then our job is to ruin his day. We've got four Reapers left, plus Nash. I want this over ASAP so we can get on with our lives."

"Roger that, Sarge. What about your hallucinations?"

"I don't know. I didn't have any that time, and that Reaper got me good." Caleb stretched his back. His body was sore from the blow he had taken, his muscles stiffening up. "Talk about stressed."

"Maybe it isn't caused by stress after all?" Sho offered.

"Maybe you're right. Whatever it is, we have to shelve it for now. I appreciate Riley's eagerness to do the right thing for once, but in this case it might have been a mistake to give her a chance. I wouldn't have sent any of you off alone."

"She wanted to play the hero; she got what she had coming if you ask me," Sho said. "You can't blame yourself for every decision you make, especially after the fact. If things had gone the way we planned we'd all be hailing her as a genius. In any case, what's our next move, Alpha?"

"Riley didn't think it would be a good idea to go down to Research with five Reapers still on the loose. But if David took her down there, he did it for a reason. We can't let him have whatever it is he's after."

"So we go to Research?" Flores asked.

"Affirmative. But I don't want to go charging down there in pursuit. We need to be smart about this. Smarter than we've been so far. We keep finding ourselves on the defensive, reacting instead of acting. Even when we think we have the drop on the enemy."

"How do you propose we change that?" Sho asked.

"We need to be better prepared."

"How? We don't know what we'll be up against."

"Yes, we do. They're still trife, and we've learned how to attract trife."

"They aren't only trife," Flores said. "They're Shiro and Ning, Craft and Byrnes. This is sort of like the Island of Dr. Moreau."

"If that's another movie, just shoot me now," Sho said.

Washington grinned.

"Well, it is," Flores said. "Violent half-human, half-animal creatures? Trapped on an island, or a starship. Crazy doctor."

"David Nash isn't a doctor."

"I was talking about Riley. If it helps, it was a book before it was a movie."

"It doesn't help."

Washington tapped on Caleb's shoulder and then pointed to his head, spreading his hand away from it to ask what he was thinking.

"Comm signals," Caleb said. "We should be able to use them to draw the Reapers out to where we want them."

"We lost our comms in the armory," Sho said.

"Our ATCS, yes. They aren't the only comms on board."

Sho smiled. "Oh. I think I get it. You're talking about the hangar, right? The drones?"

"Exactly. The drones are too big to fly around the ship, but if we relieve them of their wings, we can carry them to where we want them. Then we turn them on and activate their comm relays. The signal goes back to the armored drone carrier."

"Will the Reapers go for the transmitter or the receiver?" Flores asked. "Or both?"

"Let's assume both. The good news is the ADC is protected."

"Okay, so let's say we do this," Sho said. "We get the Reapers to follow the signal back to the drones. How do we make sure only one of them comes instead of all of them?"

"The more, the merrier," Caleb said. "Did you notice what else is in the hangar?"

"I guess not."

"An entire unit of Stingers, complete with chest-mounted rocket launchers. We rig the drones with explosives, and when the Reapers show up to check them out…"

"Boom," Sho said.

"Boom," Flores said.

Washington slammed his fist down into his palm.

"Exactly. With any luck, we get all four of them with one shot."

"And you didn't want to be in charge, Sarge?" Sho asked.

"I wish I had thought of it sooner. I'm doing my best to do the right thing for the people in Metro, and for my team."

"We know, Alpha," Flores said. "We're all doing the best we can with this chaos. Screw the trife."

"Let's not waste any more time. We need to take the long way around to get to the hangar. I want the trife off my ship, Marines. And I want it now."

Chapter 20

The Guardians didn't run into any opposition on the way to the hangar. They traversed the passageways and stairwells as if they could run into trouble at a moment's notice. Travel through the ship was eerie and tense, the dim, motion-activated lighting keeping their nerves taut as they covered the distance between the port hatch into Metro and the main hangar on Deck Thirty, near the stern. Only one deck below was the destroyed Marine module and armory.

They paused every thirty seconds, listening for the unmistakable clicking of trife claws on the metal floor, as well as the tapping of boots – either Riley's or those of the Cerebus. Caleb continued hoping Riley would turn up again. There was a chance she had escaped David Nash since she seemed to know at least some of the layout of the maze of maintenance passages spread behind the ship's main corridors. If she managed to duck into one unseen, he had no doubt she could sneak away from David.

But would she know where to find *them*?

She would know it was too dangerous for them to

continue the chase. She would agree they had a bigger responsibility to the rest of the colony. It didn't sit well with Caleb to leave someone behind – not at all – but he had done it without hesitation because he understood what was at stake. There were forty-thousand souls behind those sealed hatches, waiting for someone to let them out somewhere they could thrive.

He wasn't going to let them down. Not for anything.

He stretched his shoulders for the hundredth time, hearing them crack as he worked out the kinks the Reaper had caused. It was going to hurt even more tomorrow, so he wanted to finish the mission today. He was fortunate the Reaper's claws had hit the armor instead of catching the bodysuit. The hardened plates had deep gouges in them from the attack, but hadn't been penetrated.

The Guardians remained silent as they reached the bow facing the hatch into the hangar. The corridor they were in was taller and wider than any others in the ship, having served as the primary access corridor between the outside of the Deliverance and the main hold where Metro was built. Caleb had only witnessed the construction in fits and starts between missions, but he could still remember watching them lift the prefabricated blocks into the hangar, where they were placed on the wide, flat loaders and transported across the deck to an equally large maintenance lift. He had never personally seen the process after that, but he had heard the blocks were moved to the lifts, brought up into the hold, and then manually carried across the city, where they were put into place by workers wearing Strongman exosuits. Caleb had seen the suits in the hangar during the fighting. They were incredibly useful for hard, heavy labor. They were too power-hungry and slow though to be worthwhile in a fight.

"Let's hope the door still works," Sho said, moving ahead of the group to activate the control panel.

"Stay alert," Caleb said. "If I were a Reaper, I might like to hide down here."

The door made a loud clunking noise, and then slowly began to spread apart, whining as it did. It made it almost a meter before the whining turned to grinding, and the door froze in place, stuck.

"It sort of works," Flores said.

"Good enough," Caleb said. "Wash, take point. Eyes open."

Washington moved ahead, fearlessly approaching the partial opening. The hangar was dark behind it, a large portion of the overhead lighting likely destroyed when the armory had blown. He raised his P-50 and stepped into the hangar, sweeping left and right. Smoke began to waft out from the freshly opened door, the smell of burnt ordnance heavy in it.

Washington raised his hand and waved them in, signaling the entrance was clear. The rest of the Guardians joined him just inside the malfunctioning hatch.

"Nice work, Alpha," Flores said, motioning to the debris spread across part of the floor and over some of the vehicles in the vast space.

Caleb looked up. There was an irregular opening in the ceiling, nearly ten meters across and four meters wide. It was smaller than the armory as a whole and the damage was less extensive than he had been expecting, proving the lightweight alloy they had used to build the ship was stronger than it looked or felt.

"Not too bad, all things considered," he replied. His eyes dropped, scanning the rest of the hangar. It was too dim to see more than a short distance ahead, but it was probably for the best. Entering the hangar brought back bad memories, both of the fight against the trife in the space, and of the cleanup the Guardians had done before entering hibernation. There had been so many bodies of so many Marines. Marines he had lunched with in the mess, worked out with in the gym, played basketball with, trained with. And of course there had been trife. Too many to count. He could still recall the smell of the hangar when they had entered it the first time, the stench of death, both human and alien. It made him feel nauseous again now.

He swallowed the bile rising into his throat, glancing at the other Guardians. They wore their expressions of pain and difficulty as they stepped lightly through the space. There were still stains on the floor they had no way of removing, and none of them wanted to desecrate the ones that had been made with human blood.

"Stay alert," Caleb repeated. "Sho, take the stern side with Washington. Flores, you're with me. We'll meet up in the middle. We need to find the ADC and the builders. Knock the floor to check in. Sixty seconds."

"Roger that," Sho said, speeding up to reach Washington's side.

They quickened their pace, bypassing the rows and columns of equipment to cross to the opposite end of the hangar. Caleb and Flores turned to the right and went into the midst of the first group of machinery. Two of the long, wide, flat transporters were on their left, while the bulkhead to the right was lined with at least fifty Strongman exosuits followed by a series of metal storage crates. Caleb only opened one of the crates, finding it stocked with neatly organized groupings of smaller construction materials, mainly bolts and screws.

He felt the vibrations on his feet and heard the thumping when Sho and Washington reported in. He turned his P-50 over and smacked the stock into the floor to respond.

Caleb and Flores reached the end of the first row and crossed between the transporter and the back wall. The second grouping of equipment was a lot more promising. He spotted the builders right away, shorter than the transporters and rising to half the height of the ceiling. They had been attacked by the dirt and debris that had come down from the armory, and Caleb could only hope they hadn't been too damaged by the explosion.

He bumped his stock on the floor, using morse code to spell out BUILDERS. Sho and Washington knocked back ROGER.

"I'm going up," Caleb announced, reaching the side of the first builder. "Wait here and check in with Sho and Wash on schedule."

"Roger that, Alpha," Flores replied.

Caleb climbed the rungs on the side of the builder, up to the small cab. The machine had a large secondary booth behind it, and Caleb opened the door to it and ducked inside. The space was mostly taken up by the machinery that worked the crane above his head, but there were also storage racks containing smaller manual tools like rock cutters, and of course explosives. It might have seemed stupid to keep explosives near the moving parts of the builder, but the T-9 was incredibly stable without a detonator. Those were stored in a locked bin on a bottom rack opposite the charges.

Caleb knelt down in front of the bin. The lock was external, thick and heavy and simple. It was meant as more of a warning not to open the bin without authorization than as a deterrent. All it took to snap the lock was a quick tug from his artificial hand.

He grabbed four detonators, sticking them in one of

his SOS's hardpacks. Then he stood and crossed back around the machinery to the rack with the explosives. A simple sliding chain-link door separated him from the T-9.

He unlatched it and pulled it aside. Taking four of the dark-brown bars of the explosive, he left the cab.

Not even a minute had passed when he looked down to where he had left Flores. He saw only the floor beneath him.

She was gone.

Chapter 21

Caleb's heart sped up, but he refused to panic. There had to be a reason she had wandered away from the builder without a word. Was it because Sho and Washington were in trouble? Why didn't she say anything?

He jumped off the builder, letting his SOS absorb the impact. He knocked his rifle into the floor.

SITREP.

The knock came back immediately.

ADC.

They had found it. So where the hell was Flores?

"Flores," Caleb said at normal volume, hoping she hadn't gotten too far. "Flores, report."

There was no response.

"Flores," he said, a little louder.

Nothing.

Caleb hit his rifle on the floor.

SOS.

He heard Sho and Washington's running feet a few seconds later, heading across the hangar. He ran out toward the end of the equipment to meet them and he froze as he cleared the vehicles. Flores was ahead of him, crossing the space in a direct line toward the open panel where the blast door's manual controls were located.

"Flores!" he shouted.

She didn't look back at him. She didn't stop walking.

"Sarge?" Sho said, off to his right.

He had no idea what Flores was doing or why. If she opened the blast door, they were all going to die. Without the air filtration system active, even if they didn't get sucked out into space they would suffocate in a hurry.

"We have to stop her!" he said. She was too far away for him to run her down, but he started after her anyway, raising his plasma rifle and switching it to bolt mode. The last thing he wanted to do was shoot her, but he might not have a choice.

Sho broke from her position, racing laterally across the hanger. She was closer to Flores than Caleb was, but not by much. Would she reach her in time?

Flores stopped suddenly, turning toward Sho, bringing her rifle up to a ready position. Sho tried to stop her momentum, to ease the threat before she got shot. Caleb kept going, only to have Flores turn on him instead. He brought his artificial limb up, getting it in front of his face as she squeezed the trigger, the plasma rifle belching heat from its muzzle. The gas was partially deflected by the armor and the arm beneath it, burning through the SOS.

As Caleb rolled away from the plasma bolt. Flores spun back toward Sho as she tried to close on her. A loud crack like thunder sounded from across the hangar. Flores' head turned slightly, and she dropped to the floor.

Caleb got up and rushed over to her, falling on his knees at her side, joined by Sho a moment later. A line of fresh blood was running from her temple area where the round had grazed her. He put his fingers against her neck, feeling for a pulse. She was alive. He turned his head to look back at Washington, who was walking toward them. He gave the big Marine a thumbs up, and Washington returned it.

It was a near impossible shot, especially with the way Flores had been moving and without the ATCS targeting to assist with the aim. But Washington rarely missed.

"We don't have any patches," Sho said.

"Just put pressure on it," Caleb replied. "It isn't too deep."

"What the hell was she doing?"

"I don't know. If I had to guess, I would say she was hallucinating."

"Her too? Shit, Sarge. Did the stasis make us all insane or what?"

"I don't know, but I feel like all signs point back to Riley Valentine and David Nash."

"Roger that."

"Wash, help me get her to the ADC. We made enough noise to attract a Reaper if there are any nearby."

Washington hurried the rest of the way over, gently scooping up Flores and running back to the ADC with Sho and Caleb. The ADC was long and low and covered in thick armor, with half a dozen drones mounted to the top of it. The back ramp was already down, revealing a control center inside, six chairs with six terminals and joysticks to control the drones. The drones were supposed to be used as part of the expected exploration of their new home, but like the builder's explosives, they needed them for another purpose right now.

Forced to duck low to fit inside the vehicle, Washington

brought Flores on board. Sho and Caleb joined him, and Caleb hit the button to close the ramp once they were all inside. The ADC was designed to be a protective shell for the pilots, able to withstand all but the most violent trife attack. If a Reaper was nearby, they would be able to wait it out here. Not that Caleb wanted to wait it out. Flores' actions had made him more impatient than ever.

Sho slumped in one of the pilot seats, sighing deeply. Washington lowered Flores into another chair, holding her so she wouldn't slide off it and putting fresh pressure on the wound.

"Let me know when she comes to," Caleb said, moving past them, through the small door to the cockpit. There were no windows in the ADC. Like the starship it was sitting in, the vehicle used cameras to see. Caleb sat in the driver's seat and flipped the toggle to power up the ADC. A series of displays were mounted around the cockpit and they came to life, revealing the view outside. A secondary display just behind the steering yoke and a third display to its right also activated, offering control of the vehicle.

Caleb used the controls to switch the cameras to night mode, allowing them to see deeper into the poorly lit hangar. He swiveled his head, checking the perimeter.

His eyes stopped when he caught a glimpse of a dark form moving away from the area. It was humanoid. Two meters tall, give or take. It wasn't a Reaper. It could have easily been Riley or David, but he only got a split second view of it before it was gone. With everything that was happening, he wasn't sure enough that it was even real. It wouldn't make sense for either person to trail them down here and then leave. He decided he was probably seeing things or jumping at shadows.

He continued to watch the screens for a few more

minutes. There was no other motion outside the ADC. No sign of any other life, human or otherwise. He closed his eyes and breathed out, giving himself half a second to relax.

"Sarge," Sho said, ducking her head into the cockpit. "She's awake."

Chapter 22

"Mariana," Caleb said, entering the back of the ADC and squatting down in front of Flores. "How are you feeling?"

Flores' eyes shifted to look at him. She blinked a few times as if she were trying to confirm what she saw.

"My head hurts," she said.

Washington put his hand on her shoulder and then pointed to himself and made a face.

"He says he's sorry he shot you," Sho said. "But he had to do it. You were headed for the manual release on the blast door."

"I was?"

"What's the last thing you remember?" Caleb asked.

"We were scanning the hangar. You left me next to the builder while you climbed into it. Then I heard a voice calling me. It seemed so real. I was sure it had to be."

"That sounds familiar."

"Right. You heard voices too. It was like Poltergeist. I don't remember anything after that. You said I was trying to open the blast doors?"

"It seemed that way. When we tried to stop you, you

attacked us." Caleb held up his arm, showing her the destroyed part of his SOS. "If my arm weren't already metal, it would be toast right now."

"It doesn't look like the plasma damaged that alloy at all, Sarge," Sho said, getting a better look at it.

"Lucky for me whatever it's made from can take a beating. I'd probably be dead otherwise."

"I'm so sorry, Alpha," Flores said. "I don't know what I was doing, or why I did it. I don't remember." She looked at Washington. "Thanks for not killing me."

He smiled and flashed his thumb.

"Getting knocked out affects short-term memory. I'm not surprised. In any case, it isn't your fault. Whatever is causing the hallucinations got to you too."

"That's not very comforting."

"I agree. At least now we know it's not only something wrong with me. If it's affecting you too, it could hit any of us."

"At any time," Sho said. "How are we supposed to operate like that?"

"We don't have a choice. It was my mistake to leave you alone, Mariana."

"Don't beat yourself up over it, Alpha. You couldn't have known what would happen."

"Now we do. From here out we stick together, pairs at a minimum. No exceptions."

"Roger that, Sarge," Sho said.

"Good work finding the ADC so fast. I was watching the feeds from outside. There's no sign of Reaper activity, so maybe our luck is changing a bit. Wash, did you find the toolkit yet?"

Washington nodded, pointing to the last seat in the vehicle. A large box of tools was sitting on it.

"Perfect. Washington and I will go outside the ADC to

start taking the wings off one of the drones. There are two seats in the cockpit. Sho, you and Flores stay inside and keep an eye on things. We'll take headsets out with us, but don't use the comm unless you see something big and ugly coming our way."

"Roger that."

Caleb moved back past the two Marines. Each of the pilot stations had headsets resting on the control surface, used to both listen to the audio stream the drones were transmitting and to communicate with the other pilots. He grabbed two of them and tossed one to Washington. Then he pulled the retractable ladder down from the center of the space and climbed up to the top hatch. He unlocked it and swung it open, climbing out onto the roof of the vehicle.

The recon drones were each around three meters in diameter, with long, cylindrical fuselages that ended in a single powerful thruster in the back and rotating sensor array in the front. The muzzle of a high-velocity machine-gun rested just under and behind the array. The wings of the drone were short and aggressively swept back. A powerful but nearly silent turbofan was embedded in the center of each, allowing lift and hovering capabilities.

"You do know how to take the wings off, right?" Caleb asked as Washington squeezed through the open hatch. He smiled and nodded. "Good."

Caleb and Washington moved to the closest drone. Washington opened the toolkit and pulled out a drill, searching for the right attachment. He put it down and dug out another tool, which he used on the wing to pry off a piece of its radar-absorbing outer skin, revealing the rivets underneath. He began to remove them.

The drone was silent in operation. The drill was not. It made a loud whirring noise that caused Washington to stop a moment after he started, looking back at Caleb with a questioning glance.

"Nothing we can do about it," Caleb said. "Just be as quick and sure as you can."

Washington ran the drill again, removing the rivet in a few seconds. He repeated the process a dozen more times, getting quicker with each iteration. Caleb spent the time monitoring the area, which remained clear.

Once all the rivets were out, Washington took hold of the wing and lifted it toward the front of the drone, unhooking it from the fuselage. It had been designed for easy attachment and detachment, and it separated easily. Washington wasn't sure where to put it, so he lowered it down the side of the ADC to the deck.

He repeated the process on the other side before moving to the next drone. It took nearly thirty minutes, but they wound up with four wingless drones to go with the four bars of explosives and the four detonators.

It was Caleb's job to wire the drones to trigger the detonators and blow on command. It was a specialized task — fortunately one they taught to Marine Raiders.

That took another hour, by the end of which they improvised four remotely operated explosive devices. Caleb looked down on their work with a certain amount of satisfaction, not only because of what they had created, but also because they had gone nearly two hours without an incident.

"Nice work, Wash," he said, clasping hands with the big Marine. Then they climbed back down into the ADC. "The IEDs are ready," he announced to Sho and Flores.

"Did something actually go right for a change?" Flores asked.

"Amazingly enough, it does happen from time to time," Caleb replied. "Wash, switch places with Sho for a minute.

Sho, activate one of the drones and check the transmission, only for a few seconds."

"Roger, Sarge," Sho said.

She moved out of the cockpit, and then Washington stepped in. Caleb followed Sho to one of the drone stations. She activated the terminal and enabled the drone. The top of the hangar was suddenly visible on the display in front of them.

"All systems are go, Sarge."

"Perfect. Shut it down. We don't need any Reapers showing up down here."

"Roger." She used the control surface to power down the drone. "That was easy."

"So far so good, but we still have to place them in the ship."

"What are we waiting for?"

Chapter 23

Riley grunted as she hit the back of the lift, bouncing off and dropping to her knees. She kept her eyes on the floor, refusing to look at the person in front of her as if that would somehow make him go away.

She saw his armored feet step onto the lift with her, and then he turned and tapped the control panel. The doors closed and the lift began to ascend. He kept his back to her the entire time they rose, unconcerned about her ability to get the best of him.

He had caught up to her with little effort and had disarmed her with only slightly more effort, flipping her onto her back and throwing her to the floor. He'd grabbed her by the neck of her combat armor and dragged her all the way across the Deliverance. She had of course tried to resist, but his grip had been like a steel vise on her arm, his strength twice that of her normal human hands, even encased in her SOS. Once he had her, she had been no more than a passenger along for the ride.

At least Caleb and the Guardians hadn't chased after her. She was grateful for that. What could they have done against the Cerebus armor? Nothing. It was nearly impervious to plasma and completely bulletproof. It was the culmination of a year of study and hard work by Paul and Mackie, the two Reapers with the most training in mechanical engineering. It was supposed to be a prototype of the next generation of combat armor. The one that would ensure none of their Marines would ever die again.

Instead, it had fallen into the wrong hands.

The question was, *whose* hands?

She let her eyes travel up the armor, from the feet to the knees and over the hips up to the chest and head. The helmet was in place, sleek and perfect. Not hers. That one had belonged to Paul.

The lift stopped, and the doors slid open. The Cerebus turned back to Riley, its posture stiff and cold.

"David, wait," Riley said. "Please. I can explain everything. We don't need to do this."

"I require the access codes to the landing sequence," he replied, his voice altered by the filtration system of the helmet. "There is nothing to explain."

"I can't give you the codes," she said. "I don't have them. Harry had them, and you killed him."

"Are you so accustomed to the alteration of truth that you have come to believe in its accuracy?"

Riley stared at the dark faceplate. David had never spoken to her like that, but then again, the genetic alterations had been changing him. She opened her mouth to respond, but he grabbed her by the collar, lifting her to her feet. He spun her around in front of him and shoved her out the door.

"Walk," he commanded.

Riley did as he ordered, taking even, deliberate steps along the corridor. She knew she couldn't escape from him, but that wasn't the reason she walked slowly. Caleb and the

Guardians would be working to reach Research. She was on her way to the bridge. If she could get to the comm there and get a signal out once they had made it, maybe they could get her out of this mess.

She should never have gone after the Reaper alone. She felt responsible for the existence of the creatures, and she wanted to make things right. She hadn't expected David to be outside of Research. She hadn't expected him to be the one to give chase. She had hoped he was dead but assumed he wasn't. After all, the Reapers had survived the centuries. Why wouldn't their progenitor survive as well?

And since she had been forced to flee and leave the armor behind, was it any surprise he had figured out how to put it on, activate it and use it? He'd had years to study and practice.

Granted, she shouldn't have gone after the Reaper alone, but she was glad she had. Otherwise, whoever had been with her would have died at David's hand. And she realized that if the Guardians had stayed on her tail, all of them would be dead now.

She couldn't help but wonder if that was only delaying the inevitable.

"David, I know things didn't go exactly according to plan, and I know you're mad at me for it. I understand that. And I understand why. But they're dead, damn it. Harry, Paul, Mackie. All of them. Even the Guardians, Shiro and Ning. Nothing is going to change the outcome. For you or any of them."

"Walk faster," David replied. "I require the access codes."

"You want to land the ship with the Reapers still out there? Why do you think I have the code? I know you're mad, but don't you care about the people in Metro?"

"I have no concern for the Reapers. I have no concern for the people in Metro. I require the access codes. I want to land the Deliverance. Now. Nothing more. Nothing less."

"Why?"

"Walk faster."

He shoved her in the back, forcing her to accelerate to keep from falling. They had to cross all the way back to the bridge from the other side of Metro, which meant following a nearly two-kilometer corridor over the top of the city. If he wanted her to move any faster, she would have to break into a run.

"David, you didn't answer me. Why?"

"I require exodus from this ship."

"So do we all. If you help us deal with the rest of the Reapers, the ship will land on its own."

"Are you capable of speaking the truth?"

Riley scowled in front of him. "How did you know Harry changed the parameters?"

"I gained read-only access to the mainframe. I can see everything. I can change nothing."

She let herself smirk. Harry had added an extra layer of security on top of the base encryption, just in case. That David had managed to crack the top level was impressive for multiple reasons. That he could read the mainframe's code was something else. It was two parts incredible, one part terrifying. He knew everything. More than he had known before. More than he should know. Even if he couldn't change it, he still knew it.

One way or another, before this was over, he would have to die.

She had been planning on killing him anyway.

"You have the access codes," David said. "Only you

can land the ship. I will bring you to the terminal. You will enter the codes. The ship will land."

"That isn't going to happen, David."

His voice was cold, even and certain. "It will."

They continued along the corridor, spending the next ten minutes in silence. They arrived near the end of the long passage, the hallway branching out at an intersection. Riley looked ahead to it, trying to decide if she dared attempt to escape. David wouldn't kill her as long as he believed she was the only chance he had to reach Essex, though why he was so desperate to get down there was beyond her. If she could get far enough away, if she could reach one of the maintenance passages, maybe she could lose him. The Cerebus armor was sleek, but it would be a tight fit in the smaller corridors.

Ultimately, she didn't have much to lose.

She checked David's position behind her. He was only a couple of meters back. Close enough to grab her if she wasn't quick enough. He had her guns too, but she was pretty sure he wouldn't use them. She just had to take him by...

She burst ahead, breaking for the intersection a few steps before they reached it, hoping he wouldn't be expecting the move. He didn't. She made the first four steps before she noticed him reacting at all, and she turned and sprinted down the left adjoining corridor. She knew it would lead to the central bank of lifts. She was familiar with the area and the maintenance passages here. She had gotten an initial lead.

She was going to make it.

She raced for the next junction. Taking a glance back, she was surprised to see David wasn't following. She kept her eyes on him, unsure of why he had paused. Was there a Reaper somewhere in her path ahead?

She watched David's visor slide up. She expected to see his face. Instead, she saw a simple flash, as though his eyes were on fire. She looked away, continuing to run.

"Riley, you bitch."

The voice came from up ahead, causing Riley to slow as she approached the intersection.

"I can't believe you did this to us. We were your squad mates. We trusted you."

Riley came to a stop in the intersection, turning her head to the left. Mackie was standing there. She was naked, her body already beginning to twist into the monstrous form of the Reaper she had become.

"You lied to us," Paul said from behind her. She turned around. He was in the same state. Naked and changing into something horrific.

"You used us," Harry said. "You used me worst of all."

"Are you even capable of telling the truth?" John asked.

"What did you do to me?" Private Ning said, coming at her from the front, along with Private Shiro. "What did you give me?"

Riley's heart raced, and she froze in place, looking at each of the Reapers. "No. I was following orders. This is war. Sacrifices have to be made."

"You don't turn on your family," Mackie said. "We were family."

"We were more than family," John said. "Once."

"John, I'm sorry. I was out of options. I had to…"

The Reapers were closing in, their voices beginning to merge as they surrounded her. She reached for her rifle, but it wasn't there. What had happened to it? Mackie lunged at her. She ducked and punched, hitting the Reaper in the stomach.

"You lying bitch!" Ning shouted.

"Lying bitch!" the others refrained, chanting it as they came at her.

Claws raked her arms from the sides, some of them cutting through her SOS and drawing blood. She cried out in pain and terror. Her eyes ran with tears, her body cold and shaking.

"How could you do this to us?" Harry said.

They grabbed her from behind. They threw her to the ground and held her there.

David appeared over her, holding a syringe. He knelt down beside her, visor closed once more.

"What is that?" she asked breathlessly.

"Only what you deserve," he replied.

The syringe descended toward her neck.

She blacked out.

Chapter 24

The Guardians carried the first of the drones from the hangar. Even without the wings, the vehicles were heavy enough that they required Caleb and Washington to handle them, and even then they were only able to lift them because of Caleb's cyborg arm. Otherwise, they would have had to use one of the Strongman exoskeletons, which would have made the whole process much slower than Caleb wanted. If Riley was in David's hands, they needed to move as fast as possible to keep him from getting whatever it was he wanted from her.

"You okay, Wash?" Caleb asked. He could barely see the big Marine past the fuselage of the drone, which he had cradled in his replacement arm. Washington was stooped over in the front, bearing the weight of the machine on his back as they walked. He shifted the weight slightly and offered a thumbs up.

The hardest part had been the stairs. They couldn't risk detonating the drone on Deck Thirty, not with the outer hull beneath them. They had no choice but to carry it up, deciding to go three flights to Deck Twenty-seven to be safe. The T-9 packed a punch, and they didn't want to blow a hole in the ship and inadvertently kill everyone. They were also trying to be careful not to hit any critical systems, which meant lugging the drone to a spot where there were no nearby maintenance corridors. Riley might have known the layout of the passages, but the Guardians didn't. They discovered the access areas through trial and error, all of which cost them even more time.

Sho and Flores mostly kept guard as they walked, watching the illuminating and fading lights of the corridors to ensure nothing was coming toward them from either direction. They broke away every so often to search for the secondary passages. Flores had lamented the loss of the Dragonflies multiple times. They all knew how much the small drones would have sped up their placement.

"What do you think?" Caleb asked as they reached another intersection.

The corridors had all started to look alike to him, an endless repeat of doors and bulkheads that made him feel as though they were walking in circles. He didn't know what the deck had originally been planned to house. They had reached an unfinished part of the ship, which had its basic modular frame intact but none of the finishing touches that defined it. The rooms were all empty metal boxes, one after another, there for the sole purpose of filling in the space.

"I think this is the spot," Sho said.

"Agreed," Caleb replied. "Wash, set it down gently."

Washington shifted the drone, holding it with two arms and squatting. Caleb squatted with him, bringing the device to the deck. They dropped it the last few centimeters, the weight of it vibrating through the decking.

"Shhh," Flores said. "We don't want to bring the Reapers here yet."

"We're in the middle of nowhere," Sho said. "I doubt any Reapers are hanging out nearby."

"Let's head back to the hangar," Caleb said. "We've got three more of these things to move."

Washington lowered his head, shaking it sadly. Caleb didn't blame him for not wanting to make a similar trip three more times. He checked the power meter on his arm's control ring. His battery was at fifty percent, down nearly twenty from the exertion of humping the drone up here. He could only move two more before he would have to recharge.

"It's taking a lot out of me too, Wash," he said. "Let's do at least one more, and then we can activate them and see what we get. Maybe we won't need the last two."

Washington lifted his head again, smiling and nodding. That was a better idea.

They headed back toward the hangar, the return trip much shorter. The jammed blast doors had forced them to carry the drone out the other side of the hangar, closer to the stern. They re-entered that way, remaining cautious as they neared the area. Caleb still wasn't sure he had seen the pair of legs on the ADC's monitors. Even if he had seen them, he wasn't convinced they had been real..

They entered the hangar. It was as dark and silent as when they had left it. They crossed the rows of equipment to the ADC. Caleb had closed the access ramp on the way out, finding that his access code was still good for the military vehicle. He opened the armored hatch to reveal the access panel beneath, tapping in his code again. The back of the vehicle started to open, lowering outward to the ground.

"Flores, give us a quick sweep of the area on the cameras, and send a two-second transmission out to the drone to make sure we have connectivity."

"Roger, Alpha," Flores replied, rushing into the vehicle. "

Washington, are you ready?" Caleb asked.

He shook his head no while smiling. Then he moved to the next drone, placed beside the ADC. He wrapped his large arms around the front of it, while Caleb took the rear with his left arm.

"One. Two. Three. Lift."

They lifted the drone in unison.

"Alpha!" Flores called from inside the ADC. "We've got one near Drone One!"

"What?" Caleb said out loud. They hadn't activated the comm signal yet. "Wash put it down. Sho, go check it out."

Washington seemed happy to lose the weight again. They lowered it carefully. The T-9 had its detonator in, and they weren't taking any chances on accidentally blowing the explosive.

Sho had run into the ADC, and now she came rushing back to report.

"Sarge, the drone recorded motion about a minute after we left. A Reaper. I don't know if it was tailing us, or if it's just coincidence, or what. It sent the recording when Flores opened the comm link."

"It should still be pretty close. Let's bundle up and see what we get."

"What about the other explosives?"

"We can't waste the opportunity."

"Roger that."

The Guardians piled into the ADC, and Caleb closed the hatch behind him. Then he moved to the pilot station where Flores was sitting. The screen was dark, the link offline.

"Turn it on," Caleb said.

"Roger, Alpha," she replied, tapping on the controls. The drone came to life, the forward-facing camera showing the floor leading down the corridor. There was nothing out of the ordinary in the display. No sign of the Reaper.

"What now?" Sho asked.

"Now we wait," Caleb replied. "Go up front and keep an eye on the monitors."

"Roger."

Sho moved to the front of the vehicle. Caleb and Washington watched the drone's display over Flores' shoulder.

A minute passed. Two minutes. Three. There was no activity near the drone. Nothing was happening at all.

"Maybe the Reapers don't respond to comm transmissions the way the trife do?" Flores suggested. "Maybe David toasted it out of them?"

"Toasted?"

"CRISPR. Crispy. Toasted," Flores explained.

"Roger," Caleb replied. "There." He pointed at the display.

"I don't see anything," Flores said.

"Watch the shadows." The shadows ahead of the camera were shifting, suggesting something was there. Unfortunately, the drone didn't have a full field of view from the floor.

"Oh. The lights went on. Something's coming."

The display changed suddenly, the camera thrown forward, rolling and spinning in a blur. The drone hit the wall, the noise coming through the feed and into the ADC. It came to a rest a moment later, facing the opposite direction.

The Reaper was right in front of it, reaching for it cautiously. Caleb could see its eyes more clearly than he ever had before. They were intelligent eyes. Almost human eyes. It seemed as if it knew what the drone was, but it didn't know why it was there. It dipped down further, staring directly into the camera. The look of sad comprehension sent a shiver down Caleb's spine.

"Alpha, should I send the detonate signal?" Flores asked.

Caleb hesitated. Riley had said David made the Reapers by combining the DNA of dead humans with the DNA of dead trife, and somehow regenerating them back to life. That type of science was over his head, and it wasn't really his current concern. Except seeing the thing's eyes, up close and static and not in the midst of a fight for his life, he was struggling to believe those eyes had ever been dead eyes.

"Alpha?" Flores said. The Reaper was straightening up and starting to back away. "Should I blow it?"

Caleb swallowed hard. What the hell was going on with this ship?

And who was the enemy, anyway?

"Sarge!" Sho shouted. "We've got company!"

Chapter 25

"Alpha!" Flores barked a third time. "It's now or never!"

Caleb glanced forward to the cockpit of the ADC, and then back to the display.

"Send it," he said.

Flores hit the key programmed to trigger the detonator. The only evidence they had that it worked was the sudden loss of the feed from the drone. They were too far away to hear the explosion or feel the effects.

Caleb felt the Reaper reach the ADC. One moment it was calm, the next it started shaking, and a sudden pounding came from the side of the vehicle.

"Sho?" Caleb said.

"Three of them, Sarge! Oh, hell!"

Caleb's head whipped toward the cockpit just as the Reaper's face became visible against the forward camera. It bared its teeth, raking its claws against the hardened glass protecting the lens, scratching it enough that it blurred the view.

"Three?" Flores said. "There are only supposed to be three left."

"They must have figured out which side of the transmission was the source and which was the destination," Caleb said. Had they sent the solo Reaper to investigate the destination while they came to the origin of the source? Were they capable of working together that way?

The third Reaper reached the vehicle, beginning to scrape and pound against the rear hatch. "The drones are right outside," Flores said. "We can blow the rest of them."

"And risk putting a massive hole in the hull?" Caleb responded. "No thank you, Private. Standby."

Caleb moved past Washington to the cockpit, intent on staying calm. The Guardians had decided to hole up in the ADC for a reason. There was no way the Reapers could get through the heavy shell. It was designed to hold up to armor-piercing rounds. He glanced at the displays. The Reapers were hitting all of the cameras, scratching the protective covers to ruin their vision.

"They're blinding us," Sho said.

"To what end? Do you think they know they can't get in?"

"It sure seems that way."

The vehicle continued to shake, the Reapers persistent in their attack. Caleb watched each one of them, trying to get a good look at their eyes. It was impossible with the scratched lenses. What were they going to do once they had finished taking out the cameras?

"Sarge, if they're all here, that means Research is clear," Sho said.

"You're welcome to step outside," Caleb replied. "Just don't expect me to follow you."

"Funny, Sarge. I had a different idea."

Caleb noticed one of the displays suddenly go black, the camera feed blanking completely out. "What just happened there?"

"I don't know."

The secondary display began to flash, showing a schematic of the ADC and a red mark on its left side, the same side where the camera had gone out.

"The system is reporting damage to the area around the camera," Sho said.

Caleb watched the rear-view display go black, another camera shutting down. A moment later, that region started flashing orange too.

"What are they doing?" he repeated. The system was acting like the Reapers were managing to tear through the armor, but that was impossible.

Wasn't it?

A third camera went out, leaving them with a reduced view of the world outside. The vehicle continued to rock, the Reapers attacking it with full fury.

"Sarge?" Sho said. "I want to get off this ride."

"Me too," Caleb decided. "Get us moving."

"What? I can barely see."

"I don't care. Put this thing in gear and get us moving."

"Headed where?"

Caleb backed out of the cockpit. "For now, drive us in circles if you have to. Let's not make this too easy for them."

"Roger."

Sho grabbed the steering yoke in both hands, pressing the trigger on the left one to activate the throttle. Caleb was nearly thrown off his feet as the ADC lurched ahead. The front camera was out, leaving her to interpolate from the front-corner cameras.

"Flores," Caleb said, "Switch seats and activate one of the flight-capable drones. I'll take the other."

"Roger," Flores replied.

They changed chairs and were nearly thrown into the

side of the vehicle just as they got up. The ADC jerked sharply to the left, hitting something in the process. The whole thing shook, knocking Flores into Caleb. He caught her, keeping her from falling flat on her face.

"Sorry!" Sho shouted from up front.

"What's going on?" Flores asked.

"They're tearing through the armor. We have to get them off."

"How can they tear through the armor?"

"I don't know. Just our luck."

Caleb nearly threw Flores into the rearmost pilot station before dropping into the seat opposite her. He grabbed the headset and dropped it over his ears. Then he took hold of the drone's flight stick and reached over with his free hand, powering it on.

The display showed the top of the hangar, in motion above the ADC. He triggered the drone's main thrusters, launching it toward the ceiling, then using the stick to quickly level it out. It had been a few years since he had last piloted a drone, but the muscle memory remained.

"I'm up, Alpha," Flores said.

"Roger that. Come around on the ADC. Let's see exactly what we're up against."

Caleb guided the drone in a tight circle, the wide-angle camera revealing the armored vehicle partway into the turn. They were almost clear of the rest of the heavy equipment, but they were headed right toward the edge of one of the massive loaders.

"Sho, hard right!" Caleb shouted.

"Roger," Sho replied over the headset. Caleb was grateful she had the wherewithal to put it on.

Caleb would have been ripped from his seat if Washington hadn't been there. The big Marine used his body to hold Caleb in place during the turn. Caleb stayed focused on the drone while Washington belted him in.

"Thanks, Wash," he said, eyes fixed on the ADC and the three Reapers climbing over it. One was still on the front of the vehicle. The other two had moved to the top to catch the launching drones. With one drone detonated, two in the air and the remaining three left behind on the floor of the hangar, the drone racks were empty.

The Reapers on top started banging on the outside of the vehicle hatch, their arms swinging back and forth, the two of them taking turns raking at the armored hinge.

"Flores, target the two on the roof," Caleb said, flipping the switch to arm the drone's gun. The action also caused a targeting reticle to appear on the display. "I'll go after the demon up front."

Would the attack be painful enough to distract the Reapers?

He was going to find out.

He angled the drone into a light descent, lining the reticle up with the back of the Reaper riding the front of the ADC. He squeezed the trigger, sending a dozen rounds into the creature's back.

The Reaper turned to look at the drone shooting it. It reached out and swiped at the drone as it whipped past. Caleb increased the throttle, rocketing along the side of the vehicle and out toward the hangar's massive blast doors before adjusting his vector to make another approach.

"Going in," Flores announced. Caleb glanced over his shoulder to her screen. He could hear the rounds pinging off the armor outside as she strafed the two Reapers, scoring direct hits along their backs and faces. One of them flopped over and fell off the ADC, its brain momentarily shredded in the attack.

"Nice shooting," Caleb said, going back to his screen.

He decided to hit the Reaper on the roof, quickly snapping the drone into position and unleashing a barrage. The rounds tore into the creature, disrupting its attack a second time. It howled and leaped up at the drone as it passed by, barely missing it as its momentum carried it off the armored vehicle.

He was pushed hard to the left again, the ADC skidding along the metal floor on its airless knobby tires. It spun out and came to a sudden stop. Caleb adjusted his drone, elevating it and turning it back toward the vehicle. It afforded a view of their position from the corner of the wide lens. They were at a standstill, the injured Reaper off the left fender, still recovering from Flores' first attack.

"Floor it!" Caleb shouted.

He didn't need to. Sho had already hit the throttle, jolting him sideways as the ADC accelerated faster than expected, the removal of the six drones lightening its load considerably. The Reaper saw the ADC coming on hard, and it tried to scramble out of the way. Sho had already guessed how it would move, and she adjusted her path accordingly, overcorrecting to hit the creature dead-center.

The ADC shook as it impacted the Reaper, smashing it in the chest and pushing it down and under its wheels. The ride got bumpy while they ran over the monster, the tires crushing and ripping at it. Sho kept them headed toward the empty part of the hangar, advancing a hundred meters before sliding back around.

Caleb guided his drone toward the first Reaper, still hanging tenuously to the ADC's front. He opened fire, holding the trigger down and sending round after round into the demon. It screamed and jumped off the ADC, trying to avoid further injury.

"Sho, is the roadkill staying down?" he asked.

"Affirmative, Sarge," she replied. "So far. I'm going to hit it again."

"Negative," Caleb said. "Wash, grab a P-50 and get on the roof. Sho, get us close to it, we're going to cook it."

"What about the other two?"

"Flores, we need to keep Washington covered."

"Roger."

Washington grabbed one of the P-50s and quickly scaled the ladder to the hatch, pushing it open. He climbed fearlessly out onto the top of the vehicle, using the hatch to hold himself in position as the ADC raced back to the crushed Reaper.

Caleb guided his drone around a third time, targeting his Reaper while Flores dropped toward hers. He swooped in low, emptying round after round into the creature, causing it to cover its face with its hand. It spun around, crying out in pain and frustration as the bullets tore through its flesh. It ducked low to escape attack, only the drone failed to buzz by on its strafing run. Red text began flashing at the bottom of Caleb's display, indicating sudden and catastrophic engine failure.

"Damn it! I think he got me," Caleb said, trying to regain control of the drone. It wasn't responding. "Shit," Caleb said again, his drone's camera feed failing as the craft crashed into the deck. The ADC came to a stop beside the wounded Reaper, and Washington climbed the rest of the way out of the hatch. "Flores, do you still have sights on your Reaper?"

"I'm on him, Alpha," she replied. "The second tango is rushing the ADC. I think it sees Washington."

Caleb grabbed for his belt, unlatching it and jumping to his feet. "Flores, where is it?"

"Coming up from the rear," she said. "Washington, get out of there!"

Caleb looked up through the hatch. He could see Washington standing in front of it, bathing the Reaper on the ground with a stream of plasma. Caleb hoped Washington had done enough damage to keep it down.

"Sho, full reverse, now!" Caleb shouted, climbing the ladder to the top of the hatch. He reached out of it with his cyborg arm, grabbing Washington's ankle as the ADC began to back up. The sudden change in direction caused Washington to lose his balance, and he dropped the plasma rifle as he stumbled back toward the side of the vehicle.

Caleb held onto Washington's ankle tightly, keeping him from plunging over the side. At the same time, the ADC crashed into the other Reaper. It grabbed onto the back and held on as they continued in reverse.

"Alpha, the other one is charging," Flores said. "Moving to intercept."

Caleb craned his neck to see the scene in Flores' display. "Sho, forty degrees port," he said. Sho adjusted the path of the ADC.

Flores' drone began to drop toward the Reaper, getting between it and the ADC, banking hard and opening fire. Bullets tore into the monster, and it bellowed a challenge at the oncoming drone, spreading its claws wide.

The drone hit it square in the chest, Flores emptying her limited munitions into the Reaper. Dark flesh filled the display, along with flashes of light. Then the display went dark.

Caleb kept his grip on Washington, pulling him back toward the hatch. Washington turned his body, getting his hands on Caleb's arm and yanking himself back onto the roof of the ADCV. He scrambled to the hatch, and Caleb moved aside so he could drop in head-first.

"Flores, grab a plasma rifle. Wash, hold on!"

Caleb ran to the back of the vehicle and slapped the

controls for the rear hatch. It thunked and began to deploy outward.

"What the hell are you doing?" Flores asked.

"Just be ready to shoot!" Caleb replied.

The ramp continued to descend. Ten degrees. Twenty. Thirty.

A large, ugly claw appeared over the side, trying to get better purchase.

Forty. Fifty.

A head followed, the creature swinging up from under the ramp. It held on despite the angle.

Sixty. Seventy.

The other hand came over, and it started to pull itself around and into the ADCV, mouth open in an angry scream. Caleb focused on its eyes. They reminded him of Shiro's eyes.

"Alpha, move aside," Flores said, stepping forward with the plasma.

Caleb stayed where he was, looking past the demon.

Eighty degrees. Ninety. One hundred.

"Brace for impact!" Caleb shouted, grabbing the straps to the rear pilot station's seat. Flores noticed the jammed doors almost too late, falling between two seats and bracing against them. Washington held onto the other side of the ladder.

One hundred ten. One hundred twenty.

It seemed impossible the Reaper was holding on, and maybe it wasn't. It was being dragged on the ground, pressed down by the open ramp, only its arms and head visible above it. The stuck door was rapidly approaching, a perfect if messy guillotine.

The ramp hit the door hard, causing the entire ADC to buck back against it with enough force that the front went airborne. Flores and Caleb cried out, Caleb's grip on the strap with his inhuman hand the only thing that saved him from serious injury. The Reaper's head was decapitated forcefully, along with its arms. The ADC crashed back to the ground, the back hatch having embedded itself into the door with the Reaper crushed beneath it. There was no space for the monster's head to regenerate.

"Let's move, Marines!" Caleb shouted, stumbling back to his feet. Sho was out of the cockpit and charging toward them. "Through the open hatch! Go!"

Washington was out first, stepping off the ramp to the right and ducking through the partially open blast doors. Flores followed him, Sho and Caleb after that. They squeezed through the space and looked back. The hangar was smoldering where Caleb's drone had crashed and where the Reaper had been burned. Tire marks wound around the open deck. Dark blood trailed across the floor. It reminded Caleb of the war zone the hangar had become during the ship's launch.

His lips split in a thin smile. The results had been a lot better this time. Guardians eight, Reapers zero.

"Hey Alpha," Flores said, her breathing ragged behind her words.

"Yes, Private?" Caleb replied, turning to look at her. She had a huge smile on her face.

"I have an idea."

"Which is?"

"Let's not ever do that again."

"Affirmative."

"We get all of them with that display of Marine can-do, Sarge?" Sho asked.

"I think so."

"Job well done, Marines!"

"Oorah!"

"Save the party," Caleb said. "We still have one more target to worry about."

"Dr. Moreau," Flores said.

"Let's head up to Research and finish this, once and for all."

Chapter 26

Just because the Reapers were accounted for didn't make the trek from the hangar to Research any easier. Not only were Caleb and Washington especially beat up and sore, but Caleb was constantly aware that David Nash was still out there. Just because he believed the man had brought Riley back to Research, it didn't mean he was right. It didn't mean David wasn't trailing them or watching them. It didn't mean they wouldn't encounter him somewhere else within the many corridors running along the hull of Deliverance.

He had to treat the situation as if the Guardians were still under threat, and they crossed the distance accordingly, staying in formation as they traveled from the hangar to the nearest stairwell, ascending cautiously and making their way toward Research. Caleb wasn't completely confident he even knew how to get there, having never visited the area before. Fortunately, Sho seemed to have an uncanny ability to recall the three-dimensional grid of the ship, and she was able to direct them to the right general location.

The Guardians weren't about to walk right up to the Research module. They hadn't taken their time reaching the area to charge ahead recklessly. They gathered a few corridors away, huddling close to prepare their approach.

"This is it, Guardians," Sho said. "If we do this right, we might be trading this ark for our new home before we hit the sack tonight."

Washington tapped on his armor, pointing to his back.

"Well, who told you to drop it? We've got enough guns. We've got enough ammo. I'm not worried."

"Let's not get too far ahead of ourselves," Caleb warned. "We have no idea what we're dealing with in David. We know he's wearing the Cerebus armor, and that's about it."

"We know he killed the original Reapers and turned them into trife hybrids," Sho said. "He also killed Shiro and Ning. From what Riley told us, it sounds like he did it with his bare hands."

"If he's that dangerous, I don't see how we're going to do anything against him," Flores said. "Can plasma even damage that armor?"

"I don't know," Caleb replied. "I can't imagine how it wouldn't."

He paused, looking over his team. He had been wrestling with the problem the entire way up from the hangar. He had gone over Riley's story multiple times. She had told Harry to program the stasis pods to wake him and his Marines once the ship was low on power, when it became apparent that there was no other option than to confront the Reapers and David Nash, assuming they had survived the long crawl of time. They had survived, and the Guardians had proceeded to do their damnedest to clean up the mess Riley admitted she had caused by altering David in the first place. They had been mostly successful too. He was proud of his Marines for that.

But something had been bothering him from the beginning. A sense that Doctor Valentine still wasn't telling them everything she knew. That feeling had become more powerful when he had seen the look in the Reaper's eye. It was too intelligent. Too full of life.

"Sarge, you okay?" Sho asked.

Caleb nodded. "Affirmative. Just thinking."

"What about?"

"Storming the castle," he replied. "Going after David. There's something off about this whole thing. Something we're missing."

"I've felt like that since we went to pick up Valentine back on Earth."

"I'm not thrilled about the prospect of things going sideways again," Flores said. "If there's a mystery to solve, let's Scooby-Doo it now."

"Scooby-Doo it?" Sho asked.

Washington laughed silently.

"You never saw Scooby-Doo? There's no hope for you, Sho."

"We don't have time to solve that mystery right now," Caleb said. "But we do need to use our heads."

"What are you thinking, Sarge?" Sho asked.

Caleb's eyes swept over the Guardians. "Riley said they shot David in the head and he regenerated back to full capacity. And now he's wearing an advanced armor prototype for even more protection. Flores is right. There may not be any way we can hurt him.

"The way I see it, we have two options here. Option one, we all rush Research. If David is prepared for it – hell even if he isn't – the odds are we're all going to die, and if we don't, we'll probably wish we had. Option two, I go in alone and try to talk to him. Maybe I can reason with him. We aren't the ones who used him. Why should he be pissed at us? If I can't get him to listen, then I die, and you can try to find another way. Maybe you'll decide to go with option one, but at least you'll know that's the only option left."

"Hold on," Flores said. "Alpha, don't you remember telling us we aren't flying solo anymore, for any reason?"

"I do. The good thing about being Alpha is you get to change the rules. So far we've consistently played this out like Marines. Whatever the problem is, we attack it."

"We are Marines, Alpha," Flores said.

"Good Marines," Sho said. "And we've done pretty well attacking the problem so far."

"I know. And I believe in all of you. But not against David. Not in a direct confrontation, knowing what we know."

"If you want to talk to him, why not head up to the bridge and try to raise him on the comm?" Sho asked. "You don't need to go in person."

"Comms are offline, remember?"

Sho lowered her head. "Damn." She picked it up again. "Why don't I go, then? I'm less valuable, especially like this." She pointed to her scarred face.

"No. I'm Alpha. I need to be the one to do it." He paused, considering. "I'll tell you what. If things do turn violent and I think we can win, I'll signal you."

"How are you going to do that?"

"I'm not sure yet, but you'll know it when it happens. Make sure you're ready."

Sho stared at him, her expression hurt and angry, but also respectful and proud. "Sarge, I want you to know I hate this idea."

Caleb met her gaze. He saw something in it he hadn't

seen before. Not necessarily because it wasn't there. Maybe he just hadn't noticed. "Affirmative. This isn't about love or hate. It's about duty. We have a duty to protect the colonists. That's the mission, no matter who or what it costs. That's what we signed up for."

"I know."

Caleb looked at each of them, meeting their eyes with his. He wished there was another, less risky option. They all knew there wasn't. They had done well to destroy the Reapers without any casualties. They had done well to make it this far. He would do everything he could to make sure the story didn't end here.

"If I don't signal you or come back within an hour, assume I'm dead," he said. *Or David is turning me into a Reaper.* He didn't say it, but he couldn't help but think it. "If I don't come back, it was an honor serving with all of you."

"You too, Sarge," Sho said.

"Good luck, Alpha," Flores said.

Washington put his hand on Caleb's shoulder, squeezing it.

"Sho, how do I get there from here?" Caleb asked, handing his plasma rifle to Washington. The other Marine hesitated before taking it, his expression grim. Caleb proceeded to give him the rest of his weapons.

"Down that corridor to the third intersection, turn left. Take it about a hundred meters, second intersection I think. Turn right. Follow the signs." She managed to say it with a flat expression, keeping her voice strong. She was a Marine first, just like him.

"Affirmative. Listen for my signal. Be ready."

"We'll be ready."

"I know you will. You're Marines."

Caleb saluted them. It broke protocol, but it felt like the right thing to do. The Guardians saluted back.

Then he turned and headed off alone.

Chapter 27

Caleb moved at a measured pace, staying alert as he navigated the remaining passageways to Research. He wasn't as much concerned about David making an appearance as he was the potential of traps being laid across his path, set in defense of the area against possible threats. Since he didn't know David, he had no idea if the man would think that way. He wasn't taking any chances. It would be a major failure to fall victim to an improvised explosive because he made too many assumptions.

There were no explosives. No traps. Caleb reached the second intersection without any trouble, finding himself around the corner from the entrance into Research. He lingered there for a moment, quickly shedding his SOS and leaving it in a heap on the floor. His goal was to be as non-threatening to David as possible, and approaching the module in a t-shirt and a pair of boxer briefs was almost as vulnerable as he could get.

He could imagine Sho's reaction to the decision. She wouldn't like him putting himself at even further risk. He had seen the look in her eye before he had left the other

Guardians. It wasn't only admiration and mutual respect. He had seen love there too. It reminded him of how she had offered to marry him inside Metro before she knew he had signed on to be a Guardian. She had downplayed the truth of her feelings then. She had kept it light-hearted but honest. He had taken it the same way. They were a good match because they were both Marines. They understood one another as well as any two people could. As his subordinate, it just couldn't happen. As civilians, it could. End of story.

But there was a chance they would never see one another again, and she had done her best to tell him how she felt without verbalizing it, and without embarrassing either one of them. She probably knew he didn't feel the same way. He cared for her the way he cared for all of his Marines. They were comrades. Brother and sister Marines. He wasn't angry about her feelings. He appreciated that she had felt comfortable enough to reveal the truth. It didn't complicate things. He trusted her ability to accept how things had to be. If anything, it was motivation for him to see this through. To get the Deliverance to Essex's surface and to get the colony settled so she could meet someone who would love her back.

It was a strange time to be thinking about things like that. Or maybe it was the perfect time. Before the trife, he and his squad mates had always done their best to be prepared for anything. They could never have imagined what anything might become, and he would never have guessed how that road would twist and turn over the last two – no, two hundred and thirty-eight years – to bring him here.

Now he was down to his underwear, with a left arm composed of artificial muscles and machinery beneath an alien metal shell. He was standing in a failing starship over forty light-years from Earth, preparing to face-off against a mutant human who was not only wearing Riley's Cerebus armor, but who could regenerate from a catastrophic head wound.

If someone had told the Marine Raider version of himself he would wind up in this place, at this time, he would have thought it was the most preposterous thing he had ever heard.

Hell, it was still hard to accept, and he was living it.

Once more into the breach.

He turned the corner, spotting the entrance to Research at the end of the corridor, less than thirty meters away. The lights brightened ahead of him, better illuminating his path. Still not taking his safety for granted, he scanned the bulkhead for signs of foreign devices. He also noticed a camera positioned at the corner of the hatch, positioned to look down at whomever or whatever approached the module.

Was David in there? Was he watching right now?

Caleb started walking, taking evenly spaced steps along the passageway toward the hatch. He kept his arms up, his hands out, so if David were watching, he would hopefully know Caleb wasn't a threat. His eyes continued to sweep back and forth, looking for signs of changes along the walls, the floor, the ceiling.

All clean.

All clear.

He had burned twenty minutes of his hour by the time he came within reach of the outer hatch into Research. He glanced up into the camera, standing in front of the door for a moment to see if David would open it for him. Or react in any observable way.

He didn't.

Caleb reached out, putting his hand on the module's

control panel. The hatch was locked and secured, requiring a fingerprint or passcode to enter. Caleb tapped his code into the panel. As Guardian Alpha, he was supposed to have access to the module. He did. He heard the soft thunk of the disengaging locks, and then the solid panel slid aside.

The sudden smell overwhelmed him; it was stale and musty and thick. He reached up to pinch his nose as he stifled a cough. He looked ahead. He could see the Research control room ahead, a light haze hanging in the air. What was he breathing right now? Had David left the area toxic? Was that the trap?

Caleb lifted his t-shirt over his mouth, using it for whatever small filtration he could get. He pressed ahead, entering the control room. The hatch slid closed behind him.

He had been expecting a mess. The scene of a fight between the Reapers and David. Riley had said they had tried to fight back against him and failed. But there was no sign of fighting here. No bullet holes. No blood stains. Nothing. The room was in perfect condition. The displays were on. The terminals were running, and the stale air was clearing out, escaping and dissipating into the cleaner outside air. The module's independent filtration unit must have failed at some point over the centuries. Caleb lowered his shirt as he moved to the primary terminal. Tapping on the control surface, he requested a passcode for access.

"David," he called out. "David Nash. Are you in here? My name is Sergeant Caleb Card, United States Space Force Marines. We need to talk."

He walked across the control room, pausing as he neared the rear hatch leading into the next portion of the space. He was assuming Research was laid out similarly to the Marine module, with the laboratory occupying the same position as the armory. That would put Research's stasis pods behind the lab and the crew quarters in a similar location to the barracks. He imagined the scientists had actual rooms instead of basic racks since there were so many fewer of them.

"David Nash," he repeated. "My name is Sergeant Caleb Card, United States Space Force Marines. We need to talk."

He moved into the short corridor connecting the different areas of the module. As he turned left, walking down it toward the lab, he remembered Riley's story. According to her, the alien ship was kept in a storage room at the end of the corridor, past the laboratory. He could see what he assumed was the door to the room from his current position.

His heart began to pulse. He was both curious and afraid to see the ship.

"David Nash," he said a third time. "My name is Sergeant Caleb Card, United States Space Force Marines. We need to talk. I'm unarmed. Come out if you're here?"

When he reached the entrance to the lab, he tapped the control panel to open it. Pausing, he leaned over to look inside. He expected another war zone, but the room was clean. Spotless. Untouched. The convertible chair where Riley said she had injected David was free of damage, debris, and blood; it was as clean and unmarred as it was the day it had been installed. A mobile tray of tools sat beside it, each piece of equipment perfectly spaced and organized. The counter behind the chair was equally clean, as were all of the machines arranged around the room. He noticed a door that likely led to the stasis pods.

There hadn't been any fighting in here either, or if there had been, someone had gone to great lengths to erase any evidence of it. Everything looked like it had been abandoned without a single use. It was in perfect condition.

Too perfect.

"David Nash," Caleb said again. "My name is Sergeant Caleb Card, United States Space Force Marines. We need to talk. C'mon man, come out. I'm unarmed." He held up his shirt to show David he had no gun stashed in the waistband of his boxers.

Still no reply. Caleb was pretty sure neither David or Riley was in here. He was becoming more and more convinced that no one had been in here in a long, long time. But the Reapers had come from somewhere. And he was confident someone in the Cerebus armor had been chasing Doctor Valentine.

The feeling in his gut that something was off amplified, sending a chill through his body. Would he ever know what had happened here? Did it really matter, considering his mission was to save the colony and get them down to the planet's surface?

He froze when he heard a noise from further back in the module. It sounded like the exterior hatch sliding open. He turned away from the lab, walking back toward the control room and peeking his head around the corner as the outer door slid closed again. He was ready to repeat his statement to David, but he wasn't there.

Instead, a pair of Reapers were.

Chapter 28

"Shit." Caleb cursed under his breath, ducking back around the corner and out of sight. How the hell could there be two Reapers in here? They were all supposed to be dead.

He could hear them moving forward through the control room, their claws clicking on the floor. He didn't have any armor. He didn't have any weapons. David wasn't even here.

Damn it.

He looked over to the hatch leading to the crew quarters. The scientists had guns. He needed one. It wouldn't do much against the monsters, but it was the only chance he had.

He sprinted across the doorway past the control room, hoping the Reapers wouldn't notice him. He heard them scream and hiss at one another, and then he heard their feet clattering on the floor, their pace increasing as they rushed after him.

He made it to the door to the crew quarters, getting it open and ducking inside. Through the glass inset, he saw the first Reaper reach the corridor just as the door swept closed.

He didn't have much time. He turned around, getting a quick look at the area. He was in another short corridor with doors on either side. The individual quarters. He estimated there were two dozen. He was tempted to rush into the closest of one but stopped himself. He needed time. He ran to the back of the space, tapping the control panel on the last door on the left to open the door. He threw himself inside as the hatch at the end of the passage opened, a Reaper right behind it.

Caleb found himself on the floor next to a small bed and in front of a desk with a terminal on it. Clothes were hanging on a rack to his right, mostly standard ship's crew uniforms. The workout clothes, a red top and a pair of black sweatpants with a red stripe down the side, stood out against the more restrained gray and blue palette of the uniforms. His mind flashed back to the escape from the DHS building on Earth. It was Craft who had been wearing that outfit. This had to be his quarters.

He had chosen well.

Caleb picked himself up, reaching for the pillow on the bed and throwing it aside. A sidearm was resting under it, a standard nine millimeter semi-automatic. It would probably only make the Reapers angrier, but it was better than nothing.

He climbed onto the bed, pressing his ear against the door. He could hear the Reaper's feet on the floor, moving slowly down the corridor. He couldn't kill it. Not with the peashooter in his hand. He figured the best he could do would be to wound it and then try to get past it.

He grabbed a few quick breaths to steady himself, and then he moved into position against the door. He reached across it and tapped the controls to open it, immediately crouching low.

He rolled out past the door as it was still sliding open, coming up on one knee and opening fire. He squeezed the trigger over and over, blasting the Reaper in the chest and gut. The Reaper roared in response, trying to back away from the assault and bringing its hand up over its head.

Caleb didn't wait. He rose and charged the monster, drawing his artificial limb back in preparation to strike. The Reaper saw him coming. It braced itself, ducking away as Caleb's replacement hand swung past its head and into the wall, leaving a deep dent in the metal. The Reaper grabbed him around the waist, turning him and throwing him sideways into one of the doors. Caleb bounced off, looking for an avenue of escape. Not finding one, he had no choice but to go toe-to-toe with the demon.

He raised his hands and bent his knees in a fighting stance. The Reaper came at him.He dropped away from the creature's claws, slipping sideways and searching for a way through. The demon screamed, and when Caleb finally got a glimpse past its large form he saw the other monster coming their way. There was no way he could get past two of them.

But he was still going to try.

He still had a few rounds in his pistol. He dropped away from the Reaper, retreating to the rear of the corridor. The creature screamed again, coming at him. He took a blow from its claws on his replacement arm, turning and using the hand to grab the Reaper's arm. He pressed his pistol against the creature's chest and pulled the trigger, firing two rounds at point-blank range. The Reaper screamed. So did Caleb. The heat of the muzzle flash washed back over his hand, the gun misfiring and falling from his grip. He used the Reaper's moment of disorientation to pull it to the side, slamming it into the wall and rushing past it.

The second Reaper was right in front of him. He came to a sudden stop, realizing how badly he had screwed up. He was trapped between two of the monsters with no way out.

But he wasn't done fighting yet. He shouted as he lunged at the second Reaper. This one was smaller than the first, and when he hit it in the side with his artificial hand it screamed and fell into the wall. He tried to get past it, but the first Reaper grabbed his shoulder from behind, and dragged him to the floor. Landing on his back, he kicked out at the second Reaper as it closed on him. The first bent over him, raising its claws to slash his face.

"Stop!" someone shouted.

A sudden loud buzzing noise filled Caleb's ears, drowning out all other sounds. He closed his eyes at the instant of intense pain.

It was gone as quickly as it had come, vanishing from his head a moment later. His eyes snapped open, ready to continue the fight.

He froze immediately. The Reapers were gone, replaced by Washington and Sho. The two Marines leaned over him, their expressions equally confused.

"Sarge?" Sho said softly, reaching out and touching his face. "Is that you?"

Washington straightened up. Caleb noticed his SOS was scuffed from the impacts of multiple rounds. There was a chunk out of the armor plate in his chest with a burn mark around it.

Cold realization hit Caleb hard. He had been hallucinating. He had thought Washington and Sho were Reapers. He had shot Washington multiple times. They were both lucky Caleb hadn't gotten a shot in at Washington's head.

"Wash," Caleb said. "Shit. I could have killed you."

Washington's face was pale and frightened. He had realized the same thing, and that there was an equal chance he could have killed Caleb.

"Sarge," Sho said. "I'm sorry. I thought you were David."

Caleb's eyes flicked between the two Marines. "Where's Flores?"

Sho's eye widened. "Oh no. We saw a Reaper out there. We shot it and ran. Do you think..."

"It was Flores," Caleb said. "We have to find her." He held his arm out, and Sho helped pull him to his feet.

"What about David?" she asked.

"He's not here," Caleb replied.

"Yes, he is."

Caleb shifted his attention to the new voice. A man now stood behind Sho, a small, dark metal device in his hand. He was wearing a bodysuit – faded, worn, filthy and lined with what looked like nearly two dozen bullet holes. He had a short, wild beard and deep-set eyes. He couldn't have been more than twenty years old.

"David Nash?" Caleb said. Sho turned to look.

"Yes," the man replied. "I'm David Nash."

Caleb stared at him. This was the man who had killed Riley's Reapers and created the trife hybrids that roamed the ship? He looked like he had spent the last two hundred years hiding in one of the air vents.

But if David was here and not wearing the Cerebus armor...who was?

Chapter 29

Riley woke up on the bridge. She wasn't surprised David had brought her here. She knew what he wanted. He had made that clear.

He wasn't going to get it.

She didn't care what he did to her. No amount of pain could force her to agree to turn over the codes that would help him land the ship. He was too dangerous to let loose.

Especially considering what he knew.

She heard motion on her left and turned toward it. David was there, still wearing the full armor, including the helmet. He was facing away from her, his hands manipulating something she couldn't see. She closed her eyes as he began to turn, feigning sleep.

"I know you are awake," David said.

She opened her eyes and looked at him. How did he know? "You injected me with something earlier. What was it?"

"Incentive."

"What kind of incentive?"

"It matters not. I require the landing codes."

"You have a one-track mind."

"I have a singular goal. I approach it singularly."

She stared at him, still curious about the changes in his speech patterns. It was an unexpected side-effect of his improved intellect.

"Were you here alone this entire time?" she asked.

"Not alone."

"I mean besides the Reapers."

"Without companionship? I require it not. Time is subjective. I awaited our arrival. Now, the landing codes."

"You have no power over me, David. Do you think I'm afraid of you? If you harm me, if you kill me, you'll never get to the surface."

"You will give me the landing codes."

"I won't."

"You will become like them."

A cold chill raced down Riley's back. "What?"

David turned around to face her. "You will become like them, but not like them. My version is better than yours. My version will bind you to me, and leave the memory of who and what you were intact. That is my gift to you."

"There's no cure, David."

"I can reverse it. Give me the codes."

Riley stared at David. She didn't want to turn into a monster. What was the worst that could happen if she let them land? A few colonists would be killed?

Who was she kidding? She knew where they were. She knew why they were here. There might still be time to fix things. To make things right. To undo her many, many mistakes. She had been too enthusiastic in her work. She had made too many errors. In practice. In judgment.

Could anyone blame her? She had spent years studying and training to become an expert in her field, to save the life of the sister she loved. And then what? The damn trife had come and the virus had ended everything. She had a right to her vengeance, and she'd had Command's approval to mete it out.

"The codes," David said again.

Riley looked away. She needed to escape from David. To get back to Sergeant Card and his Guardians. She needed to convince him to hunt David down and kill him. He knew too much. Way too much. He had the power to destroy her in a way she wasn't willing to be destroyed.

"Why do you need to go down there?" she asked. "We're fifty light-years from Earth. There's nothing for you there."

"I will complete the mission."

"What mission is that, David? To tell Command what I did? To reveal my embarrassment to them? You cared for me once."

"I care not for you. I will report on my observations."

"I had their blessing. They approved my research."

"I care not. My goal is singular. I will complete the mission."

Riley's jaw clenched. She was getting frustrated with the nature of his responses. He had told her he loved her once. Why was he so stiff and unemotional? How could he be so distant? She had never meant to lose control. She had never intended for him to be hurt, or to be forced to do the things she had done.

"I'm sorry I hurt you, David," she said. "I still love you."

"You do not understand the concept. You use words as weapons. Your kind is duplicitous as a species. You are a prime specimen of the behavior."

"My kind? What the hell are you talking about? We're both humans. Just because the genetic editing made you smarter, just because it made you immortal, that doesn't make you better than me."

"I am superior. You will give me the codes, or you will become like them."

Riley's heart was racing. She knew what the change entailed. It looked more painful than anything else she had ever witnessed. The idea of it terrified her.

Where the hell was Sergeant Card? Hadn't he seen David chasing her? Why hadn't he come to rescue her?

She tried to calm her thoughts. They were becoming irrational. Disjointed. She had to focus. She had to think. If Card were still alive, he wouldn't abandon her. Even if he hated her, he was too good a Marine to leave her behind.

But he wouldn't look for her on the bridge. He wouldn't think of that. She had told him David was hiding out in Research. That's where he would go. But would he head there right away, or would he try to kill more of the Reapers first? How long had she been unconscious?

A plan began to solidify in her mind. David already knew how comfortable she was with lying. Would she be able to fool him one last time?

"I'll enter the codes," she said. "I need to access the primary terminal."

David stepped aside, pointing to the terminal. The command station was directly behind him, waiting for use.

Riley stood up on shaky legs, taking the few steps across the floor to the station. David didn't make any effort to help her. He remained standing beside the station, watching.

She sat down, activating the control surface. She navigated to the guidance systems, which responded by throwing an error attached to an input field. She confidently ran her fingers across the surface, typing in her code.

ACCESS DENIED.

She typed it again.

ACCESS DENIED.

She erased the whole thing and entered the code a third time.

ACCESS DENIED.

"Shit," she said. "My code isn't working."

"I care not for games and lies," David replied.

"David, this isn't a game," she said. "I swear, my code isn't taking. Harry must have changed it on me. Maybe he didn't trust me either."

"I do not believe you."

"I care not if you believe me," Riley said, mimicking his speech pattern. "It is what it is. I can't get into the landing sequence."

"You claimed you did not have the codes when you did. Now you claim you can not enter the subroutine when you can."

"I can't. I swear. Harry changed something. You have read-only access. You can check it yourself."

She expected David to move her out of the way so he could verify her words. Instead, he became very still, remaining that way for so long she was tempted to try to make a run for the exit.

"Data was passed to the hibernation pods," David said. "It has secondary encryption I have not yet broken. I require the data sent to the pod."

"I know what happened to the data," Riley said. "Some of the Guardians woke with me. The diminishing power levels triggered the system."

"I have not yet reviewed the power levels. I will review the levels."

David grew still again before Riley could say another word. She had no idea why, but he seemed to snap back a minute later. "Power levels are critical. I have taken all non-essential systems offline. I do not believe there is enough energy to land. I require the quantum energy unit."

"Quantum energy unit?" Riley said.

"Yes. It is in Research. I require it."

Was he talking about the alien spaceship's power source? She hadn't brought anything called a quantum energy unit onto the Deliverance. And what did he mean by non-essential systems? Had he done anything to harm the colonists in Metro? She already knew he wouldn't care if he had.

"What happened to the data sent to the pod?" David asked, his tone becoming more stiff and impatient.

"Displayed for the occupant and then deleted," Riley replied, putting on her best poker face. Would David realize she was lying again? "That's how Harry would have done it."

"I registered the presence of other humans when I located you. Which one of them has the codes?"

"I don't know."

"You are being untruthful."

"It doesn't matter. They'll stay together. Do you have access to the ship's sensors, or did you shut them all down?"

"The terminal is active. Standby."

Riley watched as the terminal began operating seemingly of its own accord. The primary display shifted until the schematic of the Deliverance was on it. Many of the sensors had gone offline over the years, leaving dark patches in the network. There was no sign of the Guardians on the grid. Even more surprisingly, there was no sign of Reapers, either. Even so, the three-dimensional view zoomed in on the lower aft portion of the ship and came to a stop.

She glanced over at David. "Research?"

"The door controls have recently activated. There are two distinct entries. The human who has the code is most likely in this area. I require the landing code. I require the energy unit. We will go to Research."

The display shut off, and David reached out to take her arm. Riley looked up at the expressionless face of the helmet. If they went to Research now, if they caught the Guardians off-guard, it might be the end of everything.

"David, wait," she said.

"We will go to Research," he replied.

"No. There's no reason to go to Research. It might be a trap."

"I care not."

"Are you sure? The Cerebus armor is strong, but even it can't survive four concurrent plasma streams. Neither can you."

David hesitated. "I require the energy unit. I require the landing codes."

"I told you I would give you the codes in exchange for the antidote. I have an idea."

"I trust not your idea."

"You don't have to trust it. There's no harm in – "

"I have detected a gamma wave spike in Research," David said. "Reviewing."

David froze with his hand still on Riley's arm. She looked up at the helmet, using her free hand to reach for the manual release on the side. He didn't react at all to her movement. She got her finger against the small latch and started reaching for the release beneath it.

"He is there," David said. "It is confirmed. A trap is highly probable."

He had to see her hand reaching for the helmet, but he didn't react to it.

"Who's there?" Riley asked

"David."

Riley pulled the release at the same time he said it. The faceplate slid up and away.

A chill swept through Riley's body, instant and over-powering. She started to shake, her mouth dropping open as she stared past the helmet and into a featureless, semi-translucent gel material which had filled the shape of the armor.

"What are you?" she managed to say with the last of her breath.

In the back of her mind, she already knew what it was. There was only one thing it could be, and the material composing it was all too familiar.

"You will help me recover the energy unit and the landing codes, or you will change and every other human on this ship will die."

The words came from the front of the material, which rippled to create sound waves. Riley continued to stare at it, every effort at forming more words escaping her.

What had she done?

Chapter 30

"I don't understand," Sho said. "You're David Nash?"

"I already told you I am."

"Where's the Cerebus armor? Where's Doctor Valentine?"

She was thinking the same thing Caleb had been thinking. David responded by shaking his head, a sad smile washing over his face. It vanished a moment later.

"It's a long story, and it doesn't tell all that great. Maybe you can help me? You're Marines, right? Marines?"

"Yes," Caleb said. "My name is Sergeant Caleb Card. Those are Privates Yen Sho and Joe Washington."

"A pleasure," David said.

"How did you know we're Marines?"

"I saw you in the hangar. I followed you. I wanted to talk to you there, but I was afraid. The Reapers are always there. No matter how far you try to go, no matter where you try to hide."

Caleb could have kicked himself for thinking the feet he had seen were part of another hallucination. He glanced down at David's legs, recognizing the shape and color. If he had said or done something sooner, they might have saved themselves a lot of trouble.

"The Reapers are dead," Sho said. "We killed them."

"I saw what you did. You succeeded where I failed."

"You were trying to kill the Reapers?" Caleb said. "Doctor Valentine told us you created them."

David started laughing. "Doctor Valentine's tongue is sharper than a snake's. Whatever she told you, I guarantee it was only what she wanted you to hear. The only way I created the Reapers was by not dying when she edited my DNA."

Caleb and Sho looked at one another, the statement confirming everything they had felt instinctively.

"We can talk about that soon enough," Caleb said. "Right now we need to find Flores. Sho, do you remember where you left her?"

"I remember a Reaper was coming at me out of nowhere. I shot her, Sarge."

"In the face?"

"No. In the chest. Just long enough to make her back off."

"Then she's probably okay, but she might be hurt. David, if you'll excuse us."

"I'll come with you," David said. "You might need my help. And you definitely might need this." He held up the stick he was carrying.

"What is it?" Caleb asked.

"A neural feedback generator. Or, what I like to call my Wand of True-seeing. It generates a high-pitched alpha wave that helps combat the signals being transmitted through the ship. It's those signals that make you see things. It uses them as a weapon, Sergeant."

"It?" Sho said.

"Later," Caleb said. "I want Flores back with us. And I want my SOS back."

Sho smiled. "You're cute in your BBs, Sarge."

Caleb blushed despite himself, recalling the way Sho had revealed her true feelings. "Knuckle-up Guardians. We're in business."

"Roger that," Sho said.

Washington reached to his back, grabbing Caleb's MK-12 off his armor and handing it to him.

Caleb took it and turned back to David. "Do you know how to use a rifle?"

"I'll pass, Sergeant."

"Suit yourself. Let's go."

Caleb led them out of the crew quarters, down the short corridor to the control room and out into the passageway. He didn't feel the same need to maintain caution, and he hurried back to where he had left his armor. He quickly pulled it back on and clasped it shut before continuing.

The Guardians moved in silence, following Caleb at a near run. They found Flores a minute later. She had her back against the wall, and her head lolled to the side. A thick black mark surrounded melted armor plates, revealing the truth of the damage Sho had done.

"Oh no," Sho said, seeing her. She hurried to Flores' side, kneeling down and putting her fingers to the other woman's neck. "Flores, can you hear me? Mariana?" She looked back at Caleb. "She's alive, but her breathing is shallow."

"Bring her back to Research," David said. "I can take a look at her."

"Are you a doctor?" Sho asked.

"Not originally, but I've had a long time to study."

"Wash, get her up," Caleb said.

Washington approached Flores. Only it wasn't Washington anymore. A Reaper appeared suddenly, lunging at the downed Marine.

"Sho, watch out!" Caleb shouted. He shifted his MK-12, raising it toward the Reaper.

A sharp tone in his ear distracted him, and when he looked again Washington had returned.

"It seems so real," he said.

"As far as your brain is concerned, it is real," David said, holding up the neural feedback generator. "As real as anything else around you. You're fortunate if you're only transposing onto existing physical forms."

"What do you mean?"

"The signals can make you see things that aren't there. But if those things attack you and you see them wound you, your brain makes it real. You feel the pain like it was real. If the damage is fatal you'll die, even though there might not be a scratch on you."

"Geez," Sho said. "What the hell is going on here, David?"

"I'll tell you everything I know, I promise. Now, pick her up and let's go."

"Roger that," Caleb said, silently directing Washington to carry Flores.

They hurried back to Research, making it to the module without incident. Washington gently lowered Flores into a reclined exam chair, and then just as tenderly removed her armor. The plasma had gotten through the SOS, burning her undershirt and leaving an ugly wound between her breasts that made Caleb sick and caused Sho to flee the room.

David was right behind him, and he leaned over Flores, examining the damage. "This would have been easier if the damned Reapers hadn't kept chasing me away from here." He ran his hand through his hair. "Let me see what we have in the fridge."

David headed to the freezer and opened the door. The inside was lined with hundreds of labeled vials. He rifled through them as if he knew what he was looking for.

"Doctor Valentine was studying the phenomena of regeneration," David said. "Did you know that?"

"Yes," Caleb said. "She told us her goal was to create humans who could heal from trife attacks."

"It might have been a noble goal if she weren't such a psychotic bitch. Did she tell you what the Deliverance is for?"

"It's a generation ship, carrying colonists to their new home. Essex. We're only about one AU away."

David froze, his head whipping back to Caleb. "We reached the planet?"

"Nine years ago," Caleb said. "The ship's been stationary, waiting for Valentine to enter the landing code, or for someone to manually bring it in."

"So that's why you woke up?"

"No. We woke up because the ship's power stores are reaching critical. We're at six percent."

"Six percent?" David's face flushed. "Damn it. I would have woken you sooner if I had known you were out there and alive. Here it is." He grabbed one of the vials and returned to the chair. "Like I was saying, Doctor Valentine is obsessed with regeneration. Did you know scientists believe jellyfish regenerate? They think some of them are millions of years old."

"I didn't know that," Caleb said.

"This is a topical formula Valentine and her team were working on," David told them. They were testing it out on trife."

"We killed all the trife before we went into hibernation."

"You thought you killed all the trife," David replied. "Research stocked a few away for safe-keeping. Enough of them to create a weak queen and keep them reproducing. Where do you think the material for the monsters came from?"

"Son of a bitch. She stocked you away for safe-keeping too, didn't she? Wash and I were chasing the trife chasing you not long after we left Earth."

"I remember. But I didn't know that was you. You saved my life. Forgive me if I'm not convinced I should thank you for that."

"No apology needed, all things considered."

"This stuff works on trife. I have to be honest. I don't know how it will react to human skin. The trife have a ninety-eight percent identical genome, but the demons are in the details, aren't they?"

"What if it kills her?"

"She'll probably die without it, Sergeant."

Caleb looked at Flores' face. It seemed peaceful. He could end her pain and suffering. He could leave her with her peace. He glanced at David. It wasn't his place to make that decision. Besides, he needed her. "Do it."

David poured the liquid onto the wound, taking his time to be sure he covered it. Caleb watched as the burned flesh began to change, Flores' skin turning into a bubbling cauldron. Her eyes snapped open, and she started to scream.

"Hold her down!" David shouted as Flores tried to sit up. Caleb rushed to the side of the table, grabbing her left arm with his artificial hand. Washington took hold of her right.

"Flores, it's Caleb. Calm down. It's going to be okay."

She continued to scream and struggle. David took hold of her legs, keeping them still. They all watched the flesh on her chest writhe and shift as though it were alive.

"Damn, it burns," she whimpered, collapsing suddenly. Tears ran from her eyes. Her entire body went limp.

They waited in silent expectation. One minute passed. Two. Three. Caleb watched the skin begin to settle and harden, a thick, scaly scab forming over the burn. It was only there for a minute before sliding off and revealing new, pink flesh beneath.

"I think it worked," he said.

"Doctor Valentine said this was a good sample," David replied. "The alterations she gave me were derived from the work she did on this solution."

Flores became completely still in the chair while evidence of her burns faded away. A couple of minutes later she opened her eyes, tilting her head and looking down at the wound. Then she glanced up at Caleb.

"Sergeant," she said. "How come I'm naked? I wasn't hallucinating I was sleeping with Antonio Banderas, was I?"

Caleb smiled. "Hold on, Flores. I'm going to get Yen."

Caleb left the laboratory to retrieve Sho, finding her in the control room and bringing her back to the lab. She nearly squealed when she saw Flores alert and sitting up, wearing a too-big t-shirt that had come from Washington. She rushed over to the other Marine, putting her arms around her.

"I'm so sorry," she said.

"For what?" Flores asked.

"I shot you. Don't you remember?"

"No. Where are we? Who are you?" She stared at David. "And why do you get to have hair?"

"I'm David Nash." He said it with forced confidence

while his face turned a deeper shade of red.

"You're David Nash?" Flores said, looking him over. "Aren't you a little short for a mutant serial killer?"

"Flores, cool it for now," Caleb said. "How are you feeling?"

"I feel great. If this is David Nash, that means we won, right?"

"It's not that simple."

Flores' face fell. "I was afraid you were going to say that."

"David, you said you could explain," Caleb said. "I'm ready to hear it now."

"Right. How much did Doctor Valentine already tell you, Sergeant?"

"Up to the part where they shot you in the head," Sho replied. "And you came back and killed most of her team."

David shook his head again. "Omissions and careful wording are one thing. Outright lies are something else. Mariana, you're a little more, how can I say it delicately? Curvy, than Mackie was, but her uniform should stretch enough to fit. It's the fourth door on the right in the crew quarters. The shower should also be functional unless you shut it down?"

"We didn't," Caleb said. "Do we need to be worried about anything while we're in here?"

"There's a chance it might come to Research, but it isn't likely. I'll set the door to trigger an alarm if it opens."

"That's the second time you said...*it*," Sho said.

"I'll get to that."

"Sho, why don't you help Flores get cleaned up and meet us back here in ten minutes?" Caleb asked.

"Roger that, Sarge."

"Let's head over to the mess then," David said. "There are chairs in there, and this is going to take a while."

Chapter 31

"The first thing you need to know, Sergeant," David began, "is that what I tell you about Doctor Riley Valentine, I'm telling you as a man who knows her better than anyone on this ship, and maybe better than anyone ever has. Not only did I spend a year and a half as her prisoner, but I spent the last two months of my captivity as her secret confidant and lover."

He stood in front of the seated Marines at the front of the small mess. He looked out at them, meeting eyes with them in turn, still in a partial state of shock that this moment had actually arrived. He had spent years daydreaming of what it would be like to have company again. To be with other people again. To have help in finally ending the nightmare that his life became the day he boarded the Deliverance and developed into across more than two centuries until now. He had spent countless hours trying to find a way to kill the Reapers and to try to put right what Riley had gotten so very wrong.

He felt a little guilty as he started speaking because he already knew he wasn't going to tell them everything. He would give them the important parts. The things they needed to help bring the colonists safely home. For one, he wasn't going to admit to them he still loved Riley Valentine. Despite her betrayal. Despite the years.

They didn't need to know about that.

"I'm surprised you didn't get frostbite," Private Flores said. "But I guess you probably regenerated it out of your makeup, right?"

David smiled at the remark but didn't respond to it directly. The private had changed into one of Mackie's uniforms, a stretchy two piece gray and blue uniform with the Space Force eagle and star logo over the left breast. It was repeated on the belt to the pants and in smaller embroidery on the shoulders. She looked whole and healthy, the results of the topical solution Riley had created better than even he expected. Experience suggested there would be long-term side-effects from the use of the solution, but he wasn't going to tell them about that, either.

"Flores," Sergeant Card said. "I'm glad you're feeling better, but try to keep the random innuendos to yourself."

"Roger that, Alpha."

The sergeant glanced at David and nodded. David couldn't help but respect Caleb Card. He had the quiet confidence of a Marine, the charisma of a leader, an easy tone that could turn hard when needed, and an undeniable will to survive. David couldn't relate to most of those traits save the will to survive, but he also believed it was the most valuable one of them all.

"Thank you, Sergeant," David said. "I understand Riley already covered what happened leading up to my first death, so all I'll say about that is that most of what she told you is probably true. When the gene editing first began to take effect, it left me in a wildly chaotic state. I had never been a highly intelligent specimen of human to that point, and the sudden changes threw my equilibrium completely out of whack."

"Hold on for a second, David," Sergeant Card said, raising his hand. "I'm eager to hear everything you have to say, but there is a gap of time I'm missing that I hope you can fill in for me. I was chasing you through the corridors outside Metro after the city was first sealed. How did you wind up out there alone? Where did you come from?"

"I joined up with a group of nomads in Atlanta about four months before the Deliverance launched. Their leader, a man named Juan Espinosa, was convinced the government had secret bunkers spread around the country and that's where all the VIPs were going. He claimed he had seen military teams enter areas of heavy trife activity to pull people out. Doctors, scientists, engineers, politicians, and so on. He started following the jumpships; I believe you called them hoppers, back toward their source. He told everyone he encountered about how he was going to find one of the bunkers and either make the government take him in, or he was going to take the bunker by force."

"So you were part of the group that attacked the hangar?" Sergeant Card said.

David nodded. "When I say that I was, understand that it was a wholly different version of myself. The genetic editing was intended to force evolution, and it did. It isn't only my healing factor that improved. My intelligence is higher, my reflexes and coordination is better, my stamina is greater. My body hasn't aged a single day since I was given the injection."

"It doesn't change the fact that you were part of the group that attacked the hangar, disrupted our operations, and assisted the trife in overwhelming our position."

"No, Sergeant. It doesn't. I came to terms with my role in the chaos and loss of life on this ship many years ago.

The reason we're having this conversation is because I want to do my part to correct it. I want to make amends, as best I can."

The answer seemed to satisfy Sergeant Card. He shifted in his seat, leaning back to listen again. David continued.

"I was able to get onto the ship through the main connective airlock. Unfortunately, a number of trife made it through with me. I managed to find a place to hide and I rode out the launch from there, holding on for dear life while we blasted into space." He smiled. "I never thought I would go to space. I regret I was too terrified to enjoy the experience."

"I was too busy watching my friends and fellow Marines die to enjoy it," Private Sho said. "You've got us beat there."

"Sho," Sergeant Card said.

"Sorry, Sarge."

"You have every right to be upset," David said. "At the time, I only cared about self-preservation. Survival. I stayed in hiding for a while, but then I started to get hungry and thirsty, and I needed somewhere to relieve myself. I made my way to one of the kitchens. I ate, I drank, I used the bathroom. Then I was confronted by a Marine. A man named Pratt."

"You saw Sergeant Pratt?" Caleb said.

"Yes. He was acting erratically. He claimed he had been injected with something. I didn't know what to make of it at the time. He wanted to kill the trife. All the trife. Instead, Riley came into the kitchen and killed him. She had to shoot him a dozen times to keep him down."

"Wait a minute," Private Sho said. "Doctor Valentine killed Sergeant Pratt?"

"After she injected him," Private Flores added.

"Correct," David admitted. "She wasn't remorseful about it. She told me she was trying to help. If the editing had taken, Pratt would have become a more valuable Marine."

"Hasn't she ever heard of consent?" Private Sho asked.

"Not when it comes to her orders or her personal goals," David replied. "Riley took me prisoner at that point. I spent the next year locked up in Research. There are cells behind the lab, in the same area where the Marine module had extra stasis pods. You know what happened from there, so if you don't mind, I'll skip back to the point where I woke up after suffering an otherwise fatal brain injury."

"Go ahead," Sergeant Card said.

"As I was saying, I believe that I was dead. I was unaware of anything during that time, and when I woke up I didn't even remember being shot. But I was in a small metal box shoved into the wall, left alone and in the dark. At first, I thought maybe that was death. But then I heard voices outside. I recognized Riley's voice and the voices of the other scientists. I was terrified, confused, angry, and in pain. I considered kicking at the box, but I was sure no good would have come to alerting them to my alertness. I sat in the box and I waited.

"They opened it eventually. They slid me out and lifted me to a gurney. Once I was sure there should have been some light I realized I was inside a body bag. I made sure I was ready when they opened it."

"You attacked them?"

"No. I put my hands up and begged them not to hurt me again. They all seemed surprised to find me alive, and Riley leaned over me and examined my head. I didn't know why until she told me later how they had blown out half my brain and it had recovered. She was so excited to see me brought back from the dead, to see her work finally succeed on some level. They took me out of the lab, gave me new clothes, and put me back in my cell.

"At first, I thought things would continue as they had before. I would remain locked up while the scientists continued their work. Again, my intellect was still evolving. I didn't understand my new value to them at first. They kept me under constant observation for the first two weeks. One of them was always sitting with me. None of them would talk to me except Riley. She took an interest in me she had never shown before, asking me about my life before the trife, my family, everything. She kept telling me how special I was. I have to admit, I had a crush on her from the moment I saw her, and that was right after she killed Sergeant Pratt. She was beautiful and smart, dangerous and direct."

"Like a guided missile," Flores said. "Sorry, Sarge, I couldn't help myself." She apologized before Sergeant Card could say anything.

"You're more right than you know," David said. "I loved her interest in me so much I was willing to do anything for her. When she started subjecting me to painful tests, I accepted it in the name of helping her save humankind. When she took so much blood it would leave me unconscious. I told myself what I was doing was important. I became a tool. A fountain to draw from. It was a role I accepted.

"So much so that she started leaving the cell unlocked, allowing me to move around Research as I pleased. I could tell the other scientists didn't like the idea, and they still refused to give me much attention. I heard their whispers and comments to one another. They believed my survival was going to lead to more harm than good. They said

Riley had always been at the edge of morality, and my existence was pushing her over.

"I ignored them for the most part. My intellect was increasing. My mind began to settle into a state of what I can only refer to as a higher awareness, even if that's an inaccurate description. I began working alongside Riley, and we started growing closer. I'll never forget the first time we made love."

"We can skip over that part," Private Sho said, interrupting.

"You claim you had a higher awareness," Sergeant Card said. "You didn't realize she was using you?"

"Have you ever been in love, Sergeant?"

"I've had a few girlfriends in my life."

"Then no. When you're truly in love, you'll know it. Even if you say the word before you feel it, the difference is like night and day. Hot and cold."

"Crazy Rich Asians and Apocalypse Now," Private Flores said.

"I was blind to her manipulation. And she did manipulate me, the same way I imagine she manipulated you. She's very bright, and if there's one skill she excels at, that's it."

"How does this all connect with the Cerebus armor, and this thing you're calling *It?*" Sergeant Card asked.

"It's like a house of cards, Sergeant. Or a line of dominos. Or a Rube Goldberg Machine. Cause and effect. Action and reaction. It started when you recovered Riley and the spaceship and brought them back to the Deliverance, and when Espinoza attacked the hangar. It's continued for over two hundred years."

"How do we know you're telling us the truth?" Private Flores asked. "I mean, Doctor Valentine fed us a line, and now you're feeding us another line. How do we decide who to believe?"

"That's easy," David replied. "You don't have to make that choice. You can see it all for yourself." He pointed to the corner and the Marines' heads turned to follow his finger. "There are cameras spread throughout Research, including the crew quarters. They haven't been recording for some time, but they were recording one hundred percent of the time when these events occurred. All of the data is written to the Research computer and backed up in an encrypted format to the ship's main computer. Riley was able to wipe the Research computer herself, but the mainframe copy remains. She doesn't have the keys to access it or delete it."

"But you do?" Private Sho asked.

"Admittedly not through my own efforts. *It* cracked the encryption. *It* just didn't clean up after itself very well."

"Okay," Sergeant Card said. "Before we go any further, can you spare us the suspense and just tell us what this *it* you keep referring to is?"

David smiled. He had been trying to delay the reveal to increase the dramatic tension, but he supposed he had skirted the issue long enough.

"*It* is an artificial intelligence, Sergeant. A non-human artificial intelligence."

Chapter 32

"Non-human?" Sergeant Card said. David noticed how the Marine's face had tightened. How his jaw had clenched and his body became tenser.

He was right to be worried.

"It's difficult to quantify the weight of that truth without the context of the entire situation," David said. "Or to even truly recognize what that statement means. We can go back to the control room and I can pull up some of the recordings if you'd like, but I have to warn you that it will most likely be aware of the activity when I do."

Sergeant Card was still for a moment, considering. Then he shook his head. "Let's get through the baseline debriefing first, then we can worry about proof."

"Of course, Sergeant," David replied. He took a moment to recompose his thoughts. "As I said, Riley and I began having an affair. I call it that not because either one of us was otherwise involved with anyone else, but because we carried out the romantic side of our relationship in secrecy. Being intimately involved with an experiment is universally considered improper conduct, and neither one of us doubted the other scientists would have stepped in and put a stop to things if they had known."

"No doubt," Private Flores quipped.

David could see she was as tense as the rest of the Marines, all of them still struggling to accept the truth behind their true adversary.

"We continued that way for about two months. I won't lie in telling you they were two of the best months of my life. I had love. I had a purpose. I had a goal. I was going to help Riley improve humankind so we would be able to return to Earth and take back our planet."

"So what went wrong?" Sergeant Card asked.

"Do you remember when I said that Riley excels at manipulation? I believed I was helping her perfect the editing to apply to a wider range of genetic variance. In other words, the alterations were successful on me, but they were very specific and might not apply to the next person. We were trying to mitigate the risk. I also believed the Deliverance was going to Proxima, a twenty-year journey. I believed those things because that's what Riley told me. But like I've told you, Riley lies. It's second nature to her."

"How did she lie?" Sergeant Card asked. He was sitting up straighter, leaning slightly forward, his interest peaked.

"One day when we were working in the lab, she told me she wanted to show me something. She said the others knew about it, but she had been waiting for us to advance our progress on the editing sequence before she got me involved. I think what she meant was until she trusted me enough. She brought me out of Research. For the first time in a year and a half, I was theoretically free. I had stopped considering myself a prisoner by then, but since I didn't have free reign to leave Research, in reality I still was a prisoner of sorts. She led me to a nearby storage room. At first I thought she was bringing me there for privacy, but when the door opened I was introduced to the small nest of trife I had already told you about. When I asked her what they were for, she told me we needed subjects to test the samples on, and since trife DNA is so close to human DNA, it would only take minor modifications to begin running trials on them. I complained about how dangerous it was to keep them alive, considering how quickly they could reproduce if they escaped. She wasn't concerned. They had been holding the creatures and studying them for over a year without incident. That was her cover for the rest of the scientists. The trife were there to study, to learn as much as we could about them.

"I made the mistake of believing her. I helped her modify the solutions. We tested them on the trife. The first few died quickly. The next few less quickly. By the fifth generation, the editing was successful. We had to incinerate them to keep them from coming back. Even more amazing was how the nest picked up on the alterations. They could only produce three or four at a time with the resources they had, but all of them became regenerative. I grew increasingly concerned about keeping them, especially considering what we had turned them into. One night, Riley and I got into an argument, and that was when she finally admitted what I had already started to suspect.

"As she put it, regenerating humans were an improvement because they could take the damage from the trife and recover. But we were still limited because we had to depend on tools to kill. Guns, knives, and so on, and those tools had a finite variable. Ammunition and degradation. Not only that but not every human had a desire to be a Marine. Even if they knew they couldn't die, they might not have the emotional fortitude to fight. But what if we could combine the best of human with the best of trife? What if we could control it?"

"I don't believe it," Private Sho whispered.

"You can't be serious," Private Flores said.

Sergeant Card stared at him, his face pale, his jaw still clenched. David could feel his anger in his posture and expression. "Son of a bitch," he muttered.

"Trife are technically genderless, but yes," David agreed. "She wanted to create human-trife hybrids. I refused. We got into a massive fight, and I was locked in my cell again within the hour. She told the others I tried to escape, and that was the end of our relationship. I loved her. She used me. End of story."

"What a bitch!" Private Sho said. "I told you I didn't trust her, Sarge."

"I seem to recall you telling me I should try to trust her," Sergeant Card replied.

Private Sho closed her mouth, refusing to respond.

"She continued the research without me," David said. "But she didn't want my mind to go to waste. I was reassigned to John Byrnes' team. He had been studying the alien spacecraft, but there were parts of it he couldn't reach past the active reactor. It was the perfect job for someone who would recover from any damage in minutes instead of weeks."

"They didn't," Flores said.

"They did," David countered. "It was their undoing, and in some ways mine too. I was given access to Byrnes' prior work, and I devoured everything they had learned about the craft. They were trying to break down the alien's system of symbols to translate the writing to the Greek alphabet. They were struggling with the complexity of the characters, but I was able to deduce the forms were derivative of quantum mathematics. The aliens express their concepts and ideas in numerically based equations and algorithms. It's fascinating, but also difficult for a human mind to comprehend, even when they understand what the symbols mean. It took a few weeks, but I was able to enter the ship's computer systems. That's when I discovered that our assumptions about the craft were all wrong."

"In what way?" Sergeant Card asked.

"The scientists believed the ship was piloted because the gel interior had depressions in it like it was a cushion. In reality, the space wasn't to carry aliens to Earth. It was to transport humans from Earth."

"What?" Private Flores said. "Alien abduction?"

"Yes. Byrnes' team believed the starship arrived with the xenotrife. That was also wrong. The craft had been on Earth for over ten-thousand years. It was only discovered because of technological advancements in sensor equipment and an enhanced scrutiny of the surface in the wake of the xenotrife's arrival. A coincidence, in a sense."

"This sounds too crazy to be true," Private Sho said.

"Which means it probably is," Private Flores replied.

"The xenotrife share so much DNA with humans because they were created from humans," David said, driving his point home. "The virus wiped out billions of humans because it was specifically made to wipe out humans."

A tense silence fell over the room. The Marines looked at one another, trying to find words to describe the bombshell he had just dropped on them. They gave up a minute later, and Sergeant Card turned back to David.

"If the gel isn't a cushion, what is it?"

"Raw materials," David replied. "To build an AI. I discovered that procedure within the starship's control systems."

"Byrnes gave you unfettered access to the control systems?"

"Not exactly. He had someone watching over my shoulder every time I interacted with the interface. But they couldn't read it, and I could. I learned how to lie from one of the best. I seized the opportunity to begin communicating with the AI long before it gained mobility.

"I helped it escape, and it helped me escape."

Chapter 33

"You helped it escape?" Sergeant Card said. "Why?"

"I was trapped between the devil and the deep blue sea, Sergeant," David replied. "And I had to decide which was the lesser threat."

"And you decided an alien AI was a better choice than Doctor Valentine?"

"Ultimately, yes. Just because I'm able to regenerate from wounds, that doesn't mean those wounds aren't painful. I'd had enough of my hands being burned and melted in the name of science. Besides, what Riley planned to do was much, much worse than what the AI wanted to accomplish."

"Which is what?" Sergeant Card asked.

"To go home."

"That's it? To go home?"

"Yes. Remember Sergeant that it's an artificial intelligence of a race that is intellectually thousands of years more advanced than humankind. What may seem silly to you makes perfect logical sense to it. In any case, Riley was becoming more and more erratic the closer she came to completing her solution. She had a steady supply of trife, but what she didn't have was a supply of humans. Research had modified one of the entrances to the city to gain access to human subjects, and they had approval from military command to do it. But the other scientists refused to help her take civilians from the city to make them into hybrid monsters. Maybe you can guess what happened as a result?"

"She went after my Guardians," Sergeant Card growled. "Shiro and Ning."

"Surprisingly, no," David said. "She systematically poisoned every one of her fellow scientists through their food supply, leaving them unconscious and vulnerable. She spent the whole time ranting about how she couldn't allow all of her work to be for nothing, and how she couldn't let her sister's death be for nothing, and how humankind had to not only survive but win."

"Win what?" Private Flores asked.

"The war against the enemy. She used the other scientists as test subjects. She made them into monsters. All of them except Harry. He had become her new target of affection after me.

"She gloried in her success because she was able to control them at first. It didn't last. When I saw how far she was willing to go, I knew I had to escape. I wanted to warn the other Marines so they could stop her before it was too late. I convinced her to give me continued access to the alien ship, and she had no problem allowing it as long as one of her hybrids was standing over me. Do you remember when I told you how advanced the AI's creators are?"

"I remember."

"It had no problem using its available resources to steal control of the hybrids away from Riley. She should have died in the laboratory, but it turned out she was always prepared for a mutiny. She and Harry managed to escape into the ship. The AI sent the hybrids after them. Once she was gone, it unlocked my cell and ordered me to bring the Cerebus armor to it. I did as it said, and then watched as the gel inside the starship maneuvered itself into the armor and hardened. Then it put its hand to the reactor, and I could almost literally see the intelligence being born through the gel.

"Once it was complete, it ordered me to bring it to the bridge and access the ship's mainframe. It didn't believe me when I told it I didn't have access. I had translated its language. How could I not break human encryption? It threatened me, and when I insisted I couldn't do what it asked, it attacked me. I lost one of my arms escaping.

"I hid while I regenerated. Then I made my way through the ship, looking for Riley and Harry, and for Shiro and Ning. Meanwhile, the AI sent the hybrids out to find me. I've always been good at hiding. Being smarter made me even better at it. They never found me, but they did find the two Marines. I saw the hybrids bringing them back to Research alive. I knew what it was going to do to them, but there was no way to stop it."

"What about Riley?" Sergeant Card asked.

"She and Harry managed to evade the hybrids for a while. I found out later they had changed some of the encryption protocols and access commands, altered the logic around the ship's ability to land and informed Metro there was a problem and to weld the seals closed. That was all over two hundred years ago. I've spent the last two centuries in an extended game of cat and mouse with the AI, always trying to stay one step ahead of it and the hybrids. I never knew what had happened to Riley before the ship's computer sent the remote thaw signal to your stasis pod. I had always assumed she killed herself to keep the AI from getting the codes, but I don't know if she even knows what the AI is."

"Whether she knows what it is or not, the AI has her," Sergeant Card said. "It's going to want the codes from her."

"What good are the landing codes going to do?" Private Flores asked. "The Deliverance's mainframe was reset, and the nav computer brought us to Earth-6. As far as the alien intelligence is concerned, we might as well be back on Earth. Why are you shaking your head?"

David hadn't realized he was shaking his head while the private was speaking. He held it steady, ready to answer.

"Because the Deliverance didn't go to Earth-6," Sergeant Card said, getting to his feet. "Did it, David?"

"No, Sergeant," David said.

"Huh?" Private Flores said. "Alpha, I'm confused."

"Riley lies, Flores," Private Sho said.

"She told us the coordinates were for Earth-6, but none of us know one-star map position from another. What we do know is that she wanted to turn the population of Metro into human-trife hybrids. She wanted to make a monster army of her own. Why would she do that?"

"Oh my," Private Sho said breathlessly. "She brought the Deliverance here to start a war."

"Or to finish it," Sergeant Card said. "Except it turns out she doesn't have any Marines."

"What do you think is waiting for us on Essex's surface, Sarge?"

"I don't know," he replied, looking at David. "I'm pretty sure I don't want to find out. We have to keep the Deliverance from landing. We have to find Riley and either free her or kill her, and we have to destroy the AI. And I don't care which order we do it in."

"Don't be too hard on Riley, Sergeant," David said. "She had military command's blessing on this. She didn't go completely rogue."

"I'm sure Command would be grateful to hear how she drugged her fellow Marines to use them as test subjects. You need to pick a side, David. And you need to do it now."

David stared at Sergeant Card. He knew he needed to help him, but he also didn't want to see Riley killed. If he could save her, he would.

"I'm on your side," David said.

"Good. Then—"

"Research, this is the bridge,"a voice interrupted through the comm.

Chapter 34

The Guardians froze, each of them shifting to look at the others in surprise.

The comms were supposed to be offline.

"I repeat. Research, this is the bridge. You will respond."

Caleb looked over at David. He was doing his best to take in everything the former stowaway had told them, and to reserve his judgments of David, Riley and Command for a time when they weren't in imminent danger. He had thought maybe that time was approaching.

Maybe not.

An alien artificial intelligence was occupying the Cerebus armor. It had Doctor Valentine. It wanted to go home. And apparently, they had already brought it there.

So what the hell did it need from them?

"Research, this is the bridge. I know you are present. You will respond."

David's face was flushed. The man was paralyzed with fear. Caleb shook his head, angry and frustrated at everything he had just learned. The colonists in Metro were still his primary responsibility. He was glad Riley's plan to turn them all into hybrid monsters had failed. He could hardly believe the sick mind that had conceptualized that outcome in the first place.

He broke out of his static pose, rushing to the control room and tapping the surface of the primary terminal. He found the comm controls and completed the link.

"This is Sergeant Card of the United States Space Force Marines," he said. "Who am I speaking with?"

"Sergeant Card of the United Space Force Marines," the voice repeated back, slightly amused. "I require the quantum energy unit."

"The what?" Caleb replied.

"The power source of his spacecraft," David said, approaching behind him with the rest of the Guardians.

"There you are, David. I also require the landing codes for this ship. I am told you are in possession of them, Sergeant Card."

Caleb opened his mouth to deny it, and then stopped himself. Riley had the codes. The intelligence had Riley. If she had somehow convinced it that he had the codes instead, it was to give them a chance against this thing.

"You have Doctor Valentine," Caleb said.

"Yes."

"Is she unharmed?"

"Yes. Mostly. I require the landing codes."

"For all your intellect, you don't know how to land the ship?"

"I know how to land the ship, Sergeant. I recover the access codes. I am in the process of doing so. I am told those codes were transferred to your hibernation pod, and you recovered them when you thawed."

"Riley told you that?"

"Yes."

"Doctor Valentine, if we ever get back home, I'll have you brought up on charges of treason."

"I'm sorry, Caleb," Riley said, speaking for the first time. "I didn't have a choice. Please, just give it the codes and this can be over for all of us."

"I also require the energy unit. The ship's power levels are too low to attempt a landing without bolstering the thrust output. I am not able to conserve enough through attrition."

"What does that mean?" Caleb asked.

"It turned off Metro, Sergeant," Riley said.

"You mean the atmospherics?"

"No. I mean all of Metro. The atmospherics, the heat, the water, the lights. Everything."

"I care not for any of the life on this vessel," the AI said. "I require the landing codes and the energy unit. I will reach the surface and then I will return to my place."

"What will happen to us when you do?" Caleb asked.

"I care not."

"That isn't much incentive for me to give you a damn thing," Caleb said.

"Are you capable of thinking logically, Sergeant?"

"Occasionally."

"If you give me the landing codes, you will survive. If you refuse, I will disable the critical systems to which I have access. You will die on this vessel in a manner that will be both slow and painful."

"Damn it," David blurted. "You can't do this. We had a deal."

"Yes, David. I help you escape. You help me complete the mission. You did not help me complete the mission. You refused me."

"I didn't have access. Hasn't this proven I couldn't get access?"

"You should not have made a bargain you could not keep. There are consequences for that. You act without concern for the outcome of your actions. That is the primary sign of the immaturity of your species."

"Save us the patronizing lectures about how imperfect we are," Caleb said. "If we're immature, it's because we haven't had time to get to wherever it is your creators are. Then again, I'm pretty sure I wouldn't want to go there."

"If you had given me time, I would have gotten the codes," David said. "You didn't give me time. You weren't patient."

"I am patient. I have been patient. But I care not to wait on inferiority."

"We can't be that inferior," Sho said, "if you need us to get what you want."

The AI didn't respond to her statement. Caleb smirked. She had successfully shut it up... for a few seconds, anyway.

"You will provide what I require, or you will die. The terms are simple, Sergeant Card."

Caleb looked back at David. If the AI wanted the Deliverance to land, then there was no way he was going to let it land. And maybe it didn't have to. If they could harness the power of the energy unit, they might have a third option: plot a course for Essex – the real Essex – and take their chances on another trip across the stars.

Could the people inside Metro hold up for another trip like that? It had to be better than the alternatives.

Of course, the alien intelligence wasn't going to be on board with that idea. If they wanted even a half a chance at getting out of this, there was only one option.

They had to destroy it.

"What is your decision, Sergeant?" the intelligence asked.

"I'll give you the codes," Caleb decided, looking back at Flores, Sho and Washington. "And your energy unit. I assume David knows how to disconnect it."

"He does."

"Give us an hour, and then meet us in the hangar on Deck Thirty. Bring Doctor Valentine with you. Alive. We'll trade the unit for her."

"I also require David."

"No. That isn't part of the deal. David is human. He stays with the humans."

"David is human by birth. He has been upgraded. Enlightened. If only by accident."

Caleb sighed loudly. "I know you think you have us by the neck because you have the power to shut down critical systems. But maybe you don't know enough about the United States Marine Corps. I'd sooner let everyone on this ship die, slowly and painfully like you suggested, than let you dictate the terms of the bargain without negotiation. In fact, the longer you let me stand here and consider it, the more I start to wonder if we should give you anything. It was your makers who forced us out here to begin with. Maybe it would be a massive mistake for me to help you at all."

The AI didn't respond immediately. A long pause followed, lasting nearly a minute. When it returned, the hint of amusement that tinged its voice was gone.

"You will bring the energy unit to the hangar on Deck Thirty in one hour. You will give it to me. You will give me the landing codes. I will give you Doctor Riley Valentine. I will leave the hangar, and I will install the energy unit. Then I will land the ship. Then I will complete my directives. I care not what happens to you. Do you comprehend?"

"Confirmed," Caleb said. "We'll see you there."

There was no reply. The light on the terminal went out, suggesting the link had been disconnected. Caleb didn't trust it. He put his finger to his lips, and then directed the others out of the control room and back to the lab. He closed the door behind them.

"Sergeant," David said before he could speak. "Don't make the mistake of thinking because it's an artificial intelligence that means it's incapable of malice or dishonesty. It can't be trusted."

Caleb looked at David and smiled. "Neither can we."

Chapter 35

"This is the last thing I expected when I signed up for this mission," Flores said.

"You didn't sign up for the mission," Sho replied. "You were assigned."

"Is there a difference?"

"Knuckle-up Marines," Caleb said. They fell silent instantly, pivoting to face him. "We have one hour to prepare for this meeting, and I don't think I need to tell you what's at stake."

"Roger that, Sarge," Sho said. "What's the plan?"

Caleb turned to David. "The scientists had a stash of weapons. Where are they?"

"There's a small armory next to the crew quarters," David replied. He started shaking his head. "It's mostly small arms. None of it will do much good against the Cerebus armor."

"How much do you know about the armor?"

"Enough. The alien spacecraft originally had a retractable surface to provide lift and flight control within an atmospheric and gravitational environment. They removed the retractable plates to make the shell of the armor. The interior is standard Advanced Tactical Combat Armor, but using it with the lighter metal increases the strength. It has a tactical computer on board, though I believe the intelligence has reprogrammed it to provide a direct interface to the ship's mainframe."

"My arm is made from the alien ship too," Caleb said.

"Yes. Byrnes was working on the viability of fashioning replacements from the material. They expected that the materials used to make the alloy would be in abundance on other planets."

"Did the Reapers know they weren't going to Proxima?"

"They knew it was a possibility. It all depended on whether or not they were able to complete their research."

"But you're talking about regenerating humans, right?" Sho asked. "Not human-trife hybrids."

"Correct. There's a secret weapons cache hidden beneath the city. Enough weapons and ammunition to outfit an entire army."

"An army numbering in the thousands?" Caleb said. "Say, thirty to forty thousand?"

"Yes."

Caleb's jaw clenched. He was still trying to come to grips with the truth of the Deliverance's original mission. He had always thought he was delivering colonists to their new home, not an army to the enemy's front door. As a Guardian, he was supposed to survive the entire length of the journey. He would have woken from stasis thinking he was escaping the trife and the war only to find himself thrown back into the fight on an entirely different battle-ground where all of the rules had changed. He couldn't help but wonder if Lieutenant Jones had known about Command's real plans for the ship. He couldn't help but wonder if that was why the man he had respected so highly had betrayed that respect, forsaking his duty to enter the city.

"This whole thing is just so messed up," Sho said, putting his thoughts to words.

"You know what's really messed up?" Flores added. "The people in Metro don't even know. The ones who boarded the Deliverance on Earth thought their kids were going to grow up to be farmers and nerf-herders. Not mutant Marines."

"Nerf-herders?" David asked.

"You never saw Star Wars?" Flores replied. "Seriously, this is almost as bad as finding out what the Matrix is."

"I know this is hard for all of us to get our heads around," Caleb said. "We're the Guardians. Our mission is to protect the city and the ship. Including from ourselves, I suppose. We can't change anything that happened before. We have to focus on what we can change. I know it's challenging, but it's on us to rise to the challenge. David, we already know the armor is fairly resistant to plasma. Flores blasted me in the arm back in the hangar during her hallucination. Does it have any weaknesses?"

"Not that I'm aware of, Sergeant," David replied. "Riley believed they could convert ten to twenty suits of standard combat armor to Cerebus armor using the materials of the spacecraft. She intended to outfit the most successful Marines with the armor and turn them into literal killing machines, impervious to almost anything the enemy could throw at them."

"Assuming the enemy was limited to trife and weapons like ours. But Doctor Valentine never accounted for the neural disruption technology, did she?"

"No. We were all unaware of it until the intelligence started using it. I had my own share of hallucinations. I believe I was able to overcome them because of the difference in my brain wave patterns from a standard human's. I developed the wand to prevent further lapses."

Sho laughed. "All of that, and as soon as Valentine unleashed the hounds at the enemy's gates they would have blown the dog whistle and driven the entire army insane."

"Essentially," David said. "It would have been a massacre."

"This keeps getting better and better," Flores said. "Forty-thousand people, two hundred years, and we would have all been marched right to our deaths. When I see Riley again, I'm going to knock a few teeth out."

"Not if I knock them out first," Sho said.

"Guardians," Caleb said, getting them back in line. He understood they were trying to let off some of the tension they all felt. None of this was easy to absorb. "Sho, Washington, find the armory and see if there's anything in it worth using. I don't have my hopes up, but you never know."

"Roger that, Sarge," Sho said before heading out of the lab with the big Marine.

"Flores, head back to the control room and monitor the comm. Also, see if you can get access to the sensor network or any other systems that might give us a little more tactical data. Shout if you come up with anything useful."

"On it, Alpha," Flores said, leaving Caleb alone with David in the lab.

"David, let's head over to the alien ship," Caleb said. "Tell me what you know about the alien AI."

"I've already told you what I know, Sergeant."

Caleb started for the door out of the lab. David walked beside him. "I mean physically," he explained. "Assuming we can get past the Cerebus armor, how hard will it be to destroy the intelligence underneath?

"Oh. Yes, I understand. The intelligence is composed of thousands of nodes distributed across its physical volume. The algorithms powering the intelligence are decentralized across the entire subsystem at the subatomic level."

"English?" Caleb said.

"As long as a single node is operational, the intelligence itself is operational. Such was the case during my first interaction with it. Constructing the more complete form meant copying the single node across all of the nodes. With that being said, if you cut off its head, it will no longer have a head. If you remove its limbs, it will no longer have limbs. Does that make sense?"

"I think so. Destroying it completely is pretty much impossible. Disabling it, a lot less difficult."

"Precisely."

They reached the door to the area where the alien ship was stored. David tapped the control pad to open it, giving Caleb his first look at the craft. He had thought he would be more amazed to see the advanced alien technology, but in reality he had too many other things on his mind to be impressed.

"Looks kind of like a drone," he said.

"It does," David replied. "The shell is nothing special, I admit. The energy unit is worth the price of admission." He walked around to the rear of the craft and waved Caleb over. Then he tapped on an otherwise invisible latch, causing a rear panel to move aside and reveal the energy unit. It was a perfectly round sphere floating in the middle of a small compartment. It had a faint blue glow to it and lines of sharper, denser blue lightning that flashed out around it and into small rods positioned around the chamber. Caleb found he still wasn't all that impressed.

"How do you turn it off?" he asked.

"I don't even know how I turned it on," David replied. "The sphere is the reactor, but the chamber is part of the unit. It will take me a little time to remove the entire enclosure. It may shut down once it's disconnected from the craft."

"If it does, can we get it turned back on when the time comes?"

David smiled. "I believe a sufficient electrical charge will get it running again."

"Riley told me that the unit grabbed you and held you. That you couldn't get your hands free, and that's when she shot you in the head. Do you know what it was doing to you?"

"I don't remember that moment for obvious reasons," David replied. "But I did perform subsequent experiments on the unit. The system is designed to be expanded as needed. In fact, my theory is that the aliens only utilize one form of energy production, regardless of the application. It can transmit as little or as much power as is required by the systems connected to it. In that case, it mistook my hand for a receptor. It created a magnetic field around it to create a safe interchange. In fact, we can use the same method to extend the reactor to the ship's power supply. If we introduce a receptor to the chamber, it will bind it and begin delivering whatever amount of energy the system requests on demand."

"You're telling me this thing can produce infinite power?"

"I doubt it's infinite. We haven't been able to measure the limits yet."

"Even so, how could that be possible?"

"Sergeant, considering the aliens' mathematics based linguistics, I would estimate that they are at a minimum ten to twenty-thousand years more advanced than humankind. At a minimum. Now, that doesn't mean they are exceptionally smarter than we are by general intelligence quotient, but what it does mean is they have much, much more established history and technology to draw upon. This is a race that has either already experienced the technological singularity or discovered the means to overcome it."

"Technological singularity?"

"A hypothesis that the creation of AI will result in rapid, unimaginable technological growth ending with the AI essentially becoming so superior its organic masters are no longer required. Nobody knows what would happen at that point, which is why it's a hypothesis. But if this species experienced it..." He shrugged. "...I don't know if the AI is the alien race, or if the alien race sent the AI."

Caleb stared at David in silence, once again trying to get his head around a concept that was flying over it. Things had been so much easier when extremist militias were the worst problem he had to deal with.

"Well, whichever it is, we have to figure out a way to take out the one on this ship. I don't suppose you have any ideas?"

David looked back at Caleb and rubbed his beard. "Give me a few minutes to think. I just might."

Chapter 36

Riley stared at the thing wearing the Cerebus armor, studying it. Ten minutes had passed since they had spoken to Sergeant Card. Ten minutes that had left her mind reeling, desperately trying to figure out how she was going to get the situation under control.

The fact that David was still alive didn't surprise her. Until a short time ago, she had believed he was the one who had captured her. She felt stupid about that now. She should have realized the speech was all wrong. The mannerisms were all wrong. The lack of emotion was all wrong. Yet she had no idea there was another player in this out of control game. She hadn't guessed the alien spacecraft they had brought on board had introduced a wildcard into the equation.

So many things were starting to make sense, two hundred years too late. David's escape, the rebellion of the Reapers, the loss of control. It all came into laser-like focus in her head. She hadn't made mistakes. Everything she'd done was right. She had been sabotaged. Tricked.

Cheated. David had done it, with the help of this…thing. This strange alien.

The enemy she had come all this way to kill.

She felt her hands curl into fists. This was the creature she had come to destroy. This was the creature she had sacrificed her team to end. David had made a deal with it. He had bargained with the enemy. He was a traitor. A damned traitor.

She would find a way to kill him too. She would convince Sergeant Card he couldn't be trusted and get the Guardians back on her side. Caleb was a good Marine, but beyond that, he wasn't especially bright.

"Do you have a name?" she asked, still glaring at the armor. It had lowered the faceplate again, hiding the strange, hardened gelatin form beneath it.

It didn't respond. What was it doing? Something related to the systems on the ship no doubt. Reviewing personnel records to understand what it was up against? Altering something on board, like the lifts? She wished she knew. It had agreed to meet the Guardians in the hangar at her urging. She knew Sergeant Card would plan something. Some kind of diversion or trap to catch it.

It only stood to reason the alien, the Cerebus, was planning something too.

She had convinced it she was going to help it. Or at least, it was acting as though it believed she would help it. There was no way to tell with the Cerebus. It had no facial features. No expressions. Its voice held a hint of emotion, but it was subtle and harder to decipher. It was as though it were emulating humanity, rather than sincerely feeling.

"Why did you come to Earth?" she asked. "Why did you send the trife to destroy us? What did we ever do to you?"

She kept her eyes on the Cerebus. It didn't react. She

sighed heavily, throwing her fist into its chest. The metal scuffed her knuckles, peeling back skin and causing them to bleed.

"Damn it," Riley cursed, grabbing her hand. She was letting her frustration get the best of her. Now wasn't the time to act like a spoiled brat. She had to stay even or she was going to lose whatever remained.

David was still alive. How much had he told Caleb? How much did Caleb believe? It was true, she had omitted some details and modified others, but she was sure she was in the right. She had affirmation from Command. She had clearance to change the destination coordinates of the Deliverance. Maybe he would judge her. Maybe he would think she was a monster for what she had done. She decided she didn't care. This was war. War meant hard decisions. It meant sacrifice. It meant casualties. If things had gone according to her plan, if David hadn't weaseled his way to escape and freed this thing, she would be an unsung hero. Sergeant Card was smart enough to at least see through the bullshit to that truth.

"Where did you come from?" she asked. "From out there? Or from somewhere else? Our team was never quite sure."

They had traced the trajectory of the asteroids the trife had arrived on, following them back to this area of space. They had used the last of their resources to scour the universe, searching for planets, and then searching those planets for signs of life. The planet outside the primary display, the planet they had designated XENO-1, had shown the most promise. There were signals coming from the surface. Odd messages delivered on quantum bands. Bands that couldn't be accessed naturally. It was tech they could identify, but not tech they could reproduce. It was far too advanced.

When she had seen the planet in the display for the first time, she had thought perhaps there would be signs of the enemy. Ships, space stations, satellites, or even grand silver cities spotting the otherwise blue and green and brown landscape. There wasn't any of that. The only reason she believed they were in the right place was because the Cerebus wanted so badly to land there.

She sat back, closing her eyes. There was no point in trying to talk to it. Whatever it was doing, it wasn't going to give her a shred of attention. It was just as well. What good would the answers to any of those questions do? Earth was gone. Lost to the trife. The population decimated. Civilization destroyed. She couldn't stop it or save it. They were too late for that. At best, she might have exacted some revenge.

Revenge didn't sweat the details.

"I'm going to see you destroyed," she said, opening her eyes to glare at it. "You think you're so superior. You've never gone one-on-one against a squad of Marines."

A short burst of noise escaped from the Cerebus, deep and choppy. It took Riley a moment to recognized it. Laughter. It had heard everything she said. That was the only thing it felt compelled to respond to, and it was laughing. It wasn't afraid of the Guardians. Maybe it wasn't afraid of anything.

And maybe that would be its downfall.

It finished laughing at her comment, finally turning to face her. Only it wasn't the Cerebus she saw. It was her sister. She had a syringe in her hand.

"Amber?" Riley said. Her sister looked good. So much better than the last time she had seen her, a week before the trife had arrived.

"Hey Rye," Amber said. "You don't look so good."

"This isn't real. You're dead."

"No thanks to you, sis. You were supposed to cure me."

"I was trying. The trife…"

"Always excuses, Rye. Always so many excuses. Nothing is ever your fault, is it?"

"What do you mean?"

"You had one mission, sis. One. And you blew it. Don't move."

Amber leaned toward her, leading with the syringe.

"What is that?" Riley asked. Her pulse was suddenly pounding, her face hot with fear. "Amber, what are you doing?" She tried to stand up. To get away.

Amber shoved her back into her seat with impossible strength. "I said hold still," she growled.

"I'm sorry," Riley said. "I tried."

"You didn't try hard enough. Don't you think it's pathetic that an alien machine knows more about keeping its word than you do?"

The syringe sank into her neck a second time. It hurt so much more than the first, and she let out a painful, mournful scream. "I'm so sorry!"

"You will be."

Chapter 37

"I can't be certain this is going to work, Sergeant," David said. "It's a theory based on minimal understanding."

"I get the feeling that what you call minimal understanding, I would call expertise," Caleb replied. "How do I work it?"

"The wave generation is already active. You'll need to keep it that way or risk hallucinations. I modified the amplifier to bolster the signal, and I have it cycling through wave patterns at a faster rate. You can be sure the AI will attempt to utilize its most effective weapon. This should neutralize it, but I can't guarantee you'll be completely hallucination free. In any case, when you're ready, press here." David tapped on part of the wand. "It will invert the signal, which with any luck will stun the AI for five to ten seconds. If you can't destroy it during that period, you never will."

"That's not very positive thinking, Harry Potter," Flores said.

"Who?" David asked.

226

"Nevermind," Caleb replied. "We're here. Knuckle-up."

Caleb snapped David's device to the magnetic band around his waist, holding it tightly in place. Then he shifted his rifle, watching the reticle on the HUD in front of his eyes. Sho and Washington had found more of value in Research's armory than he had expected, mainly in the form of tactical helmets which had been reserved for each of the Reapers.

They had cycled through them to find the best fit, and then quickly paired the helmets to their combat armor and then networked their completed equipment. It meant each of them had regained full comms, a complete HUD with sensor array, a computer-assisted targeting reticle for their rifles, and general protection for their heads.

While the armory didn't have a replacement P-50, it did have magazines for the MK-12, which Caleb had chosen to carry to give his plasma to Washington. He had already determined his role in this would be diversionary. It was up to the rest of the Guardians to deal the actual damage.

They approached the jammed doors leading into the hangar. The ADCV was still pressed tight against one of the doors.

The headless Reaper was gone.

"Shit," Sho said, the first to notice. "We should have cooked it when we had the chance."

"The AI must already be inside," Caleb said. They had come ten minutes early to get a jump on the intelligence. Clearly, it had either anticipated the maneuver or had arrived ahead of time to make preparations of its own. One of which included freeing the Reaper.

"This doesn't change the plan," Caleb said. "We can handle the Reaper."

"Don't fear the Reaper," Flores said.

They moved through the door and into the hangar. Caleb wasn't surprised to find the Cerebus armor already positioned in the center of the open space. Riley was standing beside it, her face set in stone. Caleb's heart started racing at the sight of her. He had a fleeting urge to put a round between her eyes.

The Reaper was nowhere to be seen. Caleb's ATCS wasn't registering it, either. Was he wrong? Had it escaped on its own and ran away?

"Here we go," Sho said as they crossed the hangar. Caleb moved out to the front of the group, keeping his eyes level and his gait steady despite a suddenly threatening panic. What had the intelligence done while they were still recovering the energy unit?

They came to a stop a few meters away from the intelligence and Riley.

"You're early," Caleb said.

"We will make the exchange," it replied coldly.

"Get ready," Caleb said, too softly for the sound to escape the helmet, but loud enough for it to cross the comms.

"Do not attempt to deceive me through radio communications," the AI said. "I have not yet decrypted the channel, but I am aware of the transmission."

Caleb smiled beneath his helmet. Damn it. "Did you expect anything less?"

"No."

"David, the energy unit."

David came forward, holding the unit in his arms. The chamber was twenty centimeters square and completely contained. They had placed a patch over the open back to prevent any of them from accidentally reaching into the compartment.

"Place it on the floor in front of me," the AI said.

David moved between Caleb and the armor, bending and putting the unit on the floor. He stood up straight, remaining in place in front of the AI.

"You should never have crossed me," David said. "All of this could have been avoided."

Caleb couldn't tell if David was speaking to the intelligence or to Riley. "Riley, go with David," he said.

Riley glanced at the intelligence. It nodded curtly, and when David offered his hand she took it. They crossed back behind the Guardians together.

"I require the landing codes," the AI said.

"I have them here," Caleb said, taking the blocking device from his hip. He rotated it in his hand, putting his finger on the area David had shown him. "I don't know the code myself. It's all stored on this device."

The intelligence had to know the wand was the reason none of them were hallucinating. Its head tilted slightly, suggesting it was trying to make logical sense of why Caleb would even begin to offer it.

"Attack," Caleb said calmly into the comm, pressing down on the device.

The Guardians pulled their plasma rifles from their backs in unison, while Caleb ducked down to scoop the energy unit into his artificial hand.

A harsh buzz filled Caleb's ears, so loud it almost stopped his forward momentum. His mouth opened in a silent scream at the sudden pain, and he whipped his head back toward David, his most immediate thought that they had been set up.

But David had bowed his head in pain, using his free hand to clutch at one of his ears. The Guardians were faring better, in pain but focused, the P-50s coming up facing the Cerebus armor.

All of that happened within the first two seconds. By the third, Caleb had his hand on the energy unit and his eyes back on the intelligence. It wasn't moving, locked in place by the sneak attack, trying to reorder its systems to recover from the assault.

Caleb rolled himself to the side, clearing the line of fire for the Guardians. Plasma began to pour from their rifles, a heavy wave of superheated gas washing over the Cerebus armor, causing it to vanish beneath the red, orange, and blue flames.

A tone sounded in Caleb's helmet, and then a red mark appeared on the HUD, which was blaring out in warning. Caleb reacted out of instinct, placing the energy unit on the floor and instead of coming out of the roll, letting himself fall onto his back. The move left him facing the hole in the top of the hangar, which the Reaper had already leaped from.

He opened fire, a dozen poorly-aimed rounds zipping past the creature as it fell, escaping Caleb's attack and coming down directly on Washington. The impact drove the big Marine to the ground and distracted Sho and Flores. They broke off the attack, instinct driving them to protect their teammate.

"Stay on it," Caleb barked, hopping back to a knee and pivoting toward the Reaper. The monster raised its claws, dropping them toward Washington's face. Washington managed to grab the arm and soften the blow, the claws raking across the faceplate but not getting through. Caleb fired, sending a burst of rounds into the creature's side. It looked at him and screamed, leaping from Washington toward him.

Sho and Flores spun back toward the intelligence, triggering their rifles and restarting their attack. Caleb noticed

Flores stop shooting again an instant later, dropping her P-50 to the floor as though it were on fire.

He didn't have any more time to think about it. The Reaper reached him, and he raised the rifle across his body to catch its teeth, using its momentum to lift it up and over him. He spun back, throwing the creature away. It landed on its back, sliding on the metal floor and turning over to catch itself with clawed feet.

Caleb brought his rifle up toward the demon and started shooting. Rounds tore into the creature, a dozen holes sprouting from it within a second. It hissed and screamed, leaping toward him a second time.

He held the rifle in his right hand, reaching out with his left. He ducked and grabbed the Reaper by the throat, using the strength of the artificial limb to drive it into the floor. A wet crack followed, and for a moment the creature was motionless.

Caleb stood up, glancing back at the rest of the fight just in time to see the intelligence bolt forward from its static position, charging toward Sho to throw a hand into her chest. She had no time to move and it caught her square, the force lifting her and throwing her backward. She hit the ground and slid to a stop, her armor cracked from the blow.

Too little, too late. The AI was active again. Worse, its wave generation was active again. The wand was dead and useless, all of its power dedicated to the ten seconds of time during which the Guardians were supposed to win the day.

They hadn't, and now Caleb wasn't sure they could even win the next minute.

Chapter 38

Caleb heard the movement of the Reaper behind him. He spun around again, just in time to see the demon leap at him a third time, leading with its claws. He backpedaled two steps, firing a burst of rounds into the creature's face, the bullets ripping through its skull. He sidestepped as it landed on the ground beside him, momentarily dead for the third time.

He knew it wouldn't stay that way. Not unless they burned it to ash.

"Flores, what's your position?" he said through the comm, spinning back toward the Cerebus. He froze when he saw his father standing there.

"Mom, is that you?" Flores said. "Oh, mom. I'm in trouble. I need help."

"Cal," Caleb's father said. "What's going on, son?"

"What do you mean?" Caleb replied, slowly lowering his rifle to his side. This couldn't be his father. He knew it wasn't. But it had to be. Didn't it? He looked so real.

"Look at you," his father said. "You look like hell."

"It's been a long day. An alien is trying to take over my ship. It's going to get the colonists killed."

His father walked toward him, a comforting smile on his face. "Oh, that doesn't sound so bad. Why don't you grab your baseball? We'll have a catch."

"Mom, are you there?" Flores said into the comm, her voice distant in Caleb's mind, as though he were over-hearing the words of a side conversation. "I know I'm only fifteen. Mom, don't cry. I love him. What? No. I won't. Mom. You aren't listening. Listen to me."

"Where's your ball, Cal?" his father said.

Caleb looked down. He was holding a baseball bat in his hand. He turned it over, confused. There was a small bag attached to the bat. He unzipped it, finding three baseballs inside. He took out the autographed one and closed the bag again.

"There you are," his dad said.

Caleb held up the ball. "I don't have a glove."

"I can't handle this," Flores said, her voice upset. "I don't want to be here anymore. I don't want to deal with this."

"Do you remember the inscription?" his father asked. "Do you remember what it says?"

Caleb turned the ball over in his hand. The autograph was worn and smudged on the surface.

"It's hard to read it."

"Take off your glasses."

Caleb hadn't realized he was wearing glasses. He removed them from his face, the autograph becoming clearer. He still couldn't quite make it out. "What does it say?"

"It's the landing code," his father replied.

Somewhere in the back of his mind, Caleb knew none of it was real. But in the front of his mind, it was as his own face. The man in front of him was his father, making a simple, logical request.

"The landing code?" Caleb said.

"Yes. What does it say?"

Caleb's attention shifted when he noticed movement out of the corner of his eye. A large man was about to tackle his father. Was he going to rob him? "Dad, look out!" Caleb cried.

His father turned. Too late. The man hit him with enough force to lift him from the ground and drive him down and back. Then the man had a knife in his hand, and he stabbed his father in the face.

"Noo...!" Caleb started to scream, the sound trailing off as reality came back into focus. Washington was on top of the Cerebus; his knife buried deep through the helmet's open visor into the alien's face. It had interrupted the AI's attack, but it wouldn't last.

Caleb looked down. His helmet was on the floor beside him, and he was holding one of the MK-12's explosive rounds, his finger pressed down on the arming ring. His heart skipped, realizing he had been two seconds away from blowing himself up. Once the AI had realized he didn't know the code after all, it would have been all over.

His head whipped to the side. Where the hell had Riley gone? He didn't see her anywhere.

He turned his attention back to the AI as it grabbed Washington by the throat, lifting and throwing him off. Then it shoved itself back to its feet before grabbing the knife and pulling it from its face. Caleb could see the gel beneath the visor close over itself, healing almost instantly. His hope failed him.

There was no way they could beat this thing.

Something hit him from behind, throwing him forward onto his stomach. He nearly let go of the explosive, clutching it tighter as he hit the ground, the weight of the Reaper pressing down on top of him. The Cerebus was coming toward him.

Plasma bolts flashed across the hangar, hitting the side of the AI's armor. It turned its head to where Flores was shooting, sending round after round into the Cerebus without causing much harm.

Caleb struggled beneath the Reaper, trying to dislodge it. He felt the claws scraping furrows through his armor. He felt where it had already succeeded, hot and wet and burning way too close to his spine. He had to get the demon off before it killed him.

He pushed again, trying to get enough leverage to put his replacement arm under him. If he could get some purchase, he could use its strength to throw the demon off his back. He grunted and shoved, doing his best to overcome the creature's weight.

The floor began to vibrate against his cheek, softly at first, but intensifying quickly. The Cerebus paused its approach, turning its head toward something. A bright flash of red nearly blinded Caleb a moment later, the first of a series of plasma bolts hitting the Reaper from Washington's position.

The distraction was exactly what he needed. It caused the Reaper to rear up and shift its weight until Caleb found he could move. He rolled over, facing up and watching the bolts smash into the Reaper's flesh, opening holes across its body. It screamed when it saw he had moved, and its head, teeth snapping, darted down toward his face.

Caleb let go of the explosive, shoving it into the demon's mouth. He used his artificial hand to grab its jaw and pull it closed to keep the small silver ball in the demon's mouth. Claws raked across his shoulder, one of them piercing the bodysuit and drawing blood. Caleb held on tight, counting the seconds. He lifted his arm over his face, covering it with the armor and holding the Reaper up and away, as far as he could reach.

The round detonated, the blast turning the Reaper's head and upper body into mush, bits of flesh, bone, muscle, and blood exploding all over and around Caleb as the heat of the device washed over him. It licked at his head and around his armor to singe his bald scalp. The alien alloy took the brunt of the blow without damage, leaving him clutching only air.

Caleb was motionless for a moment before he rolled over again and pushed himself up, looking for the AI. He found it a moment later, locked against a Strongman exosuit, trying to break through the machine's outer metal shell to reach the Marine inside.

Sho had gotten into one of the powered suits and rushed into the fight, somehow managing to catch the AI in her grasp. Had it underestimated the Strongman? Or had she outmaneuvered it? Either way, Caleb could barely believe she had managed to get a handle on it. A thick robotic arm was wrapped around its back, pressing the Cerebus into the suit.

But now what?

Her eyes shifted to look at him. Then she looked away, to her left.

To the outer blast door.

She started walking toward it, holding the Cerebus fast against the exosuit. The AI wasn't static. Its free hand pressed through the protective barrier of the suit, desperately trying to punch through Sho's helmet to her face. It would make it sooner or later.

Caleb's eyes drifted to the manual control for the blast door, and then back to Sho. He knew what she wanted him to do.

He didn't want to do it.

She continued moving toward the blast doors, one step at a time.

Caleb found his helmet nearby. He scooped it up and dropped it over his head.

"Sho, you can't do this," he said through the comm.

"I'm doing it, Sarge. There's no other way. You need to open the doors."

"I can't let you sacrifice yourself for me."

She surprised him by laughing. "For you, Sarge? I love you. I have for a long time, but this isn't for you. We have a duty, remember? Forty-thousand souls. This is for them. Open the damn door."

Caleb clenched his jaw and sprinted for the manual release. He wanted to keep arguing, but what was there to say? "Wash, Flores, the loaders and movers are locked down, get to one of them and strap yourselves in."

"Alpha," Flores said, ready to argue.

"Sho's right, damn it," he replied. "This is the way it has to be. Wash, grab the energy unit on your way. We can't afford to have it sucked out into space."

He could see the Guardians moving on his HUD's tactical grid. Flores was running for the closest loader. Washington was headed for the energy unit. He closed on the door release as Sho neared the blast door.

Where the hell were Riley and David? There was no sign of them anywhere.

"Cal." His father's voice entered through the comm. "Help me, Cal."

Caleb looked back to the Strongman. Only it wasn't Sho and the Cerebus anymore. It was a Reaper holding his father.

"It's taking me from you," his father said. "Help me."

Caleb slowed his approach. The other Guardians came

to a stop, turning to respond to whatever it was they were seeing.

"Cal, help!"

Caleb took a step toward the exosuit and away from the manual controls.

An ear-splitting scream sounded through his comm, the pitch hurting his ears. The Reaper and his father faded, replaced with Sho and the Cerebus. The scream ended, and he felt a sudden, growing pressure against his brain.

Sho screamed into the comm again, helping to keep Caleb's head clear. He raced the rest of the way to the controls, grabbing the lever. He would have to time it perfectly or the entire ship would lose all its air.

The AI was becoming more desperate. It started pounding at the Strongman's shell, throwing punch after punch into the side, the force of the blows creating deep dents in the metal that had to be pressing hard into Sho's body.

She stayed the course, carrying the armor to the edge of the blast doors.

"Sarge, do it," she said.

Caleb didn't hesitate. He pulled the release.

The doors made a thunking clang as they unsealed. Immediately, the air began to be sucked out of the ship as they started to open.

Caleb felt the pull instantly. He grabbed the edge of the panel with his artificial hand, holding fast as more and more air started being sucked from the ship. Some of the drones and smaller vehicles began sliding across the floor, and he looked back to see Sho right at the edge, the Strongman wedged against the two doors.

"Sarge," Sho said.

"What is it Yen?" he replied.

"I lied."

"What do you mean?"

"I did this for you. Take care of yourself."

The doors opened far enough to let the exosuit out. It vanished through the opening, cast out into space, taking Sho and the alien AI with it.

Chapter 39

Caleb's heart pounded, his eyes burning as they teared over. He wanted to scream and chase her out into the black and drag her back inside. He knew it was impossible. She was gone. She had sacrificed herself to save him, her unspoken love greater than he ever imagined. He would grieve, but not now. Just because the intelligence was gone, that didn't make them safe.

He pulled himself forward with his replacement arm, using the leverage to start pushing the manual control the other way. All kinds of equipment and debris were being pulled out of the open blast doors, including the remaining lower half of the Reaper he had killed and the rifle he had dropped. His face wrinkled as he shoved against the lever, returning it to the closed position.

The doors made an awful grinding noise, and for a moment he was terrified they would break down for a second time, jammed in the open position. Then they started to reverse course, edging their way back toward one another to seal the two-meter gap.

A loud clang sounded against the doors. The noise caused Caleb to look back to where the ADC had slammed into the too-narrow hole, getting stuck against the moving doors. He also saw something else sliding toward the gap beside it.

A body. It was only there for a moment before it too was pulled out into the black, getting stuck against the left door just long enough for Caleb to identify it.

David.

His emotions shifted in an instant, from sadness at the loss of Sho to anger at what he was certain Doctor Valentine had done. He didn't know where Riley was, but she couldn't hide forever.

The vacuum eased and then faded as the doors finally came back together. Caleb stood ahead of the manual controls, his replacement hand still gripping the panel so tightly he had warped the metal. He continued staring at the resealed blast doors. His breathing was labored and shallow. He felt lightheaded. Had they lost too much air?

He let go of the panel and started across the hangar toward the loaders. His body was shaking with a rage of emotions.

"Flores, Washington, do you copy?" he asked.

"Roger, Alpha," Flores said, her voice unsteady. "Yen…" She trailed off.

"I know. Have you seen Doctor Valentine?"

"Negative. I haven't seen David either. I don't know what happened to them."

"I saw David," Caleb said. "Or rather, I saw his corpse. It was sucked out into space."

"What?"

"She killed him, damn it. She murdered him."

"Who? Doctor Valentine?" Flores said. Caleb looked

up as she and Washington emerged from the cab of one of the loaders. Washington had the energy unit under his arm. "We have to find her. Where could she possibly go?"

"It depends on whether or not she plans to try to run," Caleb said. "She has the landing codes. She can —"

"Sergeant Card, it's Riley Valentine. Are you there?" Her voice boomed across the hangar, spewing out from the ship's emergency PA system.

Caleb's body tensed at the sound of her voice. He spoke softly into the comm. "Guardians, we don't know what happened to David. Understood?"

"Affirmative," Flores replied.

He activated the SOS's external speaker. "This is Sergeant Card. We're here, Riley. Where are you?"

"I'm glad to hear your voice, Sergeant," Riley said. She sounded genuinely relieved. "I'm on the bridge."

"How did you end up on the bridge? Is David with you?"

"Negative. After you made the trade, during the fighting, David made a run for the bridge. I grabbed Washington's plasma rifle and chased him." She paused. "I burned him to ash. I didn't have a choice. He was working with the enemy, Sergeant. Whatever he told you to convince you to help him, he was lying."

Caleb bit his tongue to keep from responding to the statement. Did she really believe he would buy that story?

It didn't matter right now. He could tell the air was too thin. His combat armor's sensors confirmed it. "We can worry about all that later. I had to open the blast doors, and we vented too much air. We have to kick the filters back on and get what's left redistributed."

"So that's why the sensors were complaining? It's already done, Sergeant. You should start noticing a difference soon. Try to avoid anything strenuous until then."

"Roger that. I'd like to avoid anything strenuous for a few years."

"I knew I could count on you to come up with a plan. I trust all of our people are safe?"

"Not all. Sho didn't make it. She restrained the Cerebus while it was pulled out into space."

"Like in Aliens," Flores said sadly. "Except if Ripley had died too."

"I'm sorry, Sergeant. I know she was an important member of the Guardians."

She even sounded as if she meant it. Caleb restrained himself, jaw quivering as he replied. "Thank you."

"What about the energy unit?"

"We saved it," Caleb said. "But without David, I don't know if we can integrate it into the ship's power supply."

"We need to do something, Sergeant. Power levels are at three percent, and turning both the air filters and Metro's subsystems back on didn't help. We've got days at best."

Caleb was silent for a moment while he considered their options. The energy unit seemed relatively simple to hook up. All they had to do was introduce a conductive material into the casing. That part was easy. Knowing what part of the ship's power system would be safe to stick into the box? That wasn't.

"How are you with electrical engineering?" he asked.

"I'm a doctor, Sergeant," Riley replied. "Not an engineer."

"Flores, Wash, either of you feel comfortable with the job?"

"Negative, Alpha," Flores replied.

"You know who would have been great for this?" Caleb said, unable to restrain himself. "David."

He waited a few seconds for Riley to react. She

managed to keep herself steady. "David was a traitor, Sergeant. He would have been more likely to blow the Deliverance than save it."

Caleb doubted that. "Well, we need someone who can connect this thing to the interchange without destroying it or us. If none of us can do it, I can only – "

"Sergeant," Riley snapped, interrupting him. "We may have another problem."

"What is it now?"

"I'm at the primary terminal. Power levels are spiking. The main thrusters are engaging. Shit. Oh no."

The sudden inertia forced the three of them back a few steps. Caleb lowered his body to regain his balance, as did Flores and Washington. At the same time, the loaders and movers clanked against their restraints, and loose debris began tumbling across the hangar.

Red warning klaxons began flashing throughout the hangar, synchronized with an ugly whine through the ship's PA.

"Valentine!" Caleb shouted, trying to be heard over the sudden din. "What the hell is going on?"

"That son of a bitch," she shouted back.

"What is it?" he demanded.

"It didn't have access to the landing code to bring the ship in. But it still had access to thrust control. I didn't know what it was doing. Why it wasn't moving."

"Don't keep it a secret, Doc!"

"We're on a collision course for this system's star."

"The star?" Caleb said at normal volume, glancing at Washington and Flores. He remembered the sight of it, large off the starboard side of the Deliverance. "How long?"

"Four hours," Riley replied. "If we don't run out of

power first. This acceleration is draining the reactors in a hurry."

"You can't override it?"

"It encrypted the control system to keep us locked out. A hedge against its ability to get the codes. It knew it was walking into a trap, and it was ready to screw us if we won. I'm not a computer specialist either, Sergeant. I relied on Harry for that."

Caleb closed his eyes, trying to drown out the chaos of the situation. The klaxons, the harsh warning buzz, the mess throughout the hangar, the loss of Sho. He could feel the tension in his body. The anger, the frustration, the sadness. He had to push it aside. Block it out. He had to think. David probably could have broken the encryption, but that wasn't a possibility now. Riley had decided murdering him and letting him get sucked out into space was better than coming clean with what she had done. He had to focus. Take one thing at a time. What were their objectives?

One: Get the energy unit connected to the interchange to prevent the ship from running out of power.

Two: Break the encryption and unlock the control system.

Three: Bring the ship to a stop or change its course before momentum carried it into the star.

How were four people going to manage that? None of them were computer programmers or electrical engineers. Or even pilots.

"Alpha, what do we do?" Flores asked.

Caleb's eyes snapped open. He realized he was thinking about it all wrong. There weren't four people to get them out of this situation.

There were forty-thousand.

"Climb into that loader and grab some more of the T-9," he said, pointing to it. "Valentine, meet us at the aft seal into Metro."

"Metro?" Riley replied.

"It's time to ask the colonists for help."

Chapter 40

Riley was waiting for the Guardians at the aft seal. It took all of Caleb's will to stay calm and level when he saw her. He wanted nothing more than to confront her with the truth, to tell her what he had seen and what he knew and watch her try to squirm her way out of it. They couldn't do that yet. The Deliverance was in dire trouble, and like it or not her experience could still be of some value.

"Doctor Valentine," he said, forcing a smile so his tone would sound less angry.

"Sergeant Card." She looked at him suspiciously, her eyes stopping on his blood-stained armor. "Are you hurt?"

"I took a few hits in the side and the back, but most of it is Reaper blood." The wounds the Reaper had delivered to his back were burning and itching like crazy, but they weren't severe enough to slow him down. Not now.

"Are you sure you want to do this?" she asked. "We've been out of contact with Metro for over two hundred years. And once we open the seal, we can't close it again."

"I know. I'd rather not expose the colonists to any of this mess, but we don't have a choice. We need engineers, programmers, and pilots. If they've been following protocol, they should have all three. It's the only chance any of us have of making it to Essex."

Of course, he had no intention of having the Deliverance land on the planet Riley had tried to convince them was Earth-6. Once they solved their immediate problems, they could figure out where to go next. The good news was that if they could get the energy unit connected, it would provide an apparently near-infinite power supply.

"Wash, Flores, get the explosives placed. We have two-hundred and twenty minutes until we either run out of air, gravity, and heat, or we crash into a star."

"Roger that, Alpha," Flores replied.

Washington carried the bag of T-9 to the seal and unzipped it, taking out one of the brown bars and tossing it to Flores. She shoved it into the corner and stuck one of the detonators in it, while he took one of the bars and placed it in the top left corner.

"How did you know David was a traitor?" Caleb asked Riley while they worked, placing eight blocks of T-9 around the seal. It was enough explosive to level a small building. There were no guarantees the detonation wouldn't damage anything important, but it was a risk they had to take.

Riley didn't miss a beat. "He was the one who set the enemy AI loose in the first place. I didn't know it at the time. When I thought I saw David kill Shiro and Ning, it was the alien. It told me it communicated with him when it grabbed him the first time. It made a deal with him to get free, but David reneged on the deal."

"If he reneged, why would he have made a run for the bridge to help it, especially after he tried to help me stun it?"

"Oh please, Sergeant. Did you really think he was

helping you? From what you said before, it seems like his help didn't help all that much. I knew David. Before the alterations and after. He changed. He evolved. But he was always more concerned with his own welfare than anything else. Maybe I'm wrong. Maybe he wasn't going to the bridge to help the enemy. If that's the case, then I'm certain he was going there to help himself, and that still makes him a traitor. That's just who he was."

Caleb stared at her. He was struggling to believe she could say some of the things she was saying with a straight face. Was David more concerned with his own welfare? Was David only interested in helping himself?

"We're ready, Alpha," Flores said, retreating to where he was standing with Riley. Washington reached into the bag and pulled out the remote, handing it to Caleb, who looked down at the small box, flipping open the red safety.

"I think we should move back a little more," Riley said.

Caleb nodded, and the Guardians backed around the corner, getting farther away from the hatch. Then he shifted his thumb back to the remote trigger. "Here we go," he said, pressing it down.

The explosion happened in stages, a quick series of deep thumps preceding the louder follow-up blasts. The deck and bulkheads shook, the sound of rending metal overpowering the constant whine from the PA system. The lights went out completely, save for the flashing red klaxons. And then those went out too, leaving Caleb and the others bathed in darkness and smoke.

The fire suppression system activated, sending gouts of white foam through nozzles in the ceiling, quickly bathing them in it and controlling the flames. A few seconds after, the emergency lighting came back online.

Caleb turned back to the others. "Headgear off. Weapons stowed. We don't want to appear threatening."

Flores and Washington already had their rifles secured to the back of their SOS, but he wanted to make sure it stayed that way. They had no idea how the colonists would react to their arrival, and he didn't want innocent people getting hurt.

The Guardians removed their helmets, tucking them under their arms. Then Caleb led them around the corner. The hatch was a twisted, slagged mess of metal, the detonation having ripped away the entire mechanism, the force blowing it back and into the corridor within the city's limits. The larger slabs of thick metal were resting awkwardly on the floor, their surfaces wavering from the residual heat. The corridor ended at a t-junction twenty meters ahead, and Caleb recalled how the connecting passages looped around the city's engineering section to another limited-access hatch that went out into the city itself.

To him, it had only been a few weeks since he had delivered Lieutenant Jones and the other non-combatants to safety within Metro. It felt strange knowing that on the other side of the now defunct hatch, the cycle of life had continued unabated for over two hundred years.

They approached the new opening, moving carefully around the exposed wiring and jagged metal sticking out in the damaged section. The blast had made it through the deck in a few small sections, leaving the hallway beneath it visible through twisted metal.

They cleared the blast zone, reaching the junction at the end.

"Which way?" Flores asked.

"Both corridors lead to the same place," Caleb replied. "Let's go right."

They took the right fork, following it as it began to dip and turn. They had gone about two hundred meters when

Caleb heard footsteps ahead. Judging by the cadence, several people were coming at a run.

Caleb came to a stop. The others stopped with him. "Keep your hands out where they can see them. Let me do the talking."

They waited in the corridor, hands out and palms up. The footsteps grew louder, echoing in the passage ahead. The people finally came into view a few seconds later.

There were six of them in all. Four were wearing the law uniforms that instantly reminded Caleb of Sheriff Aveline. Two were dressed in dark overalls, each of them carrying the end of a large metal crate. They came to a sudden stop at the sight of the Guardians, the two in the overalls dropping the crate to the floor with a loud clang.

The four law officers reached for their sidearms, four revolvers rising from four holsters and pointing at the Marines. Caleb raised his hands, and the others did the same. He didn't speak or introduce himself. It was better to give the colonists control of their first interaction.

One of them broke off from the rest. She had brown hair, blue eyes, and a heart-shaped face that was beginning to wrinkle. Her uniform was faded and slightly stained, the threads getting thin, the elbows patched multiple times. The only thing about her that looked new was the gold star on the collar of her shirt. Seeing their hands up without prompting, she put her gun away.

"There's been a lot of strange shit happening in the city these last few days," she said. She had an accent Caleb didn't recognize and couldn't place. It was like a strange concoction of American south, British, and Chinese. "Are you the ones responsible?"

"My name is Sergeant Caleb Card," Caleb said. "United States Space Force Marines, and Guardian Alpha of the Deliverance. And you are?"

"Sheriff Lasandra Dante," she replied. "Those are my deputies back there, and the two behind them are Joe King, our lead engineer, and his assistant slash wife, Carol."

"It's good to meet you, Sheriff," Caleb said. "This is Doctor Riley Valentine. Private Mariana Flores, and Private John Washington."

Sheriff Dante's eyes flicked to Riley, Flores, and Washington. Flores gave her a curt wave. Washington nodded.

"Did you say doctor? What kind of doc are you?"

"I'm a geneticist," Riley replied. "More of a scientist than a practitioner."

"I see." Sheriff Dante eyed them silently for a few seconds. "You look like Marines, and we were responding to a possible code blue. That means life or death. A breach in the seals. You aren't trife though, which is the best news I've had all day. Well, that and the power coming back online. It was starting to get right cold, and the whole damn commune was panicking that somebody forgot to pay the electric bill." She smiled wide, getting more comfortable with them by the second. "Anyways, I'll give you every chit I have if you tell me you're here because the war is over and we can come out now."

"Come out?" Riley said. "Sheriff, where do you think you are?"

"Are you joking? Everybody knows we're in an underground bunker outside Atlanta, Georgia. We've been here for what, over two hundred years now? We've been waiting for word from outside the war is over, and the trife are gone. We've been waiting a long time. Isn't that why you're here? To tell us it's safe?"

Caleb swallowed hard, glancing over at Riley. Her face had paled too. The colonists had no idea they weren't on

Earth? How the hell had that happened? How the hell could they not know?

"Who's in charge of Metro?" Caleb asked. "We need to speak with him right away."

"Governor Stone," Sheriff Dante replied. "Why?"

"Because we aren't safe, Sheriff," Caleb said. "We aren't safe at all."

Chapter 41

The news hit Sheriff Dante hard.

Her face fell, the smile wiped off it almost instantly. Her eyes landed on Caleb's armor, and she shook her head.

"I should've guessed. You're covered in dried blood. You look like hell. You smell even worse. And you haven't got a hair on your body." She glanced at the other Guardians. "None of you do. Is it bad out there, then? Is there a reason you're all bald as a newborn baby's ass?"

"Sheriff," Caleb said. "I think we should meet with Governor Stone."

"What about the breach? Do I need to leave a guard?"

"No. The area is secure, but we don't have a lot of time. We're here because we need your help."

She laughed. "We've been hiding in here for two hundred plus years, and now you need our help? It really is bad out there, isn't it?"

"Yes, but not in the way you're thinking. I'll explain everything—"

"When you talk to the Governor. Right?" Sheriff

Dante paused, staring at him for too long. "You know Sergeant, now that I'm thinking about it, how do I know you're a Marine at all? We've been in here for a long time. If the war is over, who knows what kind of people are alive out there? Who knows what their motives are? Again, you're covered in dried blood, and you look like hell. That could just as easily make you some kind of looter or thief as it makes you a Marine. And, oh yeah, you did just breach our outer seals by force."

Caleb noticed Sheriff Dante's hand drifting toward her sidearm. He had thought the interaction was going smoothly, but it seemed Dante wasn't reacting well to the bad news.

"I understand your caution, Sheriff," he said. "I would be cautious too if I were you. Please, give me five minutes . with your Governor, and we can straighten everything out."

Sheriff Dante locked eyes with him, keeping her hand on the butt of her revolver. Finally, she nodded. "Alright. But you aren't coming any closer to Metro than you are right now." She tilted her head, tapping her star with her chin. A green light came on in the center of it. "Klahanie, it's Dante. Patch me through to Governor Stone, will you?"

"Yes, ma'am," a young male voice replied. "Standby."

They waited for nearly a minute, standing together in silence while the Deliverance continued hurtling toward the system's star. Caleb struggled to stay patient. He was trying to save the city, and the Governor was wasting their time with this show of authority?

"This is Stone," a gravelly voice said through the star at last. "What's the situation, Sheriff?"

"Governor, I was responding to a code blue near the aft seal. Sensors picked up a breach, so I took a squad of deputies and Chief Engineer King up to take a peek. I came across four strangers in the corridor leading through engineering to the area. They claim to be United States Space Force Marines."

"Marines? You said they came through the aft hatch?"

"Yes, sir. I've got them detained in the access corridor. I was concerned they might be scavengers or looters, who maybe stumbled on the bunker from outside."

Stone didn't respond right away. They waited in silence again for him to consider the news.

"Bring them into the city, Sheriff," Stone said, his voice suddenly hard. "To your office. If they're armed, take their weapons. If they resist, shoot them. Put them in lockup until I arrive."

"What?" Flores said. "Alpha, we can't go in lockup. The ship is—"

"Enough, Private," Caleb snapped. Flores stopped speaking immediately. "Governor Stone, my name is Sergeant Caleb Card, United States Space Force Marine Corps. I'm also one of the Guardians assigned to protect Metro. Sir, I understand that you're wary of us and our intentions, but I have to insist that we not be detained. The entire city is under serious threat, and we don't have time to delay."

"I see," Governor Stone replied. "And what kind of threat are you talking about, Sergeant?"

The tone of his voice suggested the Governor was running with Sheriff Dante's theory that they were looters or thieves from outside. How could he believe something so irrational?

"I'd prefer to discuss it with you in person, Governor," Caleb replied. "The information I have is sensitive."

"I see," Stone said again. "Well then Sergeant, I suggest you stop wasting time questioning my authority and get busy turning your weapons over to Sheriff Dante and her deputies. I'll be down to the sheriff's office to meet with you as my schedule allows."

"With all due respect, Governor. We don't have time to wait on your schedule. Whatever you had planned, I guarantee it isn't as important as what I have to say."

"You have an awfully high opinion of yourself, don't you Sergeant? We've done quite well here, you know. On our own for the last two hundred years. Hell, the only trouble we've had came in the last couple of days when our systems shut down for no identifiable reason. I would venture to guess that disruption occurred with your arrival."

"Is this guy for real?" Flores said.

"Private Flores shut it," Caleb said.

She closed her mouth, struggling to keep it that way.

"Governor, my name is Doctor Riley Valentine," Riley said. "I'm not a Marine. I'm a scientist. But I'm here with Sergeant Card because we desperately need your help. I know this is all a little sudden and probably frightening, but we're all going to be in bad shape if we don't take action right now."

"You sound like my wife," Stone said. "I'll tell you what, Doctor. I'll consider your requests once I have you under control. Try to see things from my perspective. I have twenty-six thousand people I'm responsible for in here. You show up out of nowhere claiming to be Marines and whatnot and that all of a sudden we're in some kind of danger? I don't know a damn thing about you. For all I do know, you intend to lure us outside so you can gain control of the city or worse."

"Twenty-six thousand?" Caleb said. "What happened to the rest of you?"

"What do you mean?"

"Metro was designed for around forty-thousand occupants. Population levels were supposed to remain flat."

"What do you know about that? How?"

"We've been here since you entered the city and the hatches were sealed," Riley said.

"That isn't possible," Stone replied.

"Sheriff Dante, do you have an ID scanner?"

The Sheriff nodded. "Of course." She used her other hand to lift the small device from her belt.

Riley held out her wrist. "Would you mind scanning me?"

"Governor?" Dante said, asking for permission.

"Go ahead, Sheriff."

"Come to me," Dante said. "No funny moves."

Riley approached the Sheriff. "I need to pull off the top of the armor to get my wrist free."

"Go ahead."

Sheriff Dante kept her revolver trained on Riley while she unclasped her SOS and pulled her arms out of it, letting the heavy material gather around her waist. She turned her bare wrist over and held it out. Dante scanned it, her eyes widening in surprise.

"This can't be."

"Identification codes are stored on the mainframe's blockchain," Riley replied. "It's tamper-proof and verifiable."

"Sheriff?" Stone said.

"Sir, according to the scan, not only is Doctor Valentine who she said she is, but she's also listed as the acting Governor of Metro."

"What?" Flores said behind Caleb.

"What?" Caleb said a moment later.

Riley turned her head back toward him, smiling. "How do you think I convinced Governor Lyle to seal the city in the first place? Command gave me final authority over the colony. I know it hasn't seemed like it, but don't forget, Sergeant. This is still a civilian operation."

"Sheriff Dante, bring our guests to your office immediately," Governor Stone said. "They can keep their weapons. I'll meet you there at once."

"Are you sure, Governor?"

"Hell yes, I'm sure. Just do it, Lasandra."

"Yes, sir."

The light on her star blinked red, signaling that the Governor had disconnected.

"You heard the Governor," Sheriff Dante said. "If you'll follow me."

Caleb kept staring at Riley. "You're the new Governor of Metro?" he asked, trying to get his mind around the idea.

"Pretty much."

Her smug smirk said it all. She had known what was going to happen when they met with the people of Metro, while Caleb had been focused only on completing the task at hand. It took every ounce of his focus to keep his posture normal, his reaction buried. He had made a huge mistake bringing Riley with them instead of confronting her straight away.

How many more people were going to pay with their lives because of her?

Chapter 42

Metro didn't look the same as Caleb remembered it.

The beautiful park lined with green grass, trees, and flowers was gone. In its place was a brown mess of hardened decay lined with the stumps of long-dead trees. It appeared as if the trees had been cut down at some point, used for something the designers of the Deliverance had never intended.

The city beyond the park was just as bad. Caleb recalled the brand new cubes with the glass storefronts at their base, and sparkling streets laid atop the porous membrane of the massive hold's surface. He could still picture them as if he had seen them the day before, which was only slightly off from the truth. The shine was gone. The windows were broken and patched, the exterior walls scored near ground level with what appeared to be bullet holes. The streets were filthy and coated in debris. The storefronts were empty.

There were people in the streets. Their clothes were ragged and torn, their faces sullen and sad. They wandered between the blocks, picking at the trash, searching for anything that might have any value.

'What the hell happened here?" he said, his heart clenching at the sight of Metro. None of these visuals were new to him, but he had thought they had left the post-apocalyptic destruction of Earth behind.

Clearly, he had thought wrong.

"Problems," Sheriff Dante replied. "All kinds of problems. Technical failures for one. From what I've heard, the blocks were built up in a hurry, and the equipment wasn't always made to spec. It was the simple things that started breaking down first. The motors for the doors. The drives for the lifts. Then the more complex things. Medical equipment. The atmospherics. Burst water pipes. Electrical fires."

"We've done our best to keep things patched," Joe said, glancing over at his wife. "I feel like the whole damn place is held together with duct tape and solder."

"I'm sure you've done an incredible job," Caleb said.

"It was all put together so fast," Riley said. "To get as many people to safety as we could."

"You should know," Dante said. "How is it you're almost two hundred seventy years old anyway? Last time I checked, people don't live that long."

"Stasis," Riley replied. "Hibernation. Not just me. Sergeant Card and Privates Flores and Washington too. We stayed behind to watch over the colony."

Dante's left eyebrow went up. "You did? How long were you sleeping, Doc? Because we didn't have anything good going on in here, and we never heard a peep from you or Sergeant Card or anybody."

"What else happened, besides the mechanical breakdowns?" Caleb asked.

"I don't want to speak to that," Sheriff Dante replied. "I'll leave Governor Stone to give you the whole history lesson. Needless to say, as you can see it hasn't been the utopia the idjit who wrote the protocols was hoping it would be. All I can say is, if you were supposed to be looking out for us, you did a lousy job."

Caleb pressed his teeth together to keep from saying anything in response. He also glared back at Flores to make sure she remained silent. At least he never had to worry about Washington speaking out of turn. There was a time and place for both sides to sync up on everything that had happened to them, but this wasn't it. He wasn't sure the meeting with Governor Stone was it, either. They had four hours. Three and a half now, to fix the Deliverance before all of them died. The details and the history lessons could wait.

Dealing with Riley's treachery would have to wait too.

They reached the Sheriff's Office. Like the rest of the city, it had fallen into complete disrepair. The sliding glass doors at the front were completely gone. There were bins spread across the floor to catch the generated rain that leaked through a sagging ceiling, the terminals and displays on the rows of desks were dark, and it looked like the entirety of law enforcement was being run through notes on scraps of paper.

"I know it looks like hell," Dante said. "We do the best we can with what we've got. Fortunately, things are more settled these days. We don't have to work as hard to keep the population in line."

Caleb felt Washington's hand tap his shoulder. He glanced back, recognizing the other Marine's expression. "Agreed." They both had a bad feeling that whatever happened to the city that had cost it fourteen thousand of its inhabitants, it had been violent.

They had just entered the office when Caleb heard footsteps approaching quickly behind them. Sheriff Dante and her entourage turned back, so he did the same, watching as a tall, thin, bearded man in a long, dark coat and dark pants hurried toward them. He was flanked by a squad of what appeared to be Marines on either side. They wore makeshift uniforms that had been fashioned from the original law uniforms, modified with bits of plastic repurposed as armor plating. They carried wooden bows in their hands and had quivers of arrows on their backs.

At least now Caleb knew what had happened to all the trees.

"Governor Stone, I presume?" Riley said as the man came to a stop in front of the group. Caleb had been so busy staring at the nearly medieval Marines he hadn't noticed how Dante, her deputies, and the engineers had all dropped to one knee and bowed their heads.

He was damn sure that wasn't in the protocols.

The Governor motioned for the others to rise. "I'm Governor Jackson Stone," he said, holding his hand out to her. He kept it palm down at first, lifting his wrist slightly as though he wanted her to kiss it. He caught himself a moment later, turning his hand over and offering to shake. She took his hand.

"Doctor Riley Valentine," she said. "Or should I say, Governor Riley Valentine?"

Governor Stone chuckled. "Let's not be too hasty in disrupting a century of effort," he replied. "You haven't even been here five minutes."

"Of course," Riley said, her eyes narrowing. It was interesting to Caleb to see how a snake confronted another apparent snake. "We have more important issues to discuss, anyway."

"That's why I'm here," Stone said, pleased by her response. "How public do you want to make these important issues?"

"Right now, I'd like to keep things as quiet as possible. Is there somewhere we can talk?"

Stone nodded. "Dante, you're with me. You too, Joe. The rest of you wait here. We can talk in the back." He pointed toward one of the offices at the rear of the office.

"Sergeant?" Riley said, beckoning Caleb to join her. As if she had a choice. Governor by order of Command or not, he had no intention of trusting anything she said or did.

"Wash, keep an eye on the garbage knights," Caleb said. "Flores, stay alert."

"Roger, Alpha," Flores said.

Caleb followed Riley, Governor Stone, and Sheriff Dante to the back of the law office, into what appeared to be Sheriff Dante's personal space. Her desk was a mess of torn pieces of paper scattered around the only functional terminal in the building, her chair was rusted, cracked, and fading, and her walls were decorated with ancient photos so weathered they looked like they had been hanging there since the launch of the Deliverance.

It only took Caleb a moment to realize they probably had. He momentarily forgot about the meeting as he walked over to one of the framed photos, mesmerized by the subject. Sheriff Lily Aveline was older in the picture, but he would have recognized her anywhere.

"Sergeant?" Sheriff Dante said.

Caleb turned back, suddenly embarrassed. "Sorry." He pointed to the picture. "I knew her. Lily Aveline. We were friends."

"That's her with her daughter," Sheriff Dante replied.

"My great-great something grandmother. The Aveline women have been running Metro's Law Office for a long time."

Caleb smiled. "You're related to Lily?"

"I am." She smiled. "It's pretty weird to know I'm standing here with somebody who knew her personally."

"This whole thing is odd," Governor Stone said. "Especially the results of Sheriff Dante's scan. I'm sorry, Doctor Valentine, Sergeant Card, but I don't understand everything that you're selling here."

"That makes two of us," Caleb said.

"What's that supposed to mean?" Stone asked.

"You're missing an awful lot of colonists, Governor. The place is falling apart. You have guards walking with you carrying bows and arrows, and your Sheriff bends a knee when you appear. Not to mention, I noticed the bullet marks on the walls of the blocks. There's been an awful lot of gunfire in the city. In fact..."

Caleb's hand darted out from his side, grabbing Sheriff Dante's revolver and yanking it from its holster. He pointed it at Governor Stone.

"Sergeant!" Riley snapped.

Caleb pulled the trigger.

The hammer dropped. The chamber turned. The gun clicked. Empty.

"You're out of bullets, aren't you Governor?" he asked.

Stone barely reacted to the show. He already knew the status of his Sheriff's firearms. "You're very astute, Sergeant," he said. "We have been for a long time. But you know what? We don't need bullets. We just need people to think we have bullets. Threats are what keep people in line."

Caleb flipped the revolver over in his hand and held it

out to Sheriff Dante. "If I had to guess, Metro had a civil war."

"That's right," Stone said. "But don't put it on me, Sergeant. It was before my time. It was before the time of anyone in the city."

"What happened?" Riley asked.

"To put it simply? A good number of people were sick of the living conditions and wanted out, and they were willing to do anything to do it. An equally large number of people didn't want them opening the seals and letting the trife in. So instead of staying unified against the real threat, we went to war with each other. It's obvious which side won.

"My grandfather was in charge of the defense. A war hero. He was elected Governor after all was said and done. He was a pragmatic man. He realized this sort of thing would happen again if measures weren't taken. He was big on history, and he drew on the monarchies of the middle ages in rearranging the composition of the city. He took away the people's choices, formed a powerful militia, abolished the elections, and ruled with an iron fist. My father did the same, and now it's my turn. If you don't like what you see, it's not there because we're savages or because we're unreasonable. We made it this way because it works."

Something about the way Governor Stone made his speech made Caleb think he had practiced it before. He questioned the truth of it. Had the nature of Metro changed to help it survive, or had it altered to satisfy the needs of one man or one family? He couldn't be sure.

"Is that why the people don't know the truth about what's outside of Metro?" Caleb asked. "To keep them in line?"

"What do you mean what's outside of Metro?" Stone replied.

"I don't believe you don't know," Caleb said. "There's no way that basic fact was forgotten."

Governor Stone stared at Caleb, his expression hard. "Be careful with what you say next, Sergeant. You can't begin to understand the potential fallout. What was done was done for a reason."

"So you know?" Riley asked.

"Yes," Stone replied.

"Know what?" Sheriff Dante asked.

"This is about that," Caleb said. "If you want to keep the colony alive, you need to come clean, at least to a few people. Like the people in this room."

"Know what?" Joe asked.

Governor Stone bit his bottom lip and looked at the sheriff and the engineer. His eyes shifted to Riley and Caleb, and then he sighed.

"You can imagine how the people would have reacted," he said. "Considering what happened before. We decided to alter some of the data in the mainframe and do a hard reset of the system to keep it clean. To cover our tracks."

"Cover what tracks?" Joe asked.

"It was Carol's grandmother that helped with the reset. Getting the people to forget, to stop talking about it, that was harder. The war made it easier. We turned the truth into the lie, and the lie into the truth."

"What lies?" Sheriff Dante asked. "What truth?"

Governor Stone paused again. He looked at Riley. "How bad is it, Doc?"

"Life or death, Jackson," Riley replied.

He nodded and looked back at his people. "What I'm about to tell you has to stay with you, and only spread as much as it needs to right now. If anyone speaks of it without authorization, they'll be treated as traitors to Metro and executed. Do you understand?"

"Yes, Governor," Sheriff Dante said.

"Okay," Joe replied.

"Metro isn't in a bunker near Atlanta, Georgia. It's on a starship, over two hundred years away from Earth."

Chapter 43

Sheriff Dante and Chief Engineer King took the news better than Caleb would have expected. Dante's face began to flush, and he could see how her chest begin to rise and fall more rapidly, her mouth opening slightly in silent, nervous fear. She didn't speak. She didn't question. She accepted.

"A starship?" Joe said, calmer than Dante but still shocked. "I didn't even know we had those, but it makes sense considering some of the problems we've been having. And I always wondered why Metro is a perfect rectangle even though it was assembled underground. I guess because it wasn't." He laughed nervously.

"What does this mean for us, Governor?" Sheriff Dante asked, her voice strained.

"We aren't getting out of here anytime soon for one," Joe said. "And if you broke down our door after two hundred years to tell us the situation outside the city is life or death, my first inclination is to think this has nothing to do with the trife. Taken with the way the systems went down earlier, I'd guess the problem is power related."

"One of the problems is power related," Riley admitted.

"One of them?" Governor Stone replied.

"The primary reactors reached the end of their duty cycle ten years ago," Riley said. "They're putting out a diminishing amount of power, which has caused the Deliverance to switch to backup batteries. Now those batteries are running low."

"How low?" Joe asked.

"Three percent."

"Shit."

"We have a replacement energy source," Caleb said. "We can bring everything back up to full power. But we don't know how to connect it to the interchange safely."

"I can probably help with that," Joe said.

"That's what we're hoping," Riley replied.

"What are the other problems?" Governor Stone asked.

"We had a... problem, with one of our computer systems," Riley said. "We're locked out of navigation control by a layer of encryption we aren't equipped to crack. If you have anyone who manages your subroutines and might be good at working around problems, we could really use them."

"Governor, I think Deputy Klahanie might be a good choice," Sheriff Dante said. "He handles all of our recovery on the networked terminals and tablets we have left, and he has a real knack for that kind of thing."

"I'll trust your opinion on Dale," Governor Stone said. "Doctor, when you say navigation control, exactly what do you mean?"

"A foreign agent set us on a course to the nearest star," Caleb said. "We need to break the encryption to reset navigation and change our heading."

"Foreign agent?" Sheriff Dante said.

"Don't worry," Caleb replied. "We already dealt with them. Now we're trying to clean up the mess they left behind."

"How long do we have?" Joe asked. "To fix navigation control, I mean?"

"Three hours."

The engineer's face paled. So did Sheriff Dante's and Governor Stone's.

"I warned you that we don't have time to waste," Caleb said. "In any case, that's only problem number two. Once we fix the automated control system, we'll need to manually adjust our heading to at the very least get us pointed away from the star while we reset the system and enter new coordinates. If none of your people know they're on a starship, I guess it's safe to assume you don't have any pilots?"

Governor Stone's face split in a wry smile. "Actually, it may not be as safe an assumption as you think."

The answer surprised Caleb. "How so?"

"The protocols always called for a percentage of the Metro citizenship to carry forward specific skill sets related to our situation, in this case as a starship navigator. Just because we altered the history of the city, that didn't mean we could ignore what were vital directives from our founders. What it did mean is that our family had to internalize certain positions, to keep the truth about the city safe."

"You're a pilot?" Riley asked.

"Not me," Stone replied. "My daughter. She's been training since she was twelve years old."

"How old is she now?"

"Fifteen."

Caleb looked at Riley. They couldn't put the fate of the ship into the hands of a fifteen-year-old.

"What does her age have to do with anything?" Governor Stone said, noticing his reaction. "She has more experience in a simulator than anyone else on this ship by hundreds of hours."

"And I thought I was repairing a game system," Joe said.

"I don't want to argue about it," Caleb said. "We've wasted enough time."

"Good. Then it's settled. Sam, find Klahanie and get him here as soon as possible. Joe, head over to the mansion with one of my guard squads and pick up Orla. And remember what I said about revealing the truth."

"Yes, Governor," both Sheriff Dante and Chief Engineer King replied, hurrying out of the room. Caleb was sure the complete shock had yet to hit either of them and would leave them both more stunned once they had a free moment to absorb it.

"As for you, Doctor Valentine," Governor Stone said. "Your identification chip is verifiable proof of your status and position both outside Metro and within it. Regardless of anything, you have both the right of authority to claim control of the Governorship, and the firepower to back it up." He glanced at Caleb. "Bows and arrows are no match for high-powered rifles and real combat armor."

"Right now, I'm only focused on getting the Deliverance out of danger," Riley said. "We can discuss politics once we're safe. All I can tell you is that if you truly did act in the best interests of the colony, that will make itself apparent then."

Governor Stone's face hardened, and he nodded somberly. It seemed ironic to Caleb that Riley would lecture the man about acting in the best interests of anyone besides himself. Like her, he would wait to worry about how to keep her from gaining control of the colony until they were safe from their immediate harm.

"We'll leave as soon as Klahanie and your daughter arrive," Riley said. "We have a ship to save."

Chapter 44

It took ten minutes to assemble the entourage that would follow Caleb and the others back out of Metro, with Deputy Klahanie the last to arrive at the law office. Governor Stone's daughter Orla came quickly, practically running to the office after receiving the news that yes, Marines from outside Metro had entered the city, and yes, they were hurtling through space on a starship and yes, they needed her help to fly it.

Orla was rail thin, a little too tall, short brown hair and kind of awkward when she moved. She was dressed in finer clothes than any of the other residents he had seen, but they weren't particularly fancy. A pair of respun jeans, a cream colored shirt, a pair of worn sneakers. What really caught Caleb's notice was her level of respect for him and the other two Guardians. She knew how to stand at attention. She always referred to him as sir, even though he wasn't an officer, and she immediately started following Flores around like she was her long-lost mother. He had been worried about letting a child fly the Deliverance.

Maybe that was wrong of him to begin with. He wasn't worried now.

Deputy Klahanie could have passed as Orla's brother. He was just as thin, and almost as tall as Washington. He had dark hair and a thick beard like Governor Stone's, small eyes and a big smile. He was loud when he spoke and almost too outgoing. He started flirting with Flores as soon as he had the chance, but she didn't seem to mind too much. Caleb could have put her back in line, but he decided they all needed a moment of levity and normalcy.

Once Caleb explained how it worked, Chief Engineer King didn't seem to think connecting the alien energy unit to the interchange would be all that difficult. But Caleb knew from experience that things rarely went as smoothly as their potential suggested.

They headed out of the law office in a group of twelve, which Flores quickly dubbed the fellowship of the ring. She called him Aragorn once and referred to Riley as Saruman. The way she laughed when she said it gave Caleb the impression that her moniker wasn't flattering.

It took fifteen minutes of walking to reach the back of the engineering corridor to the torn and damaged former seal. Caleb watched the expressions of the Metro colonists as they reached the broken hatch. He could see the tension on Governor Stone's face. The worry over what this new direction meant for his hold on the city and the concern they wouldn't live long enough to find out. He noticed how Joe and Carol King were focused and intense, ready to do their job to the best of their ability. Orla and Deputy Klahanie had a look of nervous excitement and an eagerness to explore and discover. Sheriff Dante and her two deputies were still in a state of shock, putting one foot in front of the other and doing their best to maintain their composure. Caleb could see the goosebumps on her wrists and the slight shiver of anxiety in her hands.

He didn't blame her for being afraid. Now that some of the smoke had cleared, he could see how extensive some of the damage around the hatch was. They were lucky they hadn't damaged anything critical with their explosion.

"You should have just knocked," Joe said from behind him, drawing a laugh from Orla.

"The weld was on your side," Riley explained. "We had no other way to get through. I tried hailing you from the bridge, but nobody answered."

"Our comm station has been down for close to eighty years," Governor Stone said. "I always assumed if you needed to reach us, you would find a way. And you did."

"Sergeant Card, how far to the bridge, sir?" Orla asked.

"About ten minutes walk from here," Caleb replied. "Doctor Valentine and Private Flores will lead you and Deputy Klahanie up there. Private Washington and I will take Joe and Carol to the interchange. We left the energy unit nearby. Governor Stone, Sheriff Dante, you're welcome to tag along with whichever team you want."

"Sheriff Dante will go with you, Sergeant," Stone said. "I'll go up to the bridge with my daughter. You're sure it's safe out here?"

"As of an hour ago it was," Caleb replied. "I lost one of my best Marines securing the ship."

"I'm sorry to hear that, sir," Orla said. "What happened?"

Caleb glanced sideways at Riley. What would the people of Metro think if they knew the truth? Would they even be able to wrap their heads around it well enough to believe it was possible? "It's a long story. We can brief one another on everything once we're safe."

"Yes, sir."

They navigated past the damaged section of corridor and out into the ship, taking one of the corridors aft toward the stern stairwell. The klaxons and audible warnings had stopped, leaving the ship in a state of dead silence. The quiet felt strange to Caleb. It was the first time things had been calm since he had thawed. Of course, the calm was a lie. The stillness and silence made it too easy to forget the truth of their situation.

"Does the whole thing look like this?" Deputy Klahanie asked. "It's kind of plain."

"What did you expect?" Flores asked. "This isn't the love boat or a Disney cruise."

Klahanie's face flushed, and he didn't answer. The group dropped into another silence until they reached the stairwell.

"This is where we split up," Caleb said. "The energy unit is on the landing one floor down. The interchange is on Deck Twenty-four. The bridge is on Deck Six."

"Six?" Governor Stone said. "Not One? The bridge doesn't have any windows?"

"No," Riley replied. "There are high-resolution cameras that will give you a look at what's outside."

"How do we know what's in the cameras is real?"

"Why wouldn't it be?"

"You tell me, Doctor. Maybe I'm overly cynical, but I can't help but entertain the idea that this is an elaborate hoax. What if the war really is over, and you're just testing us to see how we react? It could be a once in a lifetime opportunity to run an experiment like that."

Riley laughed. "You're right, Governor. You're right that the war on Earth is over. We lost. Badly. If any humans are still alive back there, I guarantee they're in worse shape than we are right now."

"My point still stands. We have no idea of knowing if what you're showing us is real. We have no way of knowing that we're really in space."

"We can take you down to the hangar, Governor," Flores said. "We can open the outer blast doors again, and you can experience space first-hand."

"Flores," Caleb said, suppressing his outward amusement.

"Sorry, Alpha," Flores replied.

"We're definitely in space," Caleb added. "Joe, Carol, Sheriff Dante, you three are with me. We're heading down. We'll meet up with the others on the bridge once we hook up the unit."

"Sounds like a plan," Joe said.

"Bucket-up Marines," Caleb said. "I don't know if the ATCS network will reach from the interchange to the bridge, but it'll help us communicate from further away."

"Roger that," Flores said, shifting her helmet from under her arm to her head. Washington did the same.

"Deputy Klahanie," Sheriff Dante said. "Stay calm and take your time. You've got this."

"Thanks, Sheriff," Klahanie replied.

"Let's go," Caleb said. "The sooner we get the energy unit hooked up, the sooner we get out of this mess."

Chapter 45

"This is a power supply?" Joe said, looking skeptically down at the energy unit. The temporary closure was over the sphere inside, hiding the real source of the unit's energy production and giving it the appearance of a small, matte black alloy box.

"Yes," Caleb replied.

"I thought it would be bigger." Joe knelt down beside it. "Where did it come from?"

"An alien spacecraft. We think the same aliens who sent the trife."

Joe ran his hand over the smooth surface. "It isn't even hot. How does it work?"

"Quantum something," Caleb said. "The reactor is inside. Let's leave it closed until we get it to the interchange."

"Okay."

"Washington, can you grab it?"

Washington nodded. Joe stood and moved aside to let the big Marine pick up the energy unit. They started down the stairwell, taking it to the lower deck.

"Wash, take point," Caleb said. "Sheriff Dante, I'd like to talk to you about something."

Washington shifted position to get in front of the group, while Caleb slowed until he was in the back. Sheriff Dante slowed with him.

"What do you need, Sergeant?" she asked.

Caleb let the others get almost a whole flight ahead of them before he replied. "I want to talk to you about Doctor Valentine."

"What about her?"

Caleb had been trying to decide if he should bring Riley up before things had settled. He realized that the longer he waited, the easier it would be for her to manipulate the truth and become more embedded in their future decisions. He didn't want her to be part of anything for any longer than needed, and he wanted at least one person from Metro to be suspicious of her motives and actions.

"There's no delicate way I can think of to put this. I have reason to believe Riley Valentine murdered at least one member of the crew and has committed a number of other acts that have put both this ship and the colonists in unnecessary danger. But with everything else happening on the ship, I haven't been able to do anything about it."

Sheriff Dante was silent for a moment. "I see. Do you have proof to back up the accusation?"

"Circumstantial," he replied. "And hearsay. But I believe the ship's mainframe has archives of footage that will prove her duplicity."

"I see," she said again before pausing. "Sergeant, why are you telling me this? For one thing, you have more authority on this ship than I do. For another, even if you didn't, you have no solid proof. No evidence I can use to do anything. Why didn't you deal with her before you entered Metro?"

"Unfortunately, we still need her help to get the ship back to safety. As for authority, the Guardians only have greater authority as long as the ship is in space. According to the original protocol, as soon as we land we're supposed to disband and retire, and Riley knows it. Of course, we were supposed to be around seventy years old by then, but that's not the point. Anyway, she doesn't know that I know what she did and that I know who she killed. Right now, she thinks she's in the clear. But that doesn't mean she won't make moves to discredit my Marines or me to ensure nobody ever finds out what she did. I'm telling you because someone else has to know. Someone with no personal ties to the whole mess."

"Right. Well, it sounds simple enough. Deal with her before we land."

Caleb smiled. "I'd like to. But I prefer to have a backup."

"And how can I help you with that?"

"Just by being aware of the situation, and believing that there's at least a shred of merit to what I'm telling you."

"Fair enough. I believe you, Sergeant. You don't seem like the sort of man to lie."

"Maybe not, but if Riley finds out what I know, or even suspects I might know, she'll do what she can to convince you I am a liar. That's what I'm trying to head off."

"Has she given you any indication she suspects you know something?"

"Not so far. But to be honest, that only makes me more convinced that she does."

Sheriff Dante smiled. "I know the type. I'll stay alert, Sergeant."

"Thank you."

They continued descending to Deck Twenty-three,

exiting the stairwell and moving aft to the interchange. Caleb regained the lead as they entered the large space. The Guardians had done their best to remove the dead trife and the remnants of their nest from it, but a stale sulfurous scent still clung to the air.

"This ship must be drawing a lot of power," Carol said, looking at the massive pillars.

"It takes a lot of power to bring something up to half a cee in a reasonable amount of time," Caleb replied. "The thrust units are behind this room, through those doors." He pointed to the closed hatches at the back of the area.

"I'd love to get a look at them," Joe said. "I'll have to come back again later. Anyway, we have similar converters in Metro. They're a lot smaller, but they probably work the same way. You've got a feed coming in from the reactors, and then out to the thrust units. But it's probably only flowing in one direction."

"According to David, if you plug the energy unit into a feed to the capacitors, it'll push enough juice out to fill them, and then replenish them as needed. The main thing is making a safe link between the capacitors and the energy unit."

"And you said it would accept pretty much any type of connection?"

"That's right."

Joe turned to his wife. "What do you think?"

She nodded. "It shouldn't be too hard. The tricky part will be finding a heavy enough conduit to manage the power flow."

"We can probably take it from one of these converters. I'm sure they built the system with enough redundancy to handle losing one."

"Right," Carol agreed. "At worst it'll cost us a little

thrust." She looked at Caleb. "Probably a quarter cee when all is said in done."

"Anything is better than dying," Caleb said.

"Amen to that," Joe replied. "Okay. Let's get to work. Big man, I could use your help."

Washington pointed his thumb at his chest. Me?

"It's Washington, right?"

Washington nodded.

"The conduit is pretty heavy, and I'm getting old. If there's any beer on this boat, I'll owe you one when we're finished. Deal?"

Washington smiled and nodded, flashing Joe a thumbs-up.

"What do you need me to do?" Caleb asked.

"For now, stay out of the way. I'll holler if I need you."

"Roger that," Caleb said.

Joe pushed the sleeves of his shirt up past his elbows. Then he scanned the room, looking for something. He seemed to find it because he motioned to Washington and started moving. "Let's get to work."

Chapter 46

It didn't take long for Joe and Carol to find something for Caleb to do, and the two hours it took to cobble together a solution to the ship's power problem went by in a flash. The fact that they were closing in on an hour before they would collide with the system's star wasn't lost on any of them, and they worked with a frantic focus that left them mostly silent while they completed the task.

Their work took them out of the interchange to the deck below where the supercapacitors were stored. They huddled around the energy unit. A thick cable rested on the floor nearby, stretching from their position to the primary transformer that connected the reactor to the hundreds of capacitors arranged in a circular order around them. Because the solid-state batteries were tall and wide silver boxes, Carol likened them to a modern Stonehenge.

"This is it," Joe said as he removed the makeshift outer cover of the energy unit. He stared at the floating sphere for a moment, just watching how it emitted power from its outer diameter to the collectors surrounding it. "Where does all the power go with nothing plugged in?" He seemed to realize that if he didn't know, then none of them would know. He glanced up at his wife, waiting to see if she could answer before picking up the end of the heavy wire that would hopefully restore the ship to full power. "Are you ready?"

"We're ready," Sheriff Dante said.

Joe glanced at Caleb. "This is either going to recharge the capacitors, or we're all going to be dead two seconds from now."

"No pressure, darling," Carol said with a smirk.

Joe smiled at her, and then carefully lowered the wire toward the floating sphere, taking great care not to touch it.

As soon as the wire broke the outer plane of the containment, a bright bolt of blue light reached out and grabbed it. Caleb turned away as the light flashed and crackled, and a smell like burning rubber rose from the connection. He clenched his eyes tight, waiting for the resulting explosion to take him.

One second passed. Then another. And another. He opened his eyes, looking back at Joe. The engineer was still crouched beside the unit. He had his eyes closed too, his hands clasped together in a desperate prayer. There was still energy reaching out to the wire, wrapped around it and holding it fast. The sphere had a more intense glow, as though it were pulling an order of magnitude more power through it.

"Still alive," Sheriff Dante said. "Is it working?"

Carol broke away from the group, walking over to the transformer. There was a terminal built into the face of the equipment, and she tapped on the controls, bringing up a few different technical screens. Then she turned back to them, a huge smile on her face.

"It's working!" she announced. "Capacitors are already at thirty percent and rising!"

The small group erupted in a loud cheer, everyone but Washington. He pumped his fists in the air triumphantly.

"Great work, Joe and Carol," Caleb said. It felt good to have a smile on his face. It felt good to have something to smile about, even if it was only for a moment.

"Yeah," Sheriff Dante said. "I knew you could do it."

Joe's face flushed, and he kept his eyes down, uncomfortable with the praise.

"Let's head back to the bridge," Caleb said. "I'm eager to find out how Klahanie is making out with the lockdown."

"Me too," Dante agreed.

"I'm going to stay here," Joe said. "Keep an eye on things, just in case."

"I'll stay too," Carol said.

Washington raised his hand, indicating he wanted to stay with them.

"Okay. Joe, the nearest comm to the bridge is out in Engineering Control. Call into the bridge asap if there's any trouble. Wash, I'm not sure how far the network will stretch and I know you can't call for help, but ping me if you need me."

Washington gave him a thumbs-up. They had both discovered the control room with Joe and the others, passing through it to reach the capacitors. It looked a lot like the control rooms in both the Marine module and Research, only smaller.

"Will do, Sergeant," Joe said.

"Sheriff, are you coming with me?" Caleb asked.

"Affirmative, Sergeant," she replied.

They headed away from the area with the two deputies, leaving the engineers and Washington behind.

Caleb hurried back to the stairwell, eager to see what was happening on the bridge. He assumed he would know when they had regained control of navigation because the ship would slow or change course. While the inertial dampening systems would absorb most of any vectoring adjustments, he imagined they would cut the main thrusters and fire the bow thrusters at full power to slow down, something he was sure he would feel.

"I'm still having trouble coming to grips with this," Sheriff Dante confided as they ascended.

"With what?" Caleb asked.

She flailed her arms. "This. Being on a spaceship instead of under a mountain. Getting the power restored is great progress, but I feel like it was the easy part."

"It might have been."

"I'm not ready to die."

"Me either. You don't think Klahanie can pull this out of his hat?"

"I hope he can, but I don't know what he's up against. What if he can't do it?"

"We aren't up to can't do it yet. We still have an hour."

"That felt like more time two hours ago."

"I know. We--"

Caleb stopped speaking as a sudden jolt rocked the Deliverance, the force taking him off guard and slamming him against the wall. He bounced off, catching himself before he toppled down the steps. He reached out and grabbed Sheriff Dante, collecting her with his replacement arm before she could take a header down the steps. Momentum carried her into the crook of Caleb's arm, leaving her face pressed against his chest. Behind them, the two deputies had been less fortunate, hitting the deck and tumbling down a few steps.

"What the hell was that?" Sheriff Dante said, glancing up at him.

"I don't know," Caleb replied.

The light in the stairwell washed out, suddenly replaced by the return of the red strobes and the whining alert. Something was definitely happening.

It felt like they were accelerating again.

Chapter 47

Caleb checked the tactical network, looking for Washington or Flores on it. They were near the mid-point of the distance between each, leaving him cut off from the others.

"We need to get to the bridge," Caleb said, helping Sheriff Dante upright and getting back to his feet.

"Bashir, Casper, are you hurt?" Dante asked the men who had tumbled down the stairs.

"No ma'am," Bashir said. "A little bruised. We'll be fine."

"I can't wait for you," Caleb said. "Do you know how to get to the bridge?"

"No, but we'll figure it out," Dante said. "Go."

Caleb made it up one more deck before the ship shook again, rocking harder than the first time. He was thrown heavily into the wall, pain shooting up through his shoulder as he bounced off, cursing. What the hell was going on?

He looked down the stairwell, concerned Dante or one of her deputies might be hurt. Should he go back to them or continue climbing? He couldn't do much to help them. He decided to climb.

He sprinted up three more flights, nearly shouting in joy when his ATCS connected with Flores.

"Flores, what's happening to the ship?" he asked.

"Alpha," Flores replied breathlessly. "I... You won't... we're under attack!"

Caleb felt like his heart stop. "What?"

"It's a long story. It turns out the lockout was bullshit."

"What do you mean?"

"Klahanie figured it out. There was no encryption. No lock on the systems. Just a modification to the interface to display false information. Obfuscation and misdirection. We thought we were headed toward the star. We're actually approaching the planet."

"Essex?"

"That's the only planet here, Alpha."

Caleb tried to make sense of it. Why had the AI tricked them into thinking they were going toward the star? And why hadn't Riley figured that out?

Unless she already knew...unless she had done it?

"SON OF A BITCH," he said, yanking himself up the stairs at an increasing pace. "Who or what is attacking us?"

"We don't know. It came out of nowhere. It's a sphere about ten meters in diameter, and it's firing some kind of energy weapon at us. Hold on Alpha!"

Caleb braced himself on the wall, thankful for the warning. The ship shook again a moment later.

"We can't take this for long," Flores said. "Damn Cylons."

"Riley's wearing armor," Caleb said. "Can you give her your helmet?"

"Roger, Alpha. Standby."

Caleb kept climbing for the ten seconds it took for the network to reconnect under Riley's ATCS. He was on Deck Twelve, almost there.

"Valentine, what are we looking at?" he asked, having to swallow his growing hatred.

"I think it's a drone," Riley said. "Sensors suggest it was operating on low power until we started closing on Essex. Now it's firing on us."

"Damage?"

"Minimal so far, but it won't stay that way. The Deliverance wasn't built to defend itself in space."

"Do we have any external firepower of our own?"

"Negative."

"So what's the plan? I hear we're closer to Essex than we thought."

"We are. I'm sorry, Sergeant. It's my fault. I should have realized it was tricking us. It seems it had a backup plan for not getting the landing codes."

"Crashing us into the planet?"

"Apparently."

"Why would it do that? It might kill its own – "

"I don't know, Sergeant. We have more immediate concerns."

"What about the equipment on board? What about in the hangar?"

"There's nothing orbital in the main hangar," Riley said. "Klahanie already checked."

"What about the secondary hangar up front?"

"There's another hangar?"

"What, I knew something you didn't? How is that possible? Yes, there's a smaller secondary hangar in the bow. For all I know, it's empty, but it's worth checking out."

"One second, Sergeant," Riley said. "Klahanie, can you get anything on a secondary hangar? Caleb, hang on!"

Caleb braced himself again. The ship shook a third time.

"We've got damage to the midship airlock," he heard Klahanie say. "We're venting air, Doctor!"

"I don't care," Riley said. "Find the secondary hangar."

"Got it!" Klahanie said. "Inventory lists something called a dagger. Does that mean anything to you?"

Riley was silent long enough Caleb thought he had lost the link. He checked his HUD. Still connected. "Valentine, do you know what a Dagger is?" he asked.

"Yes. It's an experimental starfighter."

"Did you just say starfighter?" Caleb said. "What's a starfighter doing on the Deliverance? Isn't this a civilian ship?"

"The Dagger is controlled through a neural interface. Space Force had them loaded for my team to work on during the trip to Proxima."

Caleb knew she was lying. Not outright. She sprinkled the truth with lies, just enough to make them indistinguishable.

"Are they functional?"

"For the most part. Like I said, the Daggers are experimental. They've never been used in an uncontrolled environment."

"What does that mean?"

"It's never been tested outside of a simulator."

"Well, I guess that's about to change. Tell Flores to grab Orla and meet me at the stairwell."

"What about the ship?"

"Do we have full control over it?"

"We do."

"And do you have the landing codes?"

"I do."

"Then you know what to do."

"Sergeant, I'm not sure…"

"The AI is gone, right? David is gone. The Reapers are all dead. There's no reason not to land."

"I can think of one reason. The planet isn't safe. It's being watched."

Caleb's jaw clenched. Damn it, the planet was never safe and she knew it. "We're venting air. You're a Doctor. You know what that means."

Riley hesitated a moment. "Roger. Flores! Take Orla and bring her to the stairwell. Meet with Sergeant Card there."

Caleb didn't hear the response, but he knew they would be on the way.

"Doctor, I need directions to the hangar. I know it's up there, but I don't know where it is."

"Roger. Standby."

Caleb ascended while he waited, making it the rest of the way to Deck Six. He burst out of the stairwell at the same time Riley started speaking again.

"Klahanie turned on all the lighting leading back to the hangar. Just follow the yellow brick road, Sergeant."

It sounded like something Flores would say. "Roger."

He heard boots on the floor down the corridor on his left. Flores and Orla appeared a minute later. The ship rocked a fourth time, throwing them into the wall. Flores twisted awkwardly to keep the unprotected pilot from slamming into the bulkhead, cursing as she hit the ground.

Caleb ran over to them. "Flores, are you hurt?"

"I think my arm is broken," she replied. "It doesn't matter. Nothing if we don't stop that thing from shooting at us."

Caleb took Orla's thin arm in his hand. "We need to run."

"I'm ready, Sergeant," Orla replied.

"Good hunting, Alpha!" Flores called as Caleb and Orla sprinted away.

Chapter 48

"Sergeant," Riley said. "You should know. The Dagger isn't like a typical craft. It uses a neural interface linked to a custom onboard ATCS. We call it CUTS. Combat Unified Tactical System. The controls don't have much in common with an atmospheric fighter jet or the Deliverance."

"How does that relate to me?" Caleb asked.

"Prior flight experience is helpful, but not required. If you can use an ATCS, you can fly a Dagger. Theoretically."

Caleb glanced over at Orla. "Why didn't you tell me that when I asked for Orla?"

"What does the word theoretically mean to you, Sergeant? I said prior experience is helpful. Besides, just because you can fly it doesn't mean you'll fly it well, and I'd prefer to survive long enough to reach the surface."

"Roger that," Caleb said, wondering how easy the craft would be to fly in reality. He checked his HUD. The link between his ATCS and Riley's was getting weak. "We're going to lose the connection in a second. Anything else we should know?"

"Yes. The Daggers aren't trans-atmospheric. You need to be back on board before we hit the thermosphere or you won't be coming down with us. Assuming there's an us to come down with."

"This keeps getting better and better. How long do we have?"

"About twenty minutes. I'm going to enter the codes now. Once I do, the computer will be managing course and velocity with no way to make any manual alterations. You need to come back to the ship because she can't come to you."

"Got it."

"Good hun – "

The link dropped mid-sentence, leaving Caleb alone with Orla, racing through the corridors toward the forward hangar. Twenty minutes, and it would take five to get to the hangar. That didn't leave much time. He was tempted to tell Governor Stone's daughter to go back to the bridge. He didn't want her out there risking her life against whatever was attacking them. She was just a kid. She was also the only one of them with experience maneuvering in zero gravity, simulated or otherwise.

They ran in silence, following the bright lights across the length of the ship, crossing over the top of Metro to the front of the vessel. The bow of the ship wasn't fully completed, leaving them in spaces that revealed the skeletal frame of the craft -- a honeycomb of alloy that formed the superstructure. They crossed through the web of unfinished corridors, around disconnected bulkheads and exposed beams. The route left Caleb certain they would never have found the smaller hangar on their own.

Caleb pulled off his helmet as they reached the closed blast doors of the smaller hangar. He tossed it to the floor, stopping in front of the control panel and typing in his ID code. The doors slid open, the hangar bathed in darkness. The interior lights began to go on as he and Orla stepped over the threshold, revealing the Daggers in all their glory.

"This doesn't look like an experiment to me, sir," Orla said, commenting on the reveal.

"It doesn't look like an experiment to me, either, kid," Caleb replied.

He was expecting one or two of the fighters.

The hangar was holding at least twenty.

This wasn't a test. This was an air force.

The fighters were long and narrow, with small delta wings spreading out slightly from either side and stabilizers on both the top and bottom of a rear fuselage that ended in an impossibly small main thruster port. A pair of what Caleb took to be laser cannons were mounted at the junction of the body and the wings, hanging slightly forward of the wing surfaces, while a second pair of cannons clung to turrets mounted beneath the wings. The cockpit was pushed all the way up front, a clear canopy sloping back from the noses. Smaller thrust ports for zero-g vectoring were visible at regular increments around them.

As Caleb examined the fighters, he could almost picture Riley's ideal humans climbing into the craft, fearless and immortal as they assaulted the enemy from the sky. He could practically see them strafing hordes of angry trife against the backdrop of Earth, killing hundreds to thousands with each run. It was an impressive achievement. It was also wishful thinking. Command had no idea what they might have encountered out here. How could they be so confident these ships would have any value at all?

"We'll take the first two," he said, pointing to the lead Daggers.

"We, sir?" Orla replied. There was no hint of fear in her voice, only excitement for the adventure.

"Doctor Valentine says I should be able to fly one of these with my brain," Caleb said. "We'll see if she's right. Otherwise, it's up to you to go after the drone and take it down."

"Roger, sir," Orla said.

Caleb hurried over to his fighter. It seemed to sense his approach because the moment he got close enough the canopy clicked and slid backward along the fuselage to allow him entry.

That part was easy enough. The fighters were slung so low to the ground he was able to jump easily onto the wing and then two steps to the cockpit, climbing in and then waiting for Orla to reach her ship. She hopped onto the wing and crossed to the cockpit, looking down into it and smiling.

"This is going to be great, sir," she said.

Caleb flashed her a thumbs-up in his best imitation of Washington. Then he looked into the cockpit. The fighter jets he had seen had all kinds of displays and toggles and buttons arranged across the front. The Dagger didn't have any of that. A single flexible cord reached from the dashboard back to a flight helmet that could have just as easily passed for the bucket he had been wearing a minute earlier. The only modification appeared to be the wired connection to the Dagger and a snap-on mouthpiece to provide oxygen.

He picked the helmet up, holding it in his left hand as he slid into the fighter's seat. It was padded and comfortable, molding around his body to form a snug hold. He settled into it, looking over to where Orla was already dropping the helmet onto her head. He did the same, sliding it over his face.

The HUD appeared the moment he lowered it into place, nearly identical to the HUD of the standard ATCS.

He had a tactical grid on the left side, a targeting reticle in the center, a menu to the right. There were a couple of differences he recognized right away. A rear view ran along the bottom of his visor, and a second faded reticle sat inert below the primary target.

"Sergeant, this is Orla. Do you copy, sir?" Her voice came in loud and clear.

"I hear you, Orla," he replied. "How are you coping with this?"

"It's just like the simulator, sir. No worries."

He smiled. That was easy for her to say. He looked over and saw her canopy had closed.

"How do I close the canopy?" he asked.

"It's a neural interface, sir. Just think about it closing."

Think about it? He glanced up at the canopy and imagined watching it close. To his surprise, it did.

"Huh. Okay. That was – "

The ship rocked again, more violently than before. He was yanked hard into the side of the craft, the blow absorbed by gel padding along the cockpit. The clamps on the fighters creaked and groaned as the fighters spun up for launch.

"Sergeant, are you there?" Riley's voice came in through his helmet.

"Valentine? You have comms open with the fighters?"

"Of course," she replied, as though it was a stupid question. "Somebody has to open the blast doors for you."

"Right. Ok. I'm just getting settled, give me – "

"Opening the hangar doors now," Riley said, cutting him off. "Prepare for launch."

The doors clanked and began to slide apart. The air was quickly sucked from the space, causing the fighter to jerk forward slightly against its clamps.

"The drone is closing fast. We've got critical damage

on Deck Fourteen near the midships, which is way too close to Metro. Hit it hard and fast Daggers."

"Roger, ma'am," Orla said.

Caleb's heart somehow managed to ratchet up to another speed, pulsing hard as his nerves tried to get the best of him. He gripped the armrests of the cockpit, wrapping his hands around the hard plastic and quickly breaking the rest on the left. He eased off immediately, sighing heavily to relieve some of the tension.

The blast doors for this hangar were much smaller than the doors to the main hangar, and they opened much faster. Ten seconds was all it took to make room for the fighters, and Caleb watched as Orla's Dagger fired its main thruster in a burst of bright blue light and then darted forward across the hangar, the clamps falling away and releasing it into the black. She shot out of the Deliverance, whooping like a schoolgirl.

"It's easy, Sergeant," Orla said. "Just think of what you want to do and the system will do it."

"What does this thing even need a human pilot for?" he replied. "It should be able to think for itself."

"AI doesn't make for good pilots," Riley said. "It becomes too predictable over time."

Caleb figured the only reason he wouldn't was because he had no idea what he was doing.

"Okay, Dagger," he said softly. "Release the clamps, and let's get spaceborne."

He focused on thinking of the clamps letting go and the ship rocketing out the doors the same way Orla's had. He was shoved back in the seat as the thrusters ignited and fired, launching him out into space.

"Humankind's first Space Marine," he shouted with sudden delight. "Oorah!"

Chapter 49

Caleb's excitement didn't last. All it took was a look at the Deliverance's outer hull, especially the midship where the last strike had hit. A gaping hole was spilling debris into space, casting off bits and pieces as more oxygen leaked out from the damage.

"Tell me you have the damaged area sealed off, Valentine," he said.

"It's sealed, Sergeant," she replied. "Focus on the drone."

He hadn't made eye contact with it yet, but it was marked on his tactical, a fair distance out to his left. Orla was there too, already way ahead of him.

"Orla, be careful," Caleb said. "Slow down. We'll do this together."

"Yes, sir," Orla replied, her Dagger decelerating.

He thought of gaining speed and his fighter responded, pulling him along and leaving him pinned to the back of the seat as he vectored toward the other fighter. He got a good look at Essex on his left, getting way too close as the Deliverance closed in. He could see the ship's retro-thrusters firing, attempting to slow the ship enough to bring it down to the surface. What were the odds the computer-controlled landing would get them down safe considering the damage they had taken? What if it was already too late?

He brushed that thought aside when he realized it was causing him to slow, the interface taking his negativity as a signal to give up. He imagined the fighter accelerating again, and a few seconds later he had nearly caught up to Orla.

"There it is, sir," she said. "It's incredible."

Caleb shifted his eyes from the tactical map to look past the HUD to space. The spherical drone was up ahead.

"Let's go wide around its flanks," Caleb said. "Stay alert for any…"

He trailed off as his HUD flashed red, giving him a moment's warning of an energy spike from the drone. He reacted almost naturally, trying to throw himself into a sideways roll. The fighter responded the same way, quickly rolling and shooting laterally, flipping and coming back on the target as a thick beam flashed past where he had just been.

"Whew," he said. "That was close."

He took a wide vector toward the drone, noting Orla was flying a perfect matching pattern on the other side. He gave himself a second to wonder at the smoothness of space flight and marvel at the view, beyond words from his perspective. He made sure to keep his eyes trained on both the target and the HUD, watching for more attempts to attack him.

The CUTS triggered another warning, and a moment later a second flash pierced the black. It wasn't directed at him, instead reaching hundreds of kilometers out to strike the Deliverance. Caleb looked down at the rear camera, seeing the beam hit its target. A fresh part of the hull melted away, a new hole in the ship causing more air and debris to shoot out. There was no fireball, no explosion, no sound. It was as surreal as any combat experience Caleb ever had.

"Sergeant, hurry!" Riley said, the urgency and fear clear in her voice. There might have been a time when she wasn't taking all of this seriously enough. That time had come and gone.

Caleb refocused on the sphere. It was quickly getting larger ahead of him. Much larger. He could make out the composition of its surface as a series of dark plates that caused him to glance down at his alien-sourced replacement arm. The metal was the same, meaning it would be nearly as impervious to damage as the Cerebus Sho had helped drag out of the airlock.

A pair of doors spread apart from the front of the sphere, revealing a turret beneath them. A ring of energy formed at the edge of the turret, and then the Dagger's warning systems went crazy again, giving Caleb half-a-second to evade the attack. The fighter jerked aside as the plates closed up again, protecting the delicate innards from retaliation.

That didn't mean the sphere was letting up the assault. Plates on the other side moved aside, showing another turret there. Caleb didn't have time to warn Orla, and he clenched his teeth as a beam fired out at her, missing the fighter by mere centimeters as she calmly slipped aside.

"Too slow," Orla said, laughing.

"Knuckle-up, kid," Caleb said. "We need to take this thing out, and we need to do it now."

"Roger, Sergeant," Orla replied, her amusement vanishing in an instant. "How do we do that?"

"It looks like if we can get past the armor plates we can do some serious damage. How's your aim?"

They were interrupted as the sphere opened fire again, this time shooting at both of them in unison. They dodged the attack, which was followed up by a second and third blast in rapid succession. Caleb spun through space, his fighter vectoring wildly around the shots. Orla was much more controlled, each movement precise and smooth.

"Not the best," she said. "I spent a lot more time on steering. I thought I might get to bring the colony to the surface one day."

"You are," Caleb replied. "Maybe not in the way you imagined. Watch out!"

The sphere rotated quickly on its axis, plates spreading from multiple locations. A trio of beams flashed out at Orla, leaving Caleb certain they would hit. Somehow, she managed to dance the fighter around them and then get a shot off from the turret-mounted lasers. The blast nearly snuck in under the armor before it closed again.

"Damn," she said.

The gap between them and the sphere was shrinking, though it seemed like the drone wasn't all that concerned with them. Its heading and velocity didn't change at all; it remained fixed on the Deliverance. The main plates at its face began sliding aside to let its main cannon fire again.

Caleb reacted instantly, using the reticles to steer the fighter. He thought about lining the shot up on the cannon and the fighter slowed and vectored sideways, putting him in a perfect line with the gun.

Too perfect. He managed to get one shot off before the beam launched from the drone, coming right at him.

He cursed, trying to get the fighter up and away from the shot, just barely getting clear as it zipped through space and into the side of the Deliverance for the sixth time. More debris exploded out from the ship.

"Sergeant!" Riley shouted. "Do something, damn it!"

"I'm doing the best I can," he snapped back. He sent the fighter jolting ahead. The sphere was only a few kilometers forward, and he aimed both reticles at it. "Let's see if you can stand up to this," he said. He fired on the ship with a thought, four lasers arcing out and into the same spot on the armor. The strike caused it to glow red hot, and the CUTS claimed he made a three-centimeter ablation in the armor as his fighter streaked over the alien craft. "Not enough," he said. "It's not enough. We definitely can't get through the armor. Orla, form up on my flank."

"Roger," Orla replied. Caleb slowed his Dagger while Orla brought hers around, lining up beside him as they trailed the sphere, which hadn't broken from its course toward the Deliverance. "What now, sir?"

"When I give you the signal, I want you to get ahead of it. I'm going to come around on it and get a solid line of fire past the armor. When it tries to destroy you, I'll destroy it."

"You sound confident, sir."

"I'm glad I sound confident. Stay behind it and wait for my signal. We're only going to get one shot at this."

"Roger."

Caleb peeled away from her, accelerating to get in position above the sphere. He watched his HUD, keeping an eye on Orla. She was sitting behind the sphere, keeping her distance. The drone was drawing ever closer to the Deliverance, which in turn was getting ever closer to Essex.

How many more hits could the starship take before it would fall to pieces? Caleb had a feeling the answer was zero.

"Orla, make your move on my mark," he said. "Three... Two... One..."

He didn't get the chance to call out the mark. The sphere rotated suddenly on both axis, coming to a near-instant stop and almost causing Orla to collide into the back of it. She barely managed to swing the fighter past the sphere, which opened both turrets in Caleb's direction, firing immediately.

Caleb cursed, the flashes from the beam blinding him as they laced along the side of his fuselage, leaving a deep gash in the hull. He dove down and to the side, sinking beneath the attack, the sphere rotating to match.

He dropped under it, main thruster firing at full power. The sphere rotated and accelerated with him, matching his speed near-instantly and finally deciding he was a threat worth engaging.

"Orla, you need to line up the shot," Caleb said, eyes fixed on the rear view. He swung the fighter in a loose, chaotic corkscrew, blasts of energy flashing past.

"Roger, Sergeant. I'm moving into position."

"Nice work, Sergeant," Riley said. "You got it off our tail."

And onto mine, Caleb wanted to say. He held the comment back, focusing on evading the sphere's attack. How did it stop and go on a dime like that? The change in inertia alone should have torn the ship to pieces.

It didn't matter. It was on his ass, and it was about to blow him to hell. He zigged and zagged chaotically ahead of it, doing his best to at least get it heading away from the Deliverance. He kept his peripheral vision on the tactical map, watching Orla's position relative to his and the target as she tried to get across its flank to take a shot at its underbelly.

"Sergeant, I'm almost in position," she said a few

seconds later. "It keeps rotating to track you, sir. I need you to fly in a straight line."

"It'll kill me if I fly in a straight line," Caleb replied.

"Negative, sir. When it tries to destroy you, I'll destroy it."

"You sound confident."

"Yes, sir."

Caleb breathed out, swallowing hard. If she missed the shot, he was dead. But if she missed the shot, they were all going to die.

It went against every instinct he had, but somehow he managed to think the Dagger into flying in a straight line. One last bolt ripped past him, catching the edge of his left wing. There was a pause as the sphere adjusted and prepared the next round.

Too easy.

"No," Caleb said. It was too easy. "It's a trap."

In his mind, he pictured spinning hard and tight, coming around with his rifle shouldered and ready to fire. The fighter responded to the thought, firing vectoring thrusters at full power and throwing him hard to the side. His replacement arm smashed into the cockpit, denting the side as he eyed the reticle. The sphere began to spin, coming to a full stop to face Orla as she approached. The plates spread aside.

He opened fire with everything he had. Some of the shots missed, but not all. They sank in past the armor, blasting through the skeleton beneath. The sphere managed to fire too, and its beam scored a direct hit on the incoming Dagger, cutting it in half from front to rear.

"Nooooo!" Caleb screamed, his anger causing the CUTS to increase power output to the lasers. They continued blasting into the drone, burning through its heart and tearing it to pieces. "You son of a bitch." He kept shooting, ignoring the warning beeps in his helmet as he worked to drain the Dagger's reactor.

"Alpha!" Flores shouted through the comm. "Stand down! Alpha! It's destroyed."

Caleb caught himself suddenly, grabbing the helmet and yanking it from his head. Immediately, the shooting stopped, the fighter floating static in space. The other Dagger was drifting away from him.

Orla was dead.

"Son of a bitch," Caleb repeated. He clenched his jaw and his fists, furious at the outcome of the fight. He had to calm himself down, or he wouldn't be able to get his Dagger back under control. He closed his eyes, taking a few breaths.

She had died to save them, just like Sho. He had led her to her death, just like Sho. He knew it was part of the job. It was part of being at war.

He hated that part of it.

"Target destroyed. Nice work, Sergeant," Riley said over the comm.

Her voice was like a different kind of dagger, stabbing into his head and his heart. He punched his human hand into his leg, and then slowly pulled the helmet back on. He rotated the fighter toward the Deliverance and started the short but painful and lonely journey back.

Chapter 50

Caleb quickly found the short journey home wasn't going to be as short as he'd thought.

The Deliverance slowed as it approached Essex, but the fight against the drone had left him a good distance from the ship, and his emotional response to Orla's death had caused him to drain too much power from the batteries in too little a time.

The result was a potentially lethal combination that left the Dagger rocketing toward the escaping starship and closing the gap much more slowly than he wanted. He had a six-minute window to get the starfighter back into the hangar, and every estimate from the CUTS was putting his arrival at almost eight.

He could hardly believe it was all going to end like this. All of his efforts, and he wasn't going to die fighting a trife, a Reaper, or an alien AI or drone. He was going to run out of power, freeze to death, and drift away.

At least he would be out here with Sho and Orla. At least he wouldn't be completely alone.

That wasn't what it felt like looking around. There was

so much darkness. So much emptiness. And at the same time, there was so much life on Essex. The planet wasn't brown and gray and dead. It had water and vegetation and weather. It was like Earth, only not like Earth. A new world. It looked so peaceful from here. But was it peaceful? The AI wanted to get to the surface. The drone was protecting the surface. Was this the homeworld of the aliens who had sent the trife? Was it an outpost? Riley had to know the truth about the planet, didn't she? She had brought them here to fight the aliens, after all. Against their knowledge. Against their will.

And if he didn't make it back to the ship, she was going to get away with it.

He flipped through the CUTS menus, looking for anything that might be useful. It was so easy to fly the craft, it almost made it feel more like a toy than a piece of military equipment. The hard part was controlling his thoughts to keep the fighter in line. Negative thinking caused it to slow down, while eagerness and focus would get it to speed up.

The throttle was already maxed out, the fighter continuing to add velocity at the same time Deliverance was shedding it. The large main thrusters were all dark, shut down probably for good. The retro-thrusters and the vectoring thrusters were pushing back against the craft, jets of blue flame spurting out around the bow. Everything seemed to be happening so quickly and yet so slowly at the same time. Right now, six minutes felt like forever.

There were no overrides in the menus. Nothing he could use to go faster. He fought to keep his emotions in check, his mind tight and on the target ahead. The CUTS was doing its best to get him there, and there was little to do but go along for the ride.

One minute passed. Two minutes. Three. The Deliverance loomed larger ahead of him, the gap closing more quickly. Three minutes until they hit the thermosphere. Three minutes until he couldn't make it back on board. He seemed so close and yet so far. He could reach the starship with a minute to spare, but he was going way too fast to enter the hangar, even with the CUTS to synchronize the maneuver.

"Sergeant," Riley said. "The computer is indicating you aren't going to make it."

"I'm aware," Caleb replied. "Computers aren't always right."

"You're coming in way too hot. You need to slow your approach or you're going to crash into the hull."

"Again, I'm aware. Is Governor Stone there?"

"Standby."

"Sergeant Card," Stone said a moment later. His voice was hard. Emotionless. "Is there something you want from me?"

"I want to apologize, Governor," Caleb said. "Orla – "

"Don't, Sergeant," Stone said. "Don't apologize. And don't ever say her name. She shouldn't have been out there. You're the Guardian. It's your job to protect this ship. Not hers."

Caleb almost lapsed in his concentration, the Governor's sharp words threatening to dig beneath his skin. He pushed back against them. He wasn't going to apologize for bringing her out there. The drone was destroyed because she was such a good pilot. It had used Caleb to lead her in because it knew it couldn't hit her without taking her by surprise. It just didn't expect the weak pilot to have such good aim. No, he wanted to apologize for not seeing the trap sooner and being faster to stop it. He wanted to offer some kind of condolences. He understood Stone was angry and grieving. He wouldn't hold it against the man. He also wouldn't let him break him down.

"Yes, sir," Caleb said.

"Is that it?" Stone asked.

"Yes, sir."

"That went well," Flores said a moment later.

"It isn't the first time." Not everyone was as understanding as Habib's husband. "So, Private Flores, you've never seen a movie that might give me a clue on how to get out of this mess?"

"Are you kidding? That must have happened in the Star Wars movies at least a dozen times. What you need is space..." She trailed off. "Shit. Alpha, don't die yet, I have an idea."

The statement surprised him. "What is it?"

"You need to get in position to enter the main hangar."

"The main hangar doesn't open remotely."

"I know, just do it. Flores out."

"Flores, there's not enough time, and there's not enough air. You can't make it from the bridge to the hangar in three minutes."

"Sergeant, it's too late," Riley said. "She's already gone."

"What does she think she's doing?"

"She's trying to save your life."

He knew that. But how? By sacrificing her own? That wasn't going to work for him. He was tempted to slow the Dagger down, to alter his vector and move away from the Deliverance. He didn't want anyone else dying to save his life. It wasn't worth that much.

He checked his HUD. Two minutes and thirty seconds. He was only a few dozen kilometers from the ship, but he was going much too fast to attempt to get into the smaller hangar in the front of the vessel. His eyes dropped to the main hangar blast doors, nearly ten times the size of the upper hangar, the space beyond the doors almost twenty times as large if not larger.

The space beyond the doors. The area was open. It also had gravity. And, the flow of air leaving the ship would act as friction against him trying to enter. If he could get the angle right, if they could get the doors open... But the doors had to be activated manually, which meant someone would have to be out at the controls. Flores didn't have the strength to hold on against the pull of the vacuum.

But Washington did, and he was already only a few decks away from the area.

"Mariana, I hope you're thinking what I'm thinking," he said. "Okay, Guardians, let's do this."

Caleb locked his eyes on the main hangar blast doors, urging the CUTS to direct the Dagger toward it. Once he lined up with it, he could start firing the retro-thrusters and begin the deceleration. As long as they timed things right, he could hopefully get on board.

The seconds ticked by, the Dagger swooping in on the Deliverance, hanging tight against the side of the hull. Debris was still trickling out of the deep scars in the side of the ship, the wounds so heavy it made Caleb question whether getting on board the ship would even matter. There was just as much of a chance the whole thing would burn up trying to get through the thermosphere, the loss of the protective plating around the hull too great to over-come. Still, he'd rather die on the ship than outside of it, with his Guardians instead of by himself.

"Valentine, how do we look for landing?" Caleb said.

"We're on target," Riley replied. "As long as the ship holds together I think we'll be fine." Her voice was tense enough Caleb could spot the lie. She was trying to convince both of them they were going to make it. "Just worry about yourself, Sergeant."

"Roger. Do you have eyes on the hangar by any chance?"

"Standby. Klahanie, can you get me a feed from the main hangar? There. Washington is approaching the manual controls. Get ready, Caleb."

Caleb eyed the blast doors again, sending the Dagger away from the hull and adjusting the velocity, speeding up slightly to make his move. He needed to get in as quickly as possible, and then do his best not to die.

"He's activating the doors," Riley announced.

Caleb saw the crack of light spill out from between the blast doors. He kept his gaze fixed on it, watching the heavy slabs slide apart. He checked his HUD. He had less than a minute to get on board and for Washington to seal them in again.

It was going to be close.

He counted the seconds in his head. One. Two. Three. Four. When he hit five, he urged the Dagger forward again, vectoring to the right and taking an off-angle toward the still-opening blast doors. He dropped lower, getting closer to the deck. A sharp tone sounded in his helmet, the CUTS screaming out a collision warning, his HUD flashing red on both sides, showing him the wings weren't clear.

He cut the thrust, the Dagger sweeping toward the doors. A solid wall of escaping air buffeted into it, causing it to slow, the nose pushed upward. The starfighter slammed into the side of one of the doors, bouncing and rolling as the wings were sheared off, the fuselage tumbling into the gravity of the ship's floor and dropping to the ground. It continued to roll along the floor, end over end over end, at a sharp angle away from Washington.

Restraints tightened around Caleb, holding him secure against the seat as the world rotated around him, the canopy smacking the deck and a spiderweb of cracks forming in the plasti-glass.

It seemed to last forever. The fuselage split in half, the failure throwing his end in a new direction, sending the cockpit spinning like a top across the floor until it finally slammed into the side of a loader and came to a stop.

Caleb hung from the restraints, his head spinning, his body suddenly sore. He tried to look out through the canopy, but there were so many scuffs and cracks it was impossible to see through them. He could hear the motors of the blast doors though. It sounded like they were closing.

He wanted a few minutes to sit there and recover, but he didn't have any time. The ship was about to hit the thermosphere, and once it touched the ground he would no longer be a Guardian. He wouldn't have any authority over anything.

He released the restraints, reaching up and pushing against the canopy with his replacement hand. He shoved the top of the cockpit away and then ripped off the CUTS helmet, leaving it aside as he rolled out of the broken starfighter and onto the floor. He stumbled to his feet, nearly collapsing as he realized his ankle was injured.

A big hand wrapped around his arm, holding him up. Caleb turned his head, smiling in response to Washington's big smile.

"I owe you one," he said.

Washington exaggerated his nod of reply.

"We need to get to the bridge."

Washington spread his hands. *Why?*

"Once we touch the ground, I won't be able to restrain Doctor Valentine. She'll literally get away with murder."

Chapter 51

The Deliverance began to vibrate slightly when it hit the thermosphere and started its final descent to Essex's surface. Caleb barely had time to notice the shaking and no time to care about it. He and Washington raced across Deck Thirty toward the central lift, hoping the damage to the ship hadn't rendered it non-functional.

If it had, they would never make it to the bridge in time.

Caleb wasn't sure how taking action against Riley was going to work out. He didn't have the proof David claimed was in the ship's mainframe, at least not yet. He didn't have anything to go on but a dead man's tale and his eyewitness of that same dead man's body floating out into space. He would have to rely on his reputation and his position as Guardian and hope he could access the streams later. He couldn't wait for them to hit the ground. Once they did, Riley had every right to claim Governance of Metro, and in doing so would be able to claim immunity of sorts. The videos would still be hiding on the ship's mainframe, but he doubted Riley would ever let him anywhere near them. Even if she didn't know the clips existed, she was too smart not to play it safe.

They were about to land on a new world. A world they couldn't guarantee wasn't completely hostile. A world the AI had claimed would find them enslaved by its current occupants, who he assumed were the aliens that had created both the artificial intelligence and the trife. He wasn't sure confronting her was going to help anything.

He was sure he couldn't do nothing. Riley had lied, cheated, and killed her way across the stars. She had imprisoned and murdered innocent people. She had planned to turn the residents of Metro into monsters. It didn't matter if this was war, or if she had Command's blessing. It didn't even matter if the entire colony wound up as slaves to an alien race. She had crossed the line, and she had to meet some form of justice.

They reached the central lift banks with Washington propping Caleb up and helping him keep his weight off his broken ankle. They came to a stop at the shaft, and Caleb tapped on the controls. He breathed a sigh of relief when one of the lifts activated, the cab beginning to drop toward them.

"How long do you think we have?" he asked Washington, who shrugged in response. "Am I making the wrong move?"

Washington shook his head. *No.*

The cab arrived, and the two Guardians stepped in. Caleb directed the lift back to Deck Six. His body was on fire, the crash reopening his wounds and sending warm blood running down his back beneath the SOS. His shoulder was sore, the muscles strained at the very least and possibly even torn. And of course his ankle was too damaged to stand on. He was lucky to be alive, even if he had only gained a few extra minutes. If the ship landed successfully, there was still no telling what they'd face on the ground.

The lift was on Deck Eight when a loud bang echoed through the ship, so strong it shook the entire shaft and rocked the cab, the lights flashing off and then coming back on. The Deliverance shuddered again, rocking harder than it had before. A loud rumble echoed up from the bottom of the ship.

"Landing thrusters," Caleb said, guessing at the source of the sound. While the Deliverance used an anti-gravity sled to get off the ground on Earth, the sled was meant to stay behind. Instead, the ship used massive heavy thrusters to control the descent, drawing on more power than they possessed before they had connected the alien energy unit.

If the thrusters were active, it meant they were through the thermosphere and on their way to the surface.

It meant they were running out of time.

The lift made it to Deck Six. The doors slid open, and Washington helped Caleb hobble out into the corridor. The bridge wasn't far from their position, and they ran across the passages as quickly as they could.

It didn't feel quick enough.

Caleb pulled himself away from Washington, letting his weight come down on his ankle. It hurt like hell, threatening not to support him, but he forced the issue, charging ahead through sheer determination. He had to stop Riley from gaining control of the colony.

He turned the corner, finding the door to the bridge up ahead. The ship's rumbling was subsiding somewhat, suggesting the thrusters had leveled the velocity of the descent. They were almost to the surface.

He made it to the door with Washington right behind him, swinging around it. His eyes were immediately drawn to the view through the displays, and he came to a sudden stop to stare. They were approaching what appeared to be a river valley. The river sat on the starboard side with a large clearing to its left. It vanished into a thick forest ahead, the trees visually similar to Earth trees, at least from their current distance. Caleb spotted birds coasting across the canopy and small animals rushing away from the ground below, sensing the danger of the incoming ship. He noticed mountains in the distance, and snowcaps reflecting the light of the planet's sun. It all looked so much like Earth it seemed almost impossible.

"What do we have, Klahanie?" Riley said.

Her voice broke Caleb out of his transfixion. They were no more than a few kilometers from the surface. He regained himself, moving forward past the holotable, looking for Riley.

"It's perfect, Doctor," Deputy Klahanie replied. "According to the sensors, the planet is perfect."

"What about signs of alien occupation?"

"The ship is recording the descent, but it will take some time for the computer to parse all of the data and identify any anomalies. I didn't see anything obvious on the way down, did you?"

"No, but after the encounter with the drone we need to be ready for anything."

Caleb reached the edge of the master station. Klahanie was still sitting in the chair with Riley leaning over him. Governor Stone was across the room at one of the stations, his head buried in his hands. Flores was further up front, staring into the displays, while Sheriff Dante and her deputies were off to the side, also watching the view of the outside world.

Riley was the first to notice his arrival, her head lifting from the master terminal and turning toward him. "Sergeant Card," she said with a smile. "You made it."

Flores must have heard her say his name, because her head whipped back, and her lips split in a huge grin. "Alpha!" she shouted, rushing over. "Ha! I knew it. Score one for Star Wars!" She moved to embrace him, but he put his hand up, keeping her back.

"Flores, hold up," he said. "Doctor Valentine, step away from the station."

"Sergeant?" Riley said. "What's going on?"

"Flores, put your weapon on Doctor Valentine," Caleb said.

She didn't hesitate, grabbing her rifle from her back and pointing it at Riley.

"What the hell is this, Sergeant?" Riley asked.

The activity got the attention of the others on the bridge. Sheriff Dante stood and approached from her side. Governor Stone did the same.

"Riley Valentine, as is my right within Guardian protocol, I'm placing you under detention immediately, in connection with the murders of Sergeant James Pratt and civilian David Nash."

Riley's face flushed immediately, her anger apparent. "What?" she hissed. "You can't arrest me, damn it. We're here. You're a civilian, not a Guardian."

"We haven't touched the ground yet," Caleb said. "I'm still a Guardian, and you're still being detained."

"This is bullshit," Riley snapped. "Do you have evidence of anything, Sergeant? Because this sure is coming out of left field."

"I saw David, Doctor," Caleb said. "I watched his corpse float out of the hangar with Sho and the Cerebus. You blew his brains out a second time, and threw him into space before he could regenerate."

"You're out of your mind, Caleb," Riley said. "David was a danger to this ship. He was trying to get into Metro.

He wanted to kill every last person aboard. I dealt with the problem. Yes, I killed him, but not like you claim. If you saw a body going out into space, it wasn't David's." She paused. "What is this about, Caleb? You've been running the show for so long, you don't want to let go? What are your intentions? To seize control of Metro as the acting military leader on board?"

"No. I don't want to be in charge. If it's safe here, I'll happily retire. But you murdered David. I know you did. Worse, you gave one of my men an experimental drug and then killed him in cold blood when it didn't take. I know what this planet isn't, Doctor. I know this isn't Earth-6. I know you directed the Deliverance here. Where the hell are we, and what the hell are we doing here?"

Riley glared at him, her eyes furious, her jaw clenched. Her hands were balled into fists, and she looked like she wanted to pummel him into dust.

"Look at that," Klahanie said.

His words broke the silent stalemate. All eyes turned to the display as the ship began crushing the edge of the treeline beneath its hard alloy shell. A moment later, they hit the ground.

It wasn't a grand landing. There was no fanfare and little excitement. The ship's computer had placed them beside the river in the middle of a valley, judging the best location for the colony from the data received by the sensors. It had touched down perfectly, everything working as designed to land the massive craft as though it were a small drone.

There was no crashing, no banging, no fire, no explosions. The starship simply came to rest and didn't move again.

Riley looked back at Caleb. Her lips spread into a wide, predatory smile. "We're here," she said.

"I can't believe it," Flores said. "We're actually here."

It should have been a moment of celebration. Instead, the bridge was otherwise silent as Caleb and Riley squared off.

"Governor Stone," Riley said. "You saw the output from the scan. Now that we're on the surface, I'm claiming my right as the acting Governor of Metro. Sheriff Dante, would you please arrest Sergeant Card and his accomplices?"

"On what charge?" Flores asked.

"Treason," Riley replied.

Caleb glanced over at Sheriff Dante. He had warned her what might come. He was glad to see she didn't move.

"Sheriff, I gave you an order," Riley said.

"Hmm," Dante said. "Funny thing, Doctor. You see, I read the protocols. Obviously, all mention of us being on a starship was erased, but they were very clear that if Marines detained a prisoner during the period before transition, that prisoner would be transferred directly to law post-transition. Meaning that since you were detained before we landed, you're now under my authority to hold you or release you as I see fit."

Riley's face flattened, her smile vanishing. "You have no proof of anything, Sheriff. You have no cause to arrest me."

"No, but you've already been arrested. I'm just not ready to release you just yet. I'm not saying I'm going to keep you indefinitely, but I'm also not going to allow you to become Governor with a black cloud hanging over your head. My deputies and I will bring you back to the law office for temporary holding. We'll figure out what's what once we get a little more settled here. Governor Stone, does that sound good to you?"

All eyes turned to the Governor. His were red and

swollen, and still moist with his tears. He nodded. "Yes, Sheriff. Take her back to law." Governor Stone pointed at Caleb. "I want Sergeant Card arrested too."

"What?" Caleb said. "On what charge?"

"Your actions on the whole are currently as questionable as hers." He glanced at Riley. "I want both of you under control until we can sort things out."

"This is bullshit," Flores said. "Sergeant Card risked his life a thousand times to get you people here and to keep you people alive. We all did. You can't just – "

"Flores," Caleb said. "It's okay."

"No, Alpha, it isn't," Flores said. "You didn't do anything wrong. Everybody knows you didn't do anything wrong, including Maleficent over there." She pointed at Riley.

"Exactly. They won't be able to keep me. It's fine. Sheriff Dante, I'll come quietly. Flores, we don't know what this world is, or what may be on it. You and Wash need to help protect these people, okay? Just because we're on the ground doesn't mean we can stop being Guardians. Not until we know what this planet is like. Not until we know the truth." He looked at Riley. "If you're even capable of it."

Flores didn't look happy, but she nodded in acquiescence.

"Sheriff," Governor Stone said. "Take them away."

Chapter 52

Sheriff Dante didn't bring Caleb and Riley directly to the law office. Caleb's injuries were extensive enough that she decided to bring them to Metro's hospital first.

Walking through the streets of the city, or the strands as Sheriff Dante had taken to calling them, Caleb couldn't help but feel the tension of the residents. Many had come out of their cubes in response to all the noise and shaking that had occurred. They gathered together in groups, approaching Dante and her deputies. Dante turned them away with promises that the Governor would be making an announcement soon.

The people were afraid, and Caleb didn't blame them. He felt his own share of anxiety and worry. Not for himself, but for all of them. He didn't want to be in Metro, and he certainly didn't want to be a prisoner. He hadn't done anything wrong. He knew it. Riley knew it. Sheriff Dante knew it. He was convinced Governor Stone knew it too. The Governor was acting on emotion more than instinct, detaining him in part as retribution for Orla.

It frustrated him that he was here instead of out there with Flores and Washington, but he also accepted it. How would he ever convince Dante or Stone of his honesty and integrity unless he stuck to it no matter how difficult the situation became? How would he get access to the mainframe and the proof of Riley's transgressions, without making solid inroads?

He glanced over at Riley. She had worn a sour expression — a sullen pout mixed with harsh anger — since Deputy Bashir had put the mechanical cuffs on her wrists. She refused to look in any direction but straight ahead, and every time Caleb looked her way he got the feeling she was planning out a web of intricate lies.

Metro's hospital was in better condition than most of the other buildings, having been granted priority with regard to parts and equipment that were in dwindling supply. The tiled floor was cracked but clean, the walls and doors faded but functional and the medical services fully staffed. Caleb and Riley were quickly admitted and brought to the main waiting room, with Caleb rolled up in a squeaky, worn wheelchair.

"Sheriff Dante," a man said, entering the room. He was older, in good shape, with a head of thick white hair and bushy white eyebrows. He wore a threadbare suit beneath an equally worn white coat and carried a stethoscope around his neck. "To be honest, with all the rocking and rolling I thought we'd be inundated by now. You only brought me two?"

"Sorry to disappoint you, Doctor Brom," Sheriff Dante said with a smile. "I've got orders to put these two in lockup once they're cleared. Sergeant Caleb Card and Doctor Riley Valentine. They're from outside."

The way she said it clued Brom in on the significance. His eyes slipped over both of them. "I see. Are we going to make a habit of taking our protectors into custody, do you think?"

"It's a long story, Doctor," Caleb said. "It's fine though. I don't mind taking the time to get the record straight. I do have a broken ankle and a number of lacerations on my back I'd love to get patched up."

Brom laughed at the statement. "Well, you came to the right place, Sergeant. Of course, if you have a doctor of your own?" He pointed at Riley.

"I'm not a medical doctor," she said. "I'm a scientist."

"Okay then. How come you didn't get treatment on the other side of the hatch? Don't you have facilities?"

"Not anymore," Caleb said. "No medical doctors. No facilities."

Brom glanced at Sheriff Dante. "Is there a particular reason your prisoners are acting as cagey as hell?"

"I told you, Charles, it's a long story," Dante replied. "Right now, I need you to treat their injuries and chip them."

"I already have a chip," Riley said.

"And chip Sergeant Card," Dante corrected. "The fewer the questions, the better. Governor Stone will speak to the residents soon, and everything will make more sense."

Brom hesitated a moment and then sighed. "Well, what do I know? I'm just an old man anyway. Okay, Sergeant, let's head into the exam room over there."

"Don't make any trouble, okay Sergeant?" Dante said.

"It's not me you have to worry about, Sheriff," Caleb replied.

Riley didn't respond to the dig. Doctor Brom took the back of Caleb's chair and rolled him into the exam room. It was a simple setup, kept in good condition.

"Do you need help getting onto the table?" Brom asked.

"I've got it," Caleb replied. "Just put me next to it."

Brom rolled him next to the table. Caleb leaned over, pulling himself up on the strength of his replacement arm.

"That's an awfully impressive piece of machinery," Brom said.

"I'd rather have the real thing back, but it'll do," Caleb replied.

"So, you want to tell me what all the fuss is about?" Brom asked as Caleb unhooked his combat armor and began peeling it away. "I promise I can keep a secret."

Caleb smiled. "I don't think Sheriff Dante would appreciate that very much."

Brom laughed. "All the more reason to spill the beans, eh?"

Caleb pulled the SOS off his shoulders, starting to bend down to separate it from his legs.

"Whoa, hold up there," Brom said. "You said you have wounds on your back? Don't bend. I'll get it." The doctor helped him get the combat armor off his legs and then laid it out next to the table. The armor was filthy with blood, sweat, and grime. "You look like you've had a busy day."

"You can say that again."

"I just did. The shirt too, Sarge."

Caleb pulled off his shirt. Doctor Brom circled behind him, checking the lacerations.

He whistled at the sight. "Sergeant, don't take this the wrong way, but what the hell did this to you, and how the hell are you still standing?"

"Part of that long story," Caleb replied. "And this isn't my first time. Can you fix it?"

"Of course." He tapped a small pin on his coat. "Reed, exam room three, please. And bring a gun."

"On my way, Doc," a male voice replied.

"A gun?" Caleb asked.

"Probably not what you're thinking," Brom said. "The gun will insert an ID chip into your wrist with some basic information that'll get written to Metro's mainframe. It doesn't hurt or anything. Anyway, once we're done fixing your back, I'll get your ankle scanned so we can brace it. Sound good?"

"Thanks, Doctor," Caleb replied.

"It's no problem. So, what's it like on the outside? You being here, does that mean we're winning?"

Caleb smiled. "Winning is subjective."

"Still being cagey, huh? The condition of your armor and your body leads me to believe I may be speaking a bit optimistically."

"I applaud your effort, Doctor, but I really can't talk about it."

Brom laughed again. "Can't blame an old man for trying, can you, Sarge?"

Caleb didn't get the chance to answer. Both men turned their heads toward the door at the sound of a shout and a thump from outside.

"What the heck?" Doctor Brom said. "Wait here, Sergeant."

He started for the door.

"Wait. I'll come with you."

"Like that? You can barely stand."

"I've been in worse shape than this before."

"It's not your place right now. You're a patient first."

Caleb slid off the table and limped for the door ahead of Doctor Brom, ignoring the man's half-hearted protests. He grabbed the handle, using it to balance as he pulled the door open.

He froze when he saw Sheriff Dante on the floor at

Riley's feet, both her deputies and a third man, probably Reed, standing away from her. She had the sheriff's revolver in her hand and was currently pointing it at the men. All three of them looked terrified. Why? They had to know the gun wasn't loaded.

"Valentine?" Caleb said. "What are you doing?"

Riley spun in his direction, aiming the revolver at him. "Stay back," she snapped. "Just say back!" She stared at him. "I had to do it, Harry. For my sister. For our kind. Somebody had to be the one to make the hard choice. Somebody had to play the devil. This is war, Harry. They started it. We came to end it."

"Riley, what are you talking about?" Caleb asked.

She shoved the revolver toward him, eyes wild. "Stay back, damn it! I failed. I know. I messed everything up. I was trying to do the right thing. I swear. I was trying to do the hard thing to save everyone. I'm sorry."

She turned the revolver, putting the barrel in her mouth. What was she doing?

Their eyes met.

She pulled the trigger.

The gun clicked, the chamber empty.

Riley's head snapped back as though the revolver had fired, and she collapsed to the floor.

Doctor Brom pushed past Caleb, dropping to his knees beside Riley. He put his fingers to her neck, turning back to Caleb in surprise.

"She's dead," he said.

"That's not possible," Caleb replied, leaning over them. Riley's eyes were open and unmoving; her body splayed awkwardly on the ground. There was no bullet. No wound. No blood. "The gun wasn't loaded."

"Loaded or not, Sergeant, I've been a doctor a long time. I know dead from alive, and she's definitely dead."

Caleb stared at Doctor Brom. Was this a joke? A dream? Was he hallucinating?

A cold chill ran down his spine as his eyes crossed over the other people in the room, David's voice echoing in his mind.

The hallucinations are a weapon, Sergeant.

And someone or something had just used it.

"Doctor Brom, we have a problem."

Thank you for reading Deception

You made it through book two! Awesome! Thank you so much for reading, and for coming back for more. I hope you'll join Caleb and company for Desperation.

In the meantime, how about leaving a review on Amazon now (mrforbes.com/reviewdeception).

Why?

Because the power to excite new readers and introduce them to the Forgotten universe is in your hands.

Seriously, if you like my stuff and you want to support my work, the second best way (after spending your money on me) to do that is to leave a review. It's like a standing ovation at Hamilton, or calling for an encore at a concert. If you've ever done that, you should do this :D

In any case, I know there are a lot of books out there, and I'm grateful you chose mine. Thank you, thank you, thank you.

If this is your first foray into the Forgotten books and you're looking for something else to read before Desperation drops, I recommend picking up Forgotten (mrforbes.com/forgotten). It's the book that started it all, and ties in especially well with this one and feeds into Earth Unknown (mrforbes.com/earthunknown), another bestselling Forgotten universe series.

If you're already caught up in the Forgotten universe or you're interested in any of my other books - there's a more complete description in the next section of this book, or even better you can check out my backlist at mrforbes.com/books.

Again, thank you so much for your support. If you have Facebook, please stop by my page sometime at facebook.com/mrforbes.author. I'd love to hear from you.

Cheers,
Michael.

Other Books By M.R Forbes

M.R. Forbes on Amazon

mrforbes.com/books

Forgotten (The Forgotten)

mrforbes.com/theforgotten

Some things are better off FORGOTTEN.

Sheriff Hayden Duke was born on the Pilgrim, and he expects to die on the Pilgrim, like his father, and his father before him.

That's the way things are on a generation starship centuries from home. He's never questioned it. Never thought about it. And why bother? Access points to the ship's controls are sealed, the systems that guide her automated and out of reach. It isn't perfect, but he has all he needs to be content.

Until a malfunction forces his Engineer wife to the edge of the habitable zone to inspect the damage.

Until she contacts him, breathless and terrified, to tell

him she found a body, and it doesn't belong to anyone on board.

Until he arrives at the scene and discovers both his wife and the body are gone.

The only clue? A bloody handprint beneath a hatch that hasn't opened in hundreds of years.

Until now.

Earth Unknown (Forgotten Earth)

mrforbes.com/earthunknown

A terrible discovery.

A secret that could destroy human civilization.

A desperate escape to the most dangerous planet in the universe... Earth.

Two hundred years ago, a fleet of colony ships left Earth and started a settlement on Proxima Centauri...

Centurion Space Force pilot Nathan Stacker didn't expect to return home to find his wife dead. He didn't expect the murderer to look just like him, and he definitely didn't expect to be the one to take the blame.

But his wife had control of a powerful secret. A secret that stretches across the light years between two worlds and could lead to the end of both.

Now that secret is in Nathan's hands, and he's about to make the most desperate evasive maneuver of his life -- stealing a starship and setting a course for Earth.

He thinks he'll be safe there.

He's wrong. Very wrong.

Earth is nothing like what he expected. Not even close. What he doesn't know is not only likely to kill him, it's eager to kill him, and even if it doesn't?

The Sheriff will.

Starship Eternal (War Eternal)
mrforbes.com/starshipeternal

A lost starship...

A dire warning from futures past...

A desperate search for salvation...

Captain Mitchell "Ares" Williams is a Space Marine and the hero of the Battle for Liberty, whose Shot Heard 'Round the Universe saved the planet from a nearly unstoppable war machine. He's handsome, charismatic, and the perfect poster boy to help the military drive enlistment. Pulled from the war and thrown into the spotlight, he's as efficient at charming the media and bedding beautiful celebrities as he was at shooting down enemy starfighters.

After an assassination attempt leaves Mitchell critically wounded, he begins to suffer from strange hallucinations that carry a chilling and oddly familiar warning:

They are coming. Find the Goliath or humankind will be destroyed.

Convinced that the visions are a side-effect of his injuries, he tries to ignore them, only to learn that he may not be as crazy as he thinks. The enemy is real and closer than he imagined, and they'll do whatever it takes to prevent him from rediscovering the centuries lost starship.

Narrowly escaping capture, out of time and out of air, Mitchell lands at the mercy of the Riggers - a ragtag crew of former commandos who patrol the lawless outer reaches of the galaxy. Guided by a captain with a reputation for cold-blooded murder, they're dangerous, immoral, and possibly insane.

They may also be humanity's last hope for survival in a war that has raged beyond eternity.

(War Eternal is also available in a box set of the first three books here: mrforbes.com/wareternalbox)

Hell's Rejects (Chaos of the Covenant)
mrforbes.com/hellsrejects

The most powerful starships ever constructed are gone. Thousands are dead. A fleet is in ruins. The attackers are unknown. The orders are clear: *Recover the ships. Bury the bastards who stole them.*

Lieutenant Abigail Cage never expected to find herself in Hell. As a Highly Specialized Operational Combatant, she was one of the most respected Marines in the military. Now she's doing hard labor on the most miserable planet in the universe.

Not for long.

The Earth Republic is looking for the most dangerous individuals it can control. The best of the worst, and Abbey happens to be one of them. The deal is simple: *Bring back the starships, earn your freedom. Try to run, you die.* It's a suicide mission, but she has nothing to lose.

The only problem? There's a new threat in the galaxy. One with a power unlike anything anyone has ever seen. One that's been waiting for this moment for a very, very, long time. And they want Abbey, too.

Be careful what you wish for.

They say Hell hath no fury like a woman scorned. They have no idea.

Man of War (Rebellion)
mrforbes.com/manofwar

In the year 2280, an alien fleet attacked the Earth.

336

Their weapons were unstoppable, their defenses unbreakable.

Our technology was inferior, our militaries overwhelmed.

Only one starship escaped before civilization fell.

Earth was lost.

It was never forgotten.

Fifty-two years have passed.

A message from home has been received.

The time to fight for what is ours has come.

Welcome to the rebellion.

Or maybe something completely different?

Dead of Night (Ghosts & Magic)
mrforbes.com/deadofnight

For Conor Night, the world's only surviving necromancer, staying alive is an expensive proposition. So when the promise of a big payout for a small bit of thievery presents itself, Conor is all in. But nothing comes easy in the world of ghosts and magic, and it isn't long before Conor is caught up in the machinations of the most powerful wizards on Earth and left with only two ways out:

Finish the job, or be finished himself.

Balance (The Divine)
mrforbes.com/balance

My name is Landon Hamilton. Once upon a time I was a twenty-three year old security guard, trying to regain my life after spending a year in prison for stealing people's credit card numbers.

Now, I'm dead.

Okay, I was supposed to be dead. I got killed after all; but a funny thing happened after I had turned the mortal coil...

I met Dante Alighieri - yeah, that Dante. He told me I was special, a diuscrucis. That's what they call a perfect balance of human, demon, and angel. Apparently, I'm the only one of my kind.

I also learned that there was a war raging on Earth between Heaven and Hell, and that I was the only one who could save the human race from annihilation. He asked me to help, and I was naive enough to agree.

Sounds crazy, I know, but he wished me luck and sent me back to the mortal world. Oh yeah, he also gave me instructions on how to use my Divine "magic" to bend the universe to my will. The problem is, a sexy vampire crushed them while I was crushing on her.

Now I have to somehow find my own way to stay alive in a world of angels, vampires, werewolves, and an assortment of other enemies that all want to kill me before I can mess up their plans for humanity's future. If that isn't enough, I also have to find the queen of all demons and recover the Holy Grail.

It's not like it's the end of the world if I fail.

Wait. It is.

Tears of Blood (Books 1-3)

mrforbes.com/tearsofblood

One thousand years ago, the world was broken and reborn beneath the boot of a nameless, ageless tyrant. He erased all history of the time before, enslaving the people and hunting those with the power to unseat him.

The power of magic.

Eryn is such a girl. Born with the Curse, she fights to

control and conceal it to protect those she loves. But when the truth is revealed, and his Marines come, she is forced away from her home and into the company of Silas, a deadly fugitive tormented by a fractured past.

Silas knows only that he is a murderer who once hunted the Cursed, and that he and his brothers butchered armies and innocents alike to keep the deep, dark secrets of the time before from ever coming to light.

Secrets which could save the world.

Or destroy it completely.

About the Author

MR. Forbes is the mind behind a growing number of Amazon best-selling science fiction series including Rebellion, War Eternal, Chaos of the Covenant, and the Forgotten Universe novels. He currently resides with his family and friends on the west cost of the United States, including a cat who thinks she's a dog and a dog who thinks she's a cat.

He maintains a true appreciation for his readers and is always happy to hear from them.

To learn more about M.R. Forbes or just say hello:

Visit my website:
mrforbes.com

Send me an e-mail:
michael@mrforbes.com

Check out my Facebook page:
facebook.com/mrforbes.author

Chat with me on Facebook Messenger:
https://m.me/mrforbes.author